DESCENT INTO ULTHOA

BLOOD RUNS TRUE

OTHER BOOKS BY

GORDON BONNET

The Shambles	*The Fifth Day*
Signal to Noise	*Sights, Signs, and Shadows*
Slings and Arrows	*Sephirot*
Lock and Key	*Gears*
Kill Switch	*Lines of Sight*
Whistling in the Dark	*Fear no Colors*
Poison the Well	*The Dead Letter Office*
Face Value	*Past Imperfect*
Room for Wrath	*The Obituary Collector*

DESCENT INTO ULTHOA

BLOOD RUNS TRUE

GORDON BONNET

Text copyright © 2021 by Gordon Bonnet
All Rights Reserved. Printed in the United States of America

Published by Motina Books, LLC, Van Alstyne, Texas
www.MotinaBooks.com

Library of Congress Cataloguing-in-Publication Data:

Names: Bonnet, Gordon
Title: Descent Into Ulthoa
Description: First Edition. | Van Alstyne: Motina Books, 2021
Identifiers: LCCN: 2021939537 | ISBN-13: 978-1-945060-31-1 (paperback) | ISBN-13: 978-1-945060-32-8 (e-book) | ISBN-13: 978-1-945060-33-5 (hardcover)
Subjects: BISAC: Fiction > Science Fiction > General
Fiction > Thrillers > Suspense

Cover and Interior Design: Diane Windsor

PART I:

DEVIL'S GLEN

I

August 2024

Claver Road doesn't end. It withers away. First from potholed asphalt to dirt, then to a pair of parallel wheel-ruts, finally fading into a tangle of blackberry, osier, and scrub willow. If you tried following it any farther, you'd soon find yourself lost in the deep forest. There, the only paths are deer trails, and those are few in number. Even the animals shun those woods. The whole place is sunk in silence, stillness, and shadow, where a whisper sounds like a shout, and most humans foolish enough to go that far make sure to leave before nightfall.

Where the deep forest starts is only fifteen miles from the nearest town, the quaint, picture-postcard village of Guildford, New York, but most of Guildford's residents either don't know about the place's reputation or else pretend not to. It shows up on maps as a blank spot, crossed by no roads, inhabited by no one. The eighty thousand acre tract of woods is nominally owned by New York State, but they don't manage it, lease it for hunting or grazing, or even post signs at the

1

boundaries. It's not off limits to hikers and skiers, but the tacit message is clear.

Enter here, and you're on your own.

The few old timers who are willing to talk about the forest at the end of Claver Road—usually after a drink or three in Finney's Pub—will tell you in a lowered voice about people who staked out claims on the land back in the early nineteenth century when the government was encouraging people to settle the rural parts of upstate New York for logging, lumber, and farming. A few took the state up on its offer of cheap land and cleared spots for cabins and barns. For a while, it seemed that everything was going well, and the settlers were thriving. But it didn't last. Gradually their families in town stopped hearing from them, visits became fewer and fewer, and they were conveniently expunged from memory, left to their fate and the shadows under the trees.

On a summer evening I asked Frank McCormick, one of the oldest residents of Guildford, what happened to them, trying to make the question sound offhand. It wasn't until I bought him his third pint that he gave me a narrow look from under his bushy gray eyebrows, and said in a hoarse, reluctant voice, "They ain't *gone*, you understand. Not dead or moved on. There's something in those woods separated 'em from their kin, made it easy for relatives to pretend they didn't remember anyone was in there." Here his voice dropped even further. "Far as I know, they're *still* there, the grandchildren and great-grandchildren of them that settled the place almost two hundred years ago. Chances are, you go into the woods, you won't see 'em even if you look for 'em. They might see *you*, though."

"How do they survive without any contact with the outside world?"

His eyes flickered to one side and then the other. "The wood takes care of its own."

At this point, he coughed nervously, drained what was left of his pint, and changed the subject. Ten minutes later, he mumbled an excuse and left the pub—and has studiously avoided me ever since.

~

Guildford was settled in the late eighteenth century, and a great many of its houses are on the Register of Historic Homes. Walking down the maple-shaded sidewalks on the two main residential streets, Washington and Prospect, you see immaculate yards, tasteful pastel-colored façades with gingerbread and gabled roofs, widow's walks and front porches with Adirondack chairs. Not a blade of grass out of place.

It's a village that prides itself on its heritage, and makes sure that heritage is always portrayed as squeaky-clean.

Myself, I doubt the image they've built up over the years. Not only because of what I know and what I've heard hinted at in Finney's Pub, but because no place is without its scandals. You'd think that after all this time, there'd be little concern over what less-than-savory things had been done by ancestors who died over a hundred years ago, but even implying some of them may not have been the upright pillars of society everyone claimed is a sure way to get excluded from any further discussion of the matter. The Village Historical Society was once described to me—again by an old-timer, and again after a couple of pints—as being a self-aggrandizing circle jerk.

It's an unusually apt metaphor.

So I knew what I was up against, right from the outset, in trying to uncover the seedier side of Guildford's past. I started out with what was readily accessible, which turned out to be not much. The Guildford Public Library is small, but it has a wealth of information about local history and genealogy, so in my free time—I work for the Department of Public Works in Colville, the nearest good-sized town—I made the forty-five-minute drive to the little village, heading to their research room to pore over musty-smelling books and folders and tubes of plat maps that look like they haven't been opened since they were archived here.

I started on this quest for information about the forest at the end of Claver Road a month ago, but have remarkably little to show for it. There's plenty of information about the Guildford aristocracy, families that settled here in the early nineteenth century and have pretty much run things ever since. The library proudly displays books on the antecedents and contributions of the Upshaws and Vanderzees, Claypools and Larkins, but it didn't take me long to figure out that the closer the families lived to Claver Road, the less mention they got.

"What're you looking for so persistently?" Cyndy Evans, the pretty assistant librarian, greeted me with a smile and gave a quick gesture to the clock to remind me it was five minutes until closing time. "You've been in here every night this week."

I rubbed my eyes. "I'm trying to track down information on the people who settled west of the village. There's lots of stuff about families in the village itself, and east and south of here, but I'm finding almost nothing about the ones that headed into the hills to the west."

"Around Deane's Corners, you mean?"

"No, farther than that."

A flash of a frown crossed her face. I'd seen that look before when I'd asked someone too many questions about the hill country west of the village, but it still came as a surprise to see it on her. The only thing I was never sure of was if the expression conveyed annoyance, avoidance—or knowledge they'd rather didn't come to light.

But her bright smile returned, and I derided myself for reading suspicion into everyone. She gestured at the map I had unrolled on the table. "Those plats date from 1805, when the area was first settled by the whites. It should say who the area you're interested in was deeded to."

"There are a couple of parcels in the names of Bishop, Dunstan, and Craig. Not much in the way of records afterward, although it appears that some time in the late eighteen-hundreds the entire area reverted to the state because of non-payment of taxes. That's about all I can find."

"Why the interest?" Again, a hint of more than idle curiosity, there and gone in a second, leaving me wondering if it was my imagination. "Does your family come from the west part of the county?"

I chuckled. "No. I'm just curious. I was raised in Lamont."

Her smile relaxed. Relief, perhaps? "So Guildford must seem like the big city to you. Lamont's what, five houses and a crossroad?"

"Six. We're growing."

This got a laugh. "Well, anyhow, good luck in your search. Tomorrow I'll do a little digging myself and see if I can find some more resources for you. The information's got to be somewhere, it's just a matter of figuring out where."

"Thanks." I rolled up the plat map and slipped it back into its cardboard tube. "Have a nice evening. I'll see you tomorrow."

"Same to you." She picked up the tube and headed off to the archive room, and I walked out into the sultry night, alive with the whirring of cicadas and the whine of mosquitoes. When I was reaching for my car door, I heard a click from behind me, and gave a quick look over my shoulder.

Cyndy was locking the library door. In the brightly-lit window I got a glimpse of her before she turned away. Her smile was gone, replaced by an expression in which puzzlement, concern, and fear predominated. I wasn't able to talk myself out of it this time.

There was no doubt. She—like a good many other villagers I'd talked to—knew more than she was saying, and was not happy that I was digging into the area's past. The question was why she cared, and found it prudent to remain silent.

~

Cyndy Evans wasn't at the library the following evening.

I'd arrived at around seven o'clock, after getting home from work, taking a quick shower, and grabbing a pint and a bite to eat at Finney's. That'd give me a solid two hours for research, starting with finding out what Cyndy might have uncovered in her own research on my behalf.

But in her place behind the counter was an older woman I'd never seen before. She had an angular, severe face, and her thin, long-limbed frame was accentuated by a loose-fitting flower-print dress that looked several sizes too large for her. Round wire-framed glasses, dark skin, and curly jet-black hair, the latter probably accomplished with hair dye, given her age. Despite her intimidating features, she gave me a friendly smile when I came up.

"Can I help you?"

"I talked to Cyndy Evans yesterday. She was going to do some research for me on local history."

"I'm sorry, Cyndy's not here this evening."

I wasn't sure where to go with the conversation. I couldn't exactly ask where Cyndy was. It's not like she's a personal friend, and this woman—her name tag said "Melvia Shields;" I'd never seen anyone who looked more like a Melvia Shields in my life—would be perfectly in her rights to tell me it was none of my damned business.

I decided to try charm, and put on a smile of my own. "Well, did she leave anything for me?"

She gave a cursory look down at the desk, more for show than as any real effort to answer my question. "No, she doesn't appear to have left any notes for patrons."

"Oh. Okay, thanks."

She met my gaze. Her eyes were hard as flint even though her mouth was still smiling at me. Eyes that dared me to push further.

Instead, I said, "I'd like to take a look at some of the maps in the archive, if that's okay?"

"Certainly. Which ones?"

"The plat maps from the early nineteenth century, of the west part of the county."

"You realize those maps are reproductions, that the originals are too fragile to withstand handling?"

"Yes, that's no problem."

She gave me a curt nod and left the desk, heading down a hallway behind the counter toward the archives. Only a minute later, she came back.

Empty handed.

"I'm sorry, sir, but those maps appear to have been removed. They may be on interlibrary loan. It's not that unusual for historians from other facilities to request loans from our map collection. I could check to see if you'd like."

I stared at her a moment. She was still smiling, no doubt amused by her success in thwarting me. My frustration bubbled over. "Don't bother. I don't believe you anyway."

"I beg your pardon?" The smile was gone in an instant, like a camera shutter closing.

"You heard me."

"I will not tolerate rudeness. If you continue to be disrespectful, I'm going to have to ask you to leave."

"Yeah, you do that." My lip curled in a sneer. "I'll leave under my own power, thanks, once you've answered one question honestly."

"Oh?" Her voice was brittle. "And what might that be?"

"I just want to know why you don't want me to know about the people who live beyond Claver Road. I could tell Cyndy was hesitant, too, but you're outright stonewalling me, and I think I have the right to know why."

She gave me an evaluative look, as if she were trying to decide if I deserved the truth. "I am under no obligation to answer that question."

I sighed, then continued in a lower voice, in what I hoped were less threatening tones. "No. No, you aren't. But I hope you will, anyway. Okay, I've heard legends about the woods at the end of Claver Road. People who settled there a long time ago, and maybe their descendants still live there. Other stories, about how it's a dangerous place, if you go into the forest you're risking your life for some reason. I've talked to some of the older residents of Guildford, people who've lived here all their lives, and all I get are oblique hints, and damned few of those. I just want to understand why."

There was a long pause. Melvia Shields looked at me with narrowed eyes, and again I had the impression of being weighed, measured, appraised for my worthiness.

When she spoke, she had lowered her own voice. "I think the more interesting question is why *you* are so eager to find out."

I suppose it was bound to come up sooner or later. Oddly, it was not a question anyone had asked me, through all of my conversations with old-timers and hours of research in the library and local historical societies. From what I'd seen of this woman, I knew if I refused to answer, that would be the end of the conversation, and the end of any help I could expect to get from her.

"Fine." I spoke in a near-whisper. "I have a good reason for wanting to know what's out there, because my brother and his girlfriend went into those woods for a couple of nights' camping. That was ten years ago." I took a deep breath, willing my voice to remain steady. "Neither of them have been seen since."

II

"You're Brad Ellicott's brother."

It wasn't a question. But by a small degree, the old librarian's manner became less frosty.

"You know about him?"

One corner of her mouth twitched upward. "Of course I know about him. Everyone in Guildford remembers the day Brad Ellicott and Cara Marshall disappeared. There were police all over the town for weeks afterward."

"They never found a trace of them. Not a scrap of clothing, none of their camping gear. Nothing."

"Oh, I know. You live in a small town, you don't forget something like that. You'd have to go back another forty years or more to find anything that shook the village up like that did. There was a murder back in 1970 or 1971, and I think between that and your brother's disappearance, nothing newsworthy at all." She paused, giving me a quick up-and-down glance. "He must have been a younger sibling of yours, then."

If that was an insult, I decided to ignore it. I'd already pissed her off enough. "I'm younger than I look. Brad and I are twins. We were thirty-five when it happened."

She gave me another evaluative glance, and one eyebrow rose. She was clearly disposed to treat everything I said with doubt, but at least she didn't feel inclined to argue with me about my own age. In the end, she said, "What were they thinking to go in there?"

It was a good question. My brother was an accomplished hiker, mountaineer, and back-country camper. Together they did the Adirondack 46er challenge—climbed the forty-six tallest peaks in the Adirondack Range. No easy feat.

Then a friend of his asked him, offhand, what camping they'd done closer to home, and wondered about that strange patch of forest out west of Guildford. Brad had never heard of it.

"Nobody goes in there," the friend told him. "It's supposed to be haunted."

Well, that was enough for him. He's always had an odd curiosity for sites with bad reputations, and in fact told me that he'd lost his virginity as a senior in high school when he hooked up with a girl in an abandoned psychiatric hospital only a few miles down the road from our parents' house, a place that apparently got shut down about twenty years ago because one of the psychiatrists went berserk and killed several of the patients.

So a few ghosts? No problem. He told me as much as he was packing up his gear.

Twenty minutes later, he left to pick up Cara for their planned hike into the woods.

I never saw either of them again.

I told Melvia Shields an abbreviated version of Brad's plan to camp in the forest at the end of Claver Road. Leaving out, of course, the part about having sex in an abandoned psychiatric hospital.

Her expression was inscrutable. "It must have been hard for you to lose him."

I wasn't sure if the attempt at commiseration was sincere, but I decided to respond as if it were. "I still haven't recovered. We were close."

"Why did it take you ten years to start looking?"

This woman and her probing questions were getting a little too close to the bone for my comfort. "I spent years trying to forget it. My parents never wanted me to talk about it, even think about it. Losing my brother broke them. My dad died last July, and my mom only outlived him by six months. Whatever happened in those woods—it destroyed my family. It damn near destroyed me. I realized I couldn't rest until I had an explanation."

She shook her head. "I'm sorry for you. At least that explains why you want to know about the area. Although what you hope to learn from nineteenth-century plat maps and books about old settlers, I have no idea."

"I've heard that those settlers left descendants who still live in those woods."

She made a dismissive sound. "Based on what evidence?"

"I've talked to a couple of people who say they've seen people in the forest, heard things. Some even have seen cabins."

"As far as any people that have been spotted in the forest, they were undoubtedly thrill-seekers like your brother and his girlfriend. I seriously doubt anyone lives there. The cabins? There were cabins in the woods, built by the settlers, and there may still be the remains in there somewhere. But if you're implying—if your sources are implying—that any cabins in those woods are inhabited, then I'm afraid you've been duped into believing the imaginings of people who like telling wild stories to frighten the gullible."

"You sound awfully sure of yourself."

"So do you."

"You're really refusing to help me, then?"

"I am unclear about what you're expecting me to do."

"Give me information. Or tell me where I can find it. Okay, I know you think I'm on a fool's errand, or grasping at straws, or whatever cliché about a stupid and pointless effort you want to use. But I'm convinced that Brad and Cara didn't just get lost and starve to death. They were abducted and murdered in those woods, and I want to know by whom."

She regarded me in silence for a moment. "There's another possibility, you know."

"What?"

"That they're still alive, and took off for parts unknown for their own reasons."

"Seriously?" I couldn't keep the scorn out of my voice. "Leaving his car parked at the end of Claver Road? If you're saying they skipped town, why all the pretense of going off for a hike?"

She shrugged. "Keep people from searching for a while. I've heard of cases like it."

"That's not possible. I knew my brother. He was happy and settled. We're not talking about an irresponsible twenty-year-old, here. He had a good job, and he and Cara had a great relationship. There's no way they created some kind of smoke screen, took off, and are now living under assumed names in Des Moines or something."

"That's as plausible as claiming they were murdered by backwoods throwbacks who, conveniently, no one else has any evidence of."

I swore under my breath, evidently loud enough for her to hear, because both of her plucked eyebrows flew upward. "Never mind," I snarled. "I don't know why I bothered talking to you in the first place. I made the mistake of assuming you had a heart."

I pivoted, and was about to head for the door, when she hissed, "Wait."

I turned slowly. Melvia Shields was leaning on the counter, and gave me a quick come-hither. In that instant, something in her expression had changed, but why? There was a sympathy in her eyes I hadn't seen, as if something I said finally touched her, broke through her icy determination to play dumb. "Look," she whispered, as I made my reluctant way back. "I know you're upset at losing your brother, and I'm sorry for you. I will tell you, though, that you're wasting your time here. There's nothing in this library that will give you the information you want." She picked up a scrap of paper, wrote a hasty note, and pushed it across the counter toward me.

"He might be able to help you."

I looked down at the name she'd written. "Alban Bishop."

"He's a regular at Gray's Café. You'll find him there most mornings. Older gentleman, stocky, with a squarish face. Ask anyone, they'll point him out." She paused. "You will not tell him I sent you."

Once again, it wasn't a question.

"I'm not certain he'll be willing to help you. You'll have to tread lightly with him. If he thinks you're some kind of reporter looking for a colorful story about those crazy hicks up in the hills, he'll tell you to clear out so quick it'll rock your head back. Start with the truth. Tell him about your brother. He may listen, although I can't guarantee it." She paused. "You may have to butter him up. Make it clear you're talking to him because you know that on this topic, he's the most knowledgeable one around."

"Sounds like that's not wrong."

"It isn't. Whatever he's willing to say, he knows a great deal about those woods and the history of the west part of the county. Maybe something will be helpful."

Bishop. One of the families on the plat map I'd seen the previous evening. I stared at her in silence for a moment, again wondering why she'd had a change of heart. Whatever the reason, I was grateful for it. My impression was not many people got though her frosty exterior.

"Thanks." I pocketed the scrap of paper. "I'll make sure your name doesn't come up."

She gave a cursory nod, and her eyes flickered around the room to see if anyone had overheard.

The only other occupants were a woman on a couch in the reading area and a high school student using one of the computers, and neither of them gave any evidence of being interested in our conversation. If anyone else was around, they were well hidden.

She looked back down at some papers on the counter. Evidently that was all I was getting. The audience was at an end.

I made the forty-five minute drive back to the house I rent in Lamont in a fugue state. The evasions and half-truths, all I'd successfully gotten out of people, had to mean there was something to what I was asking. If it really was baseless, I wouldn't be getting all the hushed confidences and side-eyes and advice about not talking to the wrong people.

I unlocked my door, stepped inside, turned on the light—then relocked the door. I'd already done it before I even considered what I was doing, and only then caught myself, frowning. Crime was non-existent in little, secluded Lamont. A lot of people never locked their doors. I did some house-sitting for a neighbor last year, and she laughingly told me they'd lost the key to their front door three years earlier and never bothered to replace it.

"Just don't publish that in the newspaper," she'd told me.

So the reflexive locking of my door surprised me, but I didn't give it any further thought. I dropped my backpack on the floor, then slipped into my pre-bedtime routine. The familiarity of it was comforting, and by the time I climbed into bed, relishing the coolness of the sheets against my skin, I was able to put aside the bizarre conversation I'd had with Melvia Shields.

I was asleep within minutes.

~

I got up the following morning, and after a quick shower and a hasty breakfast, I called my boss and let him know I might be a little late. I'm lucky to have a flexible schedule and an understanding employer, but I've worked there for twenty years and he knows I'm reliable. After I told him I'd work late to make up any hours I missed, he said no problem.

Then I got in my car for the drive up to Guildford, to Gray's Café and—with luck—a conversation with Alban Bishop.

I spotted him right away. Elderly man with thin white hair, a craggy face, perhaps six-two—a body that had probably been powerful in his youth and still filled out his flannel shirt and stained blue jeans enough to be imposing. I asked the barista if that was indeed Alban Bishop, and he gave me a curious frown but nodded his assent.

No one else was sitting near him, and the place was noisy with the breakfast crowd, so I had some hope of speaking to him without being overheard.

I went up to his table, where he sat in front of a steaming cup of black coffee. "Hello, are you Alban Bishop?"

He squinted up at me. "Yeah." His voice was hoarse, a suspicious-sounding growl that under other circumstances I'd have found intimidating.

"I'm trying to find out some information, and I was told you might be able to help."

A long pause. "Okay."

I sat down across from him, and said, in a quiet voice, "I'm Bradley Ellicott's brother."

An even longer pause. "Yeah?"

"You know who he is, then? You know the name?"

"Yeah."

Glad I wasn't expecting an outpouring of sympathy. "I'm trying to find out where, and how, he disappeared."

"Where, I can tell you."

"Okay…?"

"The hills west of Guildford. Off the end of Claver Road. That's where they found his car."

I already knew that, of course, but I didn't say so. Best behavior, the old librarian had suggested. "Yes, sir, but I'm trying to figure it out more precisely."

"Why? They never could find a trace of him. Not for want of looking, either."

"I know. But there are rumors…"

"What rumors?" Alban Bishop's eyes narrowed, and his voice took on cold, almost hostile, tones.

"That people in those woods might have kidnapped or killed him and his girlfriend."

"Why'd'ya think I know anything about that?"

"Not that specifically, but I was told you knew more than anyone else about the people who lived out there. That if you didn't know, no one did."

15

That was a bit of an exaggeration, but Melvia Shields had told me to lay it on thick.

"Yeah?" Now he sounded wry, and he took a sip of coffee, looking at me over the rim of the cup. "Someone told you that, huh?"

"Yes."

"Lot o' bullshit." He cleared his throat, coughed. "I ain't no historian."

"Historians have been no help at all."

That must have struck a positive note, because he laughed. "No, they wouldn't be. All they care about is them as had money. Goddamn Sempronius Claypool, who bought up all the land north of the village. He and his family ran the damn place for decades, but you know where he got his money? It was cash he'd gotten for rounding up mercenaries to fight in the War of 1812. A lot o' who never made it home. You won't find that detail mentioned in any of them written histories, though."

"I haven't seen it mentioned, no."

"No. I expect not." He cleared his throat again. "You from the village?"

"No. I grew up down in Lamont. Still live there."

He frowned, as if that were not what he expected me to say. "Yeah? Where abouts?"

"Flanders Mill Road."

"Huh. Okay." He paused. "So what brought your brother and his woman up to the woods out west of here?"

"They liked hiking and camping. Thought it looked like an interesting area." A half-truth. I certainly didn't want to mention that they'd gone in there mostly because of Brad's curiosity about the forest's bad reputation.

"Okay," he said again. "So whaddya already know about the settlers up in those hills?"

Tread lightly, here. The Bishops were part of that list, so anything disparaging I said could well be taken personally. "I found land records. Some land grants, mostly late eighteenth and early nineteenth

16

centuries. The ones in the area I'm interested in were Dunstan, Craig...and Bishop."

I guess that was tactful enough, because his assent was immediate. "That's right. Two brothers, Levi and Enoch Bishop, along with their families. Abraham Dunstan and his wife, and Malcolm Craig and his wife and kids. Levi Bishop's land was the closest to the village, his brother Enoch's the farthest." He gave a rough chuckle. "I gather they didn't much get along."

"It seemed like…" I paused, looking for the right words. "Their names disappear from the maps around the mid-nineteenth century. Right before the Civil War." I didn't add that what I'd found indicated they'd lost the land to the state because they didn't pay their taxes.

"Yeah. Not for the same reasons, though. My great-great-great grandfather, Levi Bishop, he was injured. Thrown from his horse and broke his leg, never did heal proper. So he and his wife and five kids couldn't manage the farm. It wasn't producing worth shit anyhow, so he figured he didn't have that much to lose. Sold it to Abraham Dunstan, moved into the village, lived the rest of his life here. Made it to ninety-five. He's buried right here in the village cemetery, he and his wife and children, and their families as well. It's where I'll take up permanent residence once I kick the bucket."

"What happened to the others?"

There was such a long pause that I thought the old man wasn't going to answer. He stared down into the depths of his coffee cup for several minutes, forehead creased, as if he were trying to figure out a way to put my question aside. Finally he spoke, and the reluctance was obvious. "I could tell you some fancy story. Like as not, if you been asking around, you heard a few of 'em. Truth is, no one knows. The three families stayed out there. It's only fifteen miles from the village, y'know, but back then that was a half-day's ride to and from, so you didn't just go for no reason. What my grandpa said is they come into the village for a while, every so often, to buy supplies or sell what meager vegetables and meat the farm produced, but those visits got fewer and fewer. No one kept track o' when the last one was. One day one of 'em came to town, did their business, and left, and that was it, no one saw 'em again.

"You don't realize at the time, y'know? Any time you talk to someone could be the last time you'll ever see 'em, but no way to know that when it happens. People mighta asked, after six months went by, 'Hey, any of you seen Enoch Bishop or his kin? Or the Dunstans or Craigs?' But everyone woulda just shook their heads, said no, no one'd seen 'em. After a coupla years, they just forgot about 'em. They had their own families and their own concerns, y'know? Never mind that they were kin to some of the folks in the village—close kin, in the case of Levi Bishop and his brother—truth is, no one was much motivated to make a long ride in just to check in on 'em." He paused. "The village folk didn't like 'em much to start with, but it only got worse over time."

"What do you think happened to them?"

"I see where you're drivin'." The hostility was back. "You been listenin' to folk sayin' that their children's children's children are still there, and they're responsible for your brother's disappearance."

"Mr. Bishop, I've got no other leads to follow. There's been nothing else to go on. Not one of his belongings, nor his girlfriend's, was ever found. If they died, starved or injured or killed by animals, surely someone would have found some trace. I know people don't go in there much—" here the old man snorted "—but right after they vanished, the police combed those woods thoroughly, and found nothing."

"You got no cause to go stirring things up. Whaddya hope to find? Whatever you learn ain't gonna bring your brother and his woman back."

The tears sprang to my eyes. Unexpected. That hadn't happened in a long while. The blunt way he said it—that my brother was gone forever—was like a jab to a wound that hadn't healed, that might never heal. When I spoke, my voice was thick, and it must have come across although I tried to hide it. "Mr. Bishop, I just want you to ask yourself if you'd give up if it were your brother."

Silence again. Finally, he spoke, and I could see in his eyes that I had gotten to him as well. "No. No, I wouldn't."

"Then don't expect me just to say okay, they're dead, I'm moving on."

"It ain't that I haven't thought about it." Another harsh cough. "Whoever told you I was the one to talk to, they was right. Nobody knows more about the people west of town than I do. When I was young I was right obsessed with it, same as you are now, I expect, though for different reasons. Me, it was just curiosity. I went through old books, asked around—some of the old folks back then could just barely remember those who'd first come to those hills, not that they'd tell you much. There were a few families lived on the edge of the woods—still are— but they didn't want to talk, either."

"Why not?"

"My Grandpa Bishop was a Methodist. Upright, never drank or swore or lied or cheated, faithful to my grandma till his dying day. He said those families who'd stayed in the wood fell to sinful ways, and them on the edge knew about it and did nothing to stop it, or even helped 'em by going into the village and picking up food and supplies, so them inside didn't have to go in their own selves. He said them on the edge didn't even see 'em, just brought what they'd bought and left it right where the trees started, and next morning it'd be gone."

"Why'd they keep doing it, then? What did they get out of helping the ones in the forest?"

He took a deep breath, let it out slowly. "Afraid of reprisal, my grandpa said. They lived too close to the forest to take chances of angering them as dwelled within." The old man shook his head. "He told me I shouldn't pry into it, it wasn't fit knowledge for a young man to have, all it'd do is attract me like sin always does."

"What kinds of sin?"

His voice dropped to a near-whisper, so quiet I could barely understand it even when I leaned forward. "Idol worship. Callin' up Satan and his minions. Back then, they called that woods Devil's Glen, didja know that?"

"No."

"Not many do, nowadays. Most people don't want to talk about it at all. Didn't back then, either. But every generation has people who'll tell you what they know or think they know. Some of 'em it takes liquor, some of 'em money, some of 'em flattery. I used all three. What I found chilled me to the core, especially knowin' my kin was part of it. They had a stone temple, they said. It wasn't built by them, nor probably by the Indians who lived here before and worshiped them same devils. It's old, older than man himself. One old man I talked to whispered to me a name, said that the initiates called it Ulthoa."

A shudder twanged its way up my backbone. This was something I'd never heard before.

He continued, and his voice sounded tremulous. "But everyone said nothin' good came to them as inquired into it. I wouldn't listen. Headstrong young idiot, I was, and curious, curious like a dog pawing away at a rabbit's burrow. So I went into them woods."

Again, there was a long pause, and when he went on, his tough, wrinkled hands, still cradling his nearly-empty coffee cup, were visibly shaking.

"I never told nobody everything happened that night. And I'm not gonna tell it all to you now. Some things should be taken to the grave. I was alone in them woods—but I wasn't alone. I heard voices in the wind. It was dark enough I couldn't see my own hand in front of my face. Voices telling me to run, telling me to get out before it was too late. I could feel their breath on the back of my neck. I got up and run, believe that. I run like hell even though I couldn't see a damn thing. I stretched both arms out in front of me so I wouldn't slam face-first into a tree, but I got caught by branches, tearing at my clothes and skin like clutching claws. It was the first light of dawn when I got clear of them woods. Looking east, I could see light in the sky, and the shadows under the trees lay behind me. I was covered with bleeding scratches, my clothes tore like I'd fought off a wildcat. I turned around, but wasn't no one there."

"My god."

He reached forward and clutched my sleeve. "Your god and my

god ain't got nothin' to do with what's in those woods, boy. Believe it. I don't know if they're descendants of my kin and the Dunstans and Craigs who settled there two hundred years ago, or something else entirely, and I don't want to find out. I was nineteen when that happened. It took me three weeks to be able to sleep the night through, and soon as I could, I moved from my daddy's house to one on the other side of the village. His front windows faced west, y'see."

"And since then you've never…" I trailed off.

"I told you. I didn't want to know. I knew enough. I told some of what had happened to my mama and daddy—had to, when they saw the shape I was in—and a friend or two. I expect the story got passed around, which is how there're people still who know I can speak about Devil's Glen without tellin' fancy lies. I know one or two of the policemen who went in and searched when your brother went missing, and they felt it, too. Something watchful, waiting, something that would take anyone who went too deep or stayed too long."

"None of them saw anything."

"Not that I heard, no. Still, more'n one of 'em said they'd never go under those trees again, not if they were paid a million bucks, but wouldn't say why."

Frustration and grief clenched at my belly. "So you're saying I should give up."

"Not give up remembering. Not give up grieving. That'll never happen, you shouldn't expect it. But I gotta tell you, although I know it must be hard to hear. If your brother and his woman went into those woods, they're gone. Remember them and honor that memory in whatever way you see fit. But for the love o' God, don't follow in their footsteps. I only escaped because I was born with more than my fair share of dumb luck. They didn't, and I'm sorry for you and sorry for them. But you ain't gonna solve anything by prying into all this, just create more anguish for yourself. Whatever's in those woods took the two of them, took 'em right out of this world, and if you follow 'em under those trees, you'll be the next one to vanish."

III

The conversation with Alban Bishop had the effect of quelling my desire for investigating my brother's disappearance. Honesty demands that I explain why—having the first substantive lead to follow, you'd think I'd have been on it like a hound on a fox's trail.

The truth was, what Bishop said had scared the shit out of me. It was all very well to hypothesize about mysterious people out in the woods who might have abducted or killed Brad and Cara ten years ago, but it was another thing entirely to meet someone who had almost befallen the same fate. If the old man was telling the truth—and nothing he said rang false to me—he'd barely escaped with his life.

Stone temples. Families separated from their kin, forgotten under the trees. Idol worship. Voices on the wind giving warnings to run, run before it was too late.

Ulthoa.

The name had a sinister sound, like the sonorous clang of a bell. I had never heard it before nor run across it in anything I'd read, but it kept recurring in my brain, especially when I was home after dark. It resonated in my skull as I lay in bed trying to fall back to sleep, all the while listening for sounds in the night. Furtive footsteps, whispered voices, the sound of something approaching, eager to silence me, prevent me from getting any closer to the secrets of Devil's Glen.

On a whim, I drove up to the Guildford Library three days later, uncertain what I intended to accomplish. Maybe talk to Cyndy Evans or Melvia Shields about what the old man had told me. Maybe go back to my maps and old books.

But I saw neither woman in the cheerful, brightly-lit room. I asked the middle-aged volunteer behind the counter if Miss Shields was around, and got a puzzled look.

"Who?" she said.

"Oh, come on…" I started, ready to query how she could be a volunteer in a small library and not recognize the person who ran the place.

"Oh, Miss *Shields*," she said. "I misheard you."

I stared at her, waiting for her to respond.

Finally, she said, "I'm not sure. I think it's her day off."

At that, something in the woman's face seemed to close like a shutter, and I knew that was all I was going to get from her.

"Oh. Okay. No problem."

She looked relieved, but said nothing.

I turned away. After five minutes' aimless wandering around the stacks, during which the volunteer's eyes followed me continuously, I got back in my car and drove home.

Sinister. But everything was seeming sinister lately.

The story Alban Bishop told, though, was more than the sidelong hints I'd gotten from other people I'd talked to in Guildford. Far from galvanizing me, what he'd said frightened me into paralysis. I derided myself as a coward, quailing as soon as I got my first glimpse of what the danger actually was, but there was no denying the clench of terror I felt whenever I contemplated following my brother under those dark trees.

I sat in a little café in Colville, sipping my coffee, a newspaper spread out before me that I was paying little attention to. Alban Bishop had warned me about delving in too deep, that even now there were people who did not want others prying into Devil's Glen. *Them on the Edge*, who did the bidding of *Them Inside* to avoid retribution.

How cautious should I be? Was I really in any danger, here in bustling, modern Colville, or even in my little home village of Lamont? I now heartily regretted mentioning to Cyndy Evans where I lived. Had I told Melvia Shields as well? I couldn't recall. I knew I'd told Alban Bishop, and dimly remembered even telling him what road I lived on. But Cyndy was mysteriously gone from the library, after acquiescing to my request for help in researching the families that settled in the woods—and both Alban Bishop and Melvia Shields had very much given me the impression that they'd said all they were prepared to say.

I was afraid. No. What I felt was a bone-chilling terror like nothing I'd ever experienced. All around me the cheerful, everyday noises of the café went on unaffected. The bright sunshine filtered in through the windows. Men and women ordered pastries and cups of coffee before work. College students sat eating breakfast and peering at laptops or phones, seeming oblivious to the chatter and bustle around them..

I got up from the table, leaving half of my breakfast unconsumed. Once outside the café I pulled out my phone and called my boss, telling him I was sick and wouldn't be in to work that day. It wasn't so far from the truth. I felt shaken, nauseated, light-headed.

I was halfway to Lamont when I realized I might well have been safer at work than I was at home, out in my little secluded house on Flanders Mill Road. Too late to change course now.

After pulling into my driveway and shutting the engine off, I sat in my car for several minutes, looking at my house. Everything seemed quiet, just as I had left it only an hour and a half ago. I opened my door slowly, but all I heard were the familiar sounds of woodland birds and other animals, the breeze in the branches overhead, the distant noise of an airplane.

The day was still sunny and mild, which somehow made it worse.

A day like this made the existence of evil seem that much more horrific.

I walked toward the front door gingerly, almost tiptoeing, expecting it to swing open when I pushed my key into the lock.

I'd watched too many crime dramas. The lock was still secure.

Even so, I again locked my doors once inside the house, and checked each window to make sure they were securely latched. Finding my house undisturbed hadn't calmed me down. If anything, I felt more rattled than ever.

I put on a pot of coffee and sat down in my recliner. I glanced through the notes I'd hastily scrawled after my conversation with Alban Bishop, looking for anything in the way of concrete information, and finding nothing. He'd gone on at considerable length, but other than two-hundred-year-old family history and one scary visit to the woods in which nothing substantive happened, he'd told me very little in the way of concrete information.

I poured a cup of coffee, moved to the dinner table, and opened up my laptop. Tried searching their names. Lots of hits for Melvia Shields, all having to do with the library. Hardly anything for Alban Bishop, or at least nothing that seemed connected with the man I'd talked to. I tried searching their names along with my brother's name, with the name "Claver Road," with keywords like *disappearance* and *cult* and *murder*.

Nothing.

Then I put in *Ulthoa*. Immediately some connection to *Game of Thrones* and George R. R. Martin popped up, along with the question, "Do you mean *Ulthos?*" Apparently some place in Martin's fictional universe. So I clicked, "Search instead for *Ulthoa*"—and got no hits at all.

I swore under my breath and shut the laptop off. My head was splitting, and I pinched the bridge of my nose between my thumb and forefinger. My forehead felt hot, and coupled with the nausea and light-headedness I'd experienced earlier in the café, I wondered if I was getting sick. What I'd found out in talking to Alban Bishop seemed dreamlike and surreal, like something that had happened in a fever-dream. I got up, and dropped into my recliner with a grunt. I was absolutely exhausted. I'm not usually a napper, but I told myself that I'd shut my eyes for a few minutes, that it would help me focus, and maybe head off whatever strange illness I seemed to be coming down with.

Moments later I was sound asleep.

~

I was wakened by someone knocking on the door, jolted from a deep, dreamless sleep so suddenly that for a moment I couldn't figure out where I was. I stood, rubbing my eyes and wiping the drool from the corner of my mouth, and went to the door.

Tried to open it, forgetting I'd thrown the deadbolt.

Unlocked it and opened it, successfully this time, only then remembering that I probably shouldn't just open my door without finding out who was there.

I looked out, squinting and blinking in the sunshine, at a UPS delivery man. He held an obviously heavy package, his clipboard balanced on top.

"Will you sign for a package?" His expression was clear. *Adult man home and stoned in the middle of the day. Wonder what drugs he's taking.*

I tried unsuccessfully to speak and finally just nodded, took the clipboard and signed after the X, then unburdened him of the box.

"Thanks," I managed to say to his retreating figure.

No response.

Ray of freakin' sunshine, some of these guys.

I went back inside—closing and relocking the door—and dropped the package on the floor with a thud.

Still walking at a slow stumble, I got a knife out of the drawer to cut the strapping tape on the package. I moved with the same hesitant deliberation I used when I'd had too much to drink, with the drunk man's conviction that if he was careful enough, he wouldn't fall or run into something. The headache was better, but I still felt disoriented, almost disembodied. I successfully dropped into a kneeling position and cut the tape without slicing open my own hand, and only then thought to look at the return address.

It said *A. Bishop, 71 King Street, Guildford, New York.*

That was enough to shake me out of my post-nap grogginess. My heart was already pounding. I opened the lid. Inside were books—very old books, from the look of them and the musty smell—and on top of the stack was a sheet of paper with a message in a crabbed handwriting. There was no salutation, it jumped right in.

> *You'll have more use for these than I ever will, specially since I'm not long for the world. Ever since we talked I seen people following me, giving me the eye, and I suspect they want to silence my mouth before I can give away anything else they'd rather stayed a secret. I'm not afraid, I'm an old man and I'm tired and sick, couldn't'a counted on many more years anyhow. I guess they was fine with me knowing what I know as long as I didn't talk about it, but once I talked they figured I wasn't gonna stop. Doesn't matter if that's true or not, they're not gonna take the chance.*
>
> *It's all in here, what you want to know. Like I said, won't bring your brother back, but might give you some peace of mind.*
>
> *And be careful. Them that live in the woods aren't the only ones who are dangerous.*
>
> *A. H. Bishop*

I set the letter down. The hairs on the back of my neck were prickling, and my heart gave an uneven gallop.

The old man thought his life was at risk because of what he'd told me. But why? And from whom?

Them that live in the woods aren't the only ones who are dangerous.

Suddenly the diffuse, vague fears I'd felt in the café coalesced into something needle-sharp. I felt uniquely conspicuous, as if I had a target on my back. A marked man. Pursued by...whom? Any of those smiling faces in the café that morning could have been an enemy, waiting for me to look away. As soon as my head was turned, their smiles would become sly and knowing, and they would follow me, waiting for their chance to strike, playing me like a cat plays a mouse.

But which ones? Or was I letting my imagination run away with me?

No way to tell.

The top book was bound in brown leather that had once borne a gilded title, but age and wear made it illegible. I opened the cover. The front page had the title, written in an archaic typeset.

An Account of the Doings by People in the Hill Country, and the Prodigies that Followed.

The author was Zachariah Larkin. It was published in Colville in 1839.

I set it aside.

Cult Survival and Satan Worship Amongst the Indians. A Genealogical Account of the Bishop and Craig Families, Before and After the Darkness Came.

A slim tome, of seemingly newer vintage, was titled, *What Lives In The Forest?*

The oldest book was on the bottom. I hesitated even to open it, afraid the pages would crumble, but curiosity drove me to turn the cracked leather cover. Printed on the front page were words that made my heart slam against my ribcage.

In Which I Make a Descent into Ulthoa and Return Alive.

~

For the next six hours, I barely moved.

I sat crosslegged on the floor, leafing through the old books Alban Bishop had sent me, in mute astonishment at what had apparently been going on for a hundred years or more, less than an hour's drive from where I'd lived my whole life.

I only got up twice, first to grab a stack of scrap paper to copy passages I wanted to consider further, and once to take a quick pee. The grogginess and sick headache were fading gradually, but were replaced by a growing horror at what I was reading.

Doubtful minds will no doubt think me a fool at best or a liar at worst, but the doings in the wild hill country I shall here report are the unalloyed truth, as I have witnessed them with my own eyes and ears...Deep in the woods there are houses of the men who settled there twenty years ago, but deeper still is an edifice not built by human hands...A temple, like unto the holy places of Ancient Rome wherein their sacrifices were made, but here turned to a darker purpose still...The men and women still dwell within the forest, alive yet altered in subtle ways from their original forms, their souls corrupted by that which comes when summoned in that temple, sundered from and shunned by their kin who were wise enough not to entrust their families to the shadows underneath the trees...

The deepest part of those woods has been inhabited for time out of mind, and them who dwell there did not themselves know for certain how long. The place they call Ulthoa, and likewise none I spoke with knew wherefore it was so called nor whereof the name signified. It was used by the heathen Indians for their wicked practices, but the Indians were not its builders either...I spoke with half-breed men who descend from settlers who took Indians as wives, who now live on the edge of the forest and keep watch, and they trembled with fear when asked what rites were performed there, and what gods were summoned forth. "Do not speak such questions," one whispered, as if he were eager not to be overheard speaking of this, even to caution another not to inquire into it further. "My brother thought to spy on these people and that which they worship. The men saw him and gave chase, and my brother was forced to find refuge in a cave he had discovered, whereof the people of Ulthoa knew not, staying there three days. He came out a changed man, only speaking to any insofar as it took to tell us what had happened to him, and died not long afterward...Perhaps you will be brought face to face with those gods some day, but you should not hasten that moment, as others besides my brother have been brought before them and forthwith died." But what those gods might be, he would not elucidate, leaving my fearful imagination to run wild, as he no doubt intended...

Enoch Bishop and his wife Tabitha (who is sister to Malcolm Craig, about whose family q.v.) were the first to claim land in that trackless forest, to try to tame it and make it fruitful. There is a curse on that land, and never shall it be productive nor healthy, for there is a darkness lying there that sweeps over whosoever dwells upon it...Enoch Bishop fathered six children: Abel, Catherine, Mariah, Isaiah, Cora, and Ethan. Catherine died young of a fever, during the first year they lived there, before the shadows came and the curtain descended that evermore was to separate that unfortunate family from their kin. What became of the other five children, and the parents withal, no one knows, but it is rumored they still live there, albeit several decades have passed, and the children have grown to adulthood, taking unto themselves as husbands and wives the children of the other settlers in those woods, some of whom have been there far longer than the Bishops themselves have.

The worst was in *What Lives in the Forest?*, which—only a few days ago—I would have regarded as a fanciful tale to scare your friends with while sitting around the campfire.

Only a few have glimpsed it. Always at night, and always at a distance, but what they have seen made every one of them swear never to come within ten miles of those woods again. Transparent, but rippling like water, so that starlight and moonlight seen through it seems to blur and waver, shuddering as the thing moves. A man cannot tell where its edges are, to determine its shape and whether in form it is like a human or an animal. But from its movement there is no doubt; its size is that of an elephant or larger, and when its feet strike the ground the stones tremble, and its passage knocks askew trees as a man striding through a field brushes aside the stalks of weeds that stand in his way.

The most frightening of all was a single passage, near the end of that book.

If, even after reading this, you decide to go into those woods looking for those who dwell there and the evil they serve, do not ask yourself how you will find them in those trackless acres of forest. Depend upon it: they will find you. And afterward, you will wish you had fettered your curiosity and remained in safe and secure ignorance.

I only stopped reading when the light had dimmed to the point I could barely see the words on the page. I closed the book, set it atop the others, then stood and stretched, my back cracking and sore muscles loosening. The sickness I'd felt earlier was gone, but that meant the anxiety over what I had just read amplified in equal measure.

What would they do, the mysterious *they* Alban Bishop warned me about, when it became clear I was still on the trail? Try to kill me, as the old man himself had suggested? Poison, perhaps, or something more violent? I pictured myself, bleeding from knife wounds, crumpled on the floor. How long would it take before someone would find me?

Days, perhaps. I had no lover, no close friends. My boss would certainly be pissed off if I didn't show up for work and didn't call in, but it'd be a good long while before he'd be concerned enough to come to my house and see what was going on, or call the police and report me as missing. By that time, I'd be long dead, my pooled blood coagulating on the carpet...

"Stop it," I said aloud, and walked into the kitchen to find something to eat. Despite my fears, I was ravenously hungry.

As I was fixing dinner, I decided one thing—I would be a great deal more careful than I had been. May as well not give them any more reason to want my mouth silenced permanently.

IV

That evening, my fears coupled with the horrific passages I'd read in Alban Bishop's books drove me into a state of deep melancholy.

I've had bouts of depression my entire adult life, usually brought on by a sense of life being out of joint. I've always felt like the puzzle piece that didn't fit, the one who was vaguely different, the one who was on the periphery of everything. Other than a couple of relationships in high school—which, I'll be honest, were more about the sex than about having any kind of deep connection—I've only been romantically involved once, an ill-fated marriage when I was twenty-two that only lasted a year and a half.

Even then there was something missing from me, and I wasn't the only one who was aware of it. When Anna left, taking along our infant son Dan, she vanished while I was at work and left only a note saying that she couldn't spend her life with a man who didn't know who he was or where he was going. In the days afterward I more than once thought of calling her, pleading with her to come back, but very quickly it became apparent that she was right.

I was only intermittently a part of Dan's life as he was growing up, and it wasn't until he reached high school that he began to show signs of wanting a deeper relationship with me. He is, in many ways, my polar opposite. He's warm-hearted where I'm cool and reserved, quick-witted and energetic where I am cautious and hesitant. He took after his mother in looks, lean, athletic, with wavy deep brown hair and dark eyes. Standing next to me, his Mediterranean handsomeness cast against my blue eyes, sallow complexion, and hair that had once been light brown but now had gone prematurely gray, no one would have guessed we are father and son.

I looked around me, at the shadows that approaching night were drawing in my little house, wondering how I'd reached the age of forty-five still alone. Everything I'd done, up to and including this quest to find out what happened to my brother, was alienating me further, separating me from the brightly-lit world going on around me.

I sat in my recliner and flipped through the passages I'd copied from Alban's books. Did so a second time, and was no closer to understanding it all. Some of what I'd read had to be wild tales and exaggerations—I wasn't credulous enough to accept it all out of hand. Surely, though, some of it had to be the truth.

But which parts were which? And even assuming I could figure that out, how did it help me?

I gave a snort and tossed my notebook aside, pulled my phone out of my pocket, and before I could talk myself out of it, dialed my son's number.

I'm not sure why I thought to do that, other than my dark mood bringing up memories of my failed marriage and hapless attempts at parenting. But he answered after three rings.

"Hello?"

"Dan? It's Dad."

"Hi." The puzzlement in his voice was clear. "What's up?"

"I needed to talk to someone with some perspective."

"About what?" A pause, and in a wry tone, "This is about Uncle Brad, isn't it?"

"Yes."

"Dad," he said, then just finished up with a sigh.

"It's been on my mind lately."

"Lately?" Dan had made it abundantly clear more than once that he considered my obsession with my brother's disappearance a fool's errand, and that one word said volumes. "Ever since Grandma and Grandpa died, you haven't thought about anything else."

"I know. But I found something. Some new information. I wanted to discuss it with someone more objective than I am."

"That would be pretty much everybody."

The comment stung, but he wasn't wrong. "I know."

"Why me?"

"A few reasons. I trust you. You're smart, and not prone to jumping to conclusions or letting your emotions rule your brain. You know the background of the story, so you understand the context."

"Okay." Now he sounded resigned, the tone you hear in a person who knows he's in for a long, convoluted, and not very interesting story. I was quite sure he was rolling his eyes as he added, "Go ahead, what did you find out?"

I launched into an account of my conversations with Melvia Shields and Alban Bishop, and told him—in as abbreviated form as I could manage—about the frighteningly suggestive accounts I'd read in the old man's books.

To his credit, he listened patiently and without interrupting.

"So," I said, when I was done. "What do you think? Am I crazy in thinking all this is significant?"

"Well…" He drew the word out. "I don't know."

"At least you didn't say 'yes' out of hand."

"I have to admit it's a bizarre story. If I'm understanding you correctly, what you're telling me is you think Uncle Brad and his girlfriend were abducted by demon-worshiping descendants of some folks who lived in those woods two hundred years ago."

Putting it that way, I have to admit, made it sound really stupid. But essentially yes, that was what I was saying. "I guess."

I half expected he'd laugh derisively and hang up, but he didn't.

After a moment he said, in a tentative voice, "Have you considered...the practical aspects of that claim?"

"Such as?"

"Okay, let's say that these three families—the Bishops, and I forget the names of the other two you mentioned..."

"Dunstan and Craig."

"That sounds like a law firm. Anyhow, yeah. So those three families have now lived there, only fifteen miles from roads and buildings and homes and civilization, and nobody's ever seen them? How do they get food and other supplies? No way could they produce enough to live on, even assuming they somehow were able to farm there in the middle of the woods without anyone noticing. And also..." He paused. "There's only three families, you know? If their descendants still live there, and have had no contact with the outer world for all that time, wouldn't they be a little...inbred by now?"

"That happens in other places."

"I suppose. But anyway, the more salient point is the food. How haven't they been either driven out of the woods by hunger, or long ago starved to death?"

"Alban Bishop told me the people who live on the edge of the woods provide them with what they need."

The wry tone was back immediately. "Dad, I hate to put it this way...but this sounds like a crazy story told by someone who has read too much H. P. Lovecraft."

I felt needled by his scorn. He had a way of doing that to me. "Look, even if you don't believe any of the rest of it, come back to the facts. Brad and Cara disappeared. Police combed the woods and couldn't find a trace of them."

"But that's more evidence that there aren't any evil throwbacks, don't you think? If there was all the stuff you told me about—the temple, the cabins, the devil-worshiping people—why didn't the police find them?" He paused. "And it's always a possibility that they're dead. Maybe you're right that some kind of psycho was in the woods. But if so, it's more likely that he killed them and buried them somewhere in there, than that they're somehow...still in the woods, being held hostage or something."

"I don't know." My headache was coming back, and I scowled, rubbing my forehead. "So you think there's nothing to all of this, then."

"Not nothing." He sighed. "Look, Dad, I know how close you and Uncle Brad were. I know you want answers. But the problem is, there's no evidence—of *anything*. No damage to his car, no trace of his camping gear, nothing. I've been back-country camping since I was a teenager, and it just isn't that easy to leave no traces even when that's your aim. Everything you do leaves a mark. I don't see how Uncle Brad and his girlfriend can have just...evaporated."

"But that's exactly what happened. If like you said, some psycho murdered them both, the police would have found the graves. That's the kind of thing they were *looking* for." I tried to quell my rising frustration. We were talking in circles.

As usual. I wondered why I bothered to call him in the first place.

"So there has to be another explanation."

"What?"

"It could be a lot of things. Maybe they wanted to take off and start over somewhere else. Uncle Brad's girlfriend probably had a car. So she follows him out, they leave Uncle Brad's car out there, take off in hers. Change their names, live under new identities. Did anyone even look into that?"

The suggestion had come up in the days following Brad and Cara's disappearance, but since it wasn't illegal to take off for parts unknown and change your name, the police had no particular interest in trying to find out if there was anything to it. "No, I don't think anyone looked into that."

"There you go, then. C'mon, Dad, you have to admit that's more likely than all of this creepy horror movie stuff."

"I guess."

Another long pause. "You're going to keep trying to find out more, aren't you?"

"Probably."

"It's a waste of time."

I'd heard that before, and not just from him. "Look, I'll accept you might be right. But you have to admit, there could be something to all of this."

"Well, there's one way to find out."

"What way?"

"Go into the woods and see for yourself."

The words were like a breath of chilly air on the back of my neck. I shuddered. "I've actually thought of doing that."

"Didn't you tell me the old man said you'd disappear if you tried it?"

"Yes. But I don't know of anything else I can do."

"Then do it. But not alone." I heard a touch of sympathy in his voice. "Dad, I know this means a lot to you, and I know I've been pretty dismissive. I'll meet you halfway, okay? I'll go with you. Maybe we should do what Uncle Brad did. Walk into those woods and see what's there."

"I wouldn't want to put you at risk."

"Oh, for fuck's sake, I've done more dangerous back-country hiking than this. If someone dropped you in the dead center of that forest, you could walk in a straight line and a few hours at most you're back in the outside world. I've spent weeks by myself up in the Rockies and Cascades, fifty miles from the nearest road. I know what I'm doing." He laughed. "Don't worry, Dad, I'll protect you."

"You'd do that?"

"Sure. I could take a few days off from work. The lab'll survive without me for a while, and I'm overdue for a vacation. Give me a week to get things sorted, and we'll do it. Probably now's a good time, once it's fall the weather gets dicier. But, Dad..."

He trailed off.

"What?"

"If we don't find anything—and I'll be honest, I think that's the likeliest outcome—promise me you'll let this go. You haven't been yourself since Grandma and Grandpa died. It's like they took a piece of you with them, reopened the wound so you can't think about anything else. You need to get on with your life. It's not..." He stopped, cleared his throat. "Life's not just going to stop and wait for you, you know. Don't throw it away."

"Okay. I'll try."

"Do more than try."

"All right, you win."

"Not exactly an airtight promise, Dad." He gave a relieved laugh. "But I guess that's the best I could hope for. I'll give you a yell when I've got things arranged. See what you can dredge up in the way of camping gear, and drop me an email to let me know what you found. I'll take care of the rest."

"Okay. And Dan?"

"Yeah?"

"Thanks."

"No problem." There was only the slightest hesitation as he added, "Love you, Dad."

"Love you, too."

I ended the call, then sat for a while in the shadowed room, staring at nothing.

It was clear Dan's acquiescence—no, his suggesting—to accompany me on a hike into the woods at the end of Claver Road was as much to get me to give up my search as it was to find out if there was anything there. But it was a concession, far more than the half-listening he'd done when I mentioned my quest to him before.

Now, to steel myself for the inevitable call from his mother, storming at me for involving "her son" in a fool's errand.

~

The expected call from Anna didn't come. Either Dan had decided not to tell her, or she'd figured it wasn't worth the fight.

But in the days that followed, I found myself fidgeting and unable to settle. I didn't take any more time off from work, but when I was there I was constantly distracted, checking my phone over and over for any messages from Dan. It was my restlessness that prompted me to get back in touch with Alban Bishop. I needed to talk to someone, and anyone else would scoff at what I'd found. The old man was at least someone I wouldn't have to talk into believing my story.

I went by the coffee shop on Main Street in Guildford the morning after my conversation with Dan, but Alban Bishop wasn't there. The barista shrugged in a disinterested fashion when I asked him where the old man might be.

"I dunno." He gestured toward the corner of the café with one heavily-tattooed arm. "He always sits over there. I haven't seen him for a day or two, though."

First Cyndy Evans, now Alban Bishop, missing without explanation. Even Melvia Shields I hadn't seen since I'd talked to her, although to be fair I'd only been in the library a couple of times.

But the third morning I went in, Bishop was there in his accustomed place, cradling his cup of coffee in gnarled hands. He looked up at me, and the instant recognition showed in his face.

It was not a happy look.

I got my own coffee and a cream cheese danish, and sat down across from him without asking for permission.

"You're back," he said in a flat tone of voice.

"I got the books you sent."

He glared at me. "Best not to talk about them. Leastways, not when anyone can hear."

I swiveled my head to the right, then the left. "No one seems to be paying any attention."

"Sure." The words, *Believe what you want to believe, you fool,* were as clear as if he'd spoken them aloud.

"What I read scared the hell out of me."

"Good." He took a sip from his mug. "But I can tell by the look on your face, you're not ready to give it up."

"No." I took a bite of danish, and without meeting his watery blue eyes, I said, "My son and I are going to go into the woods."

"Didn't you understand a thing I told you? Or a thing you read?"

"Yes. But don't you see? If all that's true, I might finally have some answers."

"You're not gonna like the answer if you find it." He snorted. "What idiotic notion was it that made you involve your son?"

"I just wanted his advice. He's a smart guy. He's a geologist, a trained scientist, and wouldn't hesitate to tell me I'm being ridiculous." I didn't add that he'd basically told me just that. "Call it a reality check. But the idea to go into the forest was his idea, not mine."

"Stupidity must run in your family."

I considered a snarky response, but held it back. "Curiosity, not stupidity."

"That can sometimes be the same thing."

I began to question why I'd bothered trying to talk to him again. "Look, were you serious when you said you were in danger of your life?"

"Why would I have told you so if I wasn't serious?"

"I don't know."

"Me either."

"But from whom?"

He lowered his voice. "Like I told you. The ones in the woods aren't as much of a danger as the ones who do their bidding."

"*Them on the Edge*, you mean."

His eyes widened in alarm. "You really don't give a continental damn whose life you put at risk, do you?"

"I just want to understand what's going on here."

He looked down into his coffee cup for a long while, and I thought for a moment he wasn't going to answer. But finally he said, "Leave me in peace. I figure I'm already done for, but I don't want to bring it on myself any sooner than I have to, and the more I'm seen with you, the more likely it is."

I finished my danish, then stood. "Okay. But I hope you're wrong."

"So do I. But I'm not wrong." His eyes met mine in a gaze of startling intensity. "I'll be waiting to see you and your son's names in the newspaper. If you don't see mine first."

~

Two days later, I was reading the *Colville Times* in the grocery store deli on my lunch break, and saw the following.

Alban Hazen Bishop

Alban H. Bishop, 82, of Guildford, was taken into the arms of His Lord and Savior early in the morning hours at Colville General Hospital on Sunday, August 11, after being suddenly taken ill in his residence. He was one of the oldest residents of the village, and a fixture at Gray's Café, where he could often be found playing checkers or swapping stories with his many friends and acquaintances.

Alban was born in Guildford on February 2, 1942, and other than a four-year stint in the Army during which he served our country in an overseas assignment in Germany, he spent his entire life in the village. He was known as a fund of lore and village history, and was never shy about sharing his knowledge with anyone who would lend an ear.

Alban was the son of Oris and Selena (Whately) Bishop, the youngest and last surviving of seven children. His wife, the late Audrey (Marsh) Bishop, passed away ten years ago. The marriage was not blessed with children, but he was the proud uncle to many nieces and grand-nieces, nephews and grand-nephews.

A funeral service will be held Saturday morning at 10:00 a.m. in the Guildford Methodist Church, and will be followed by burial in the Vanderzee-Upshaw Cemetery on Caldwell Road.

I stared at it, my heart hammering against my ribs. Reread it, trying not to let the horror show in my face. I had just begun to get control of my breathing when I looked down at the next obituary.

Melvia Lee Shields

Miss Melvia Lee Shields, 68, of Guildford, passed away unexpectedly on Monday, August 12, at her residence. Miss Shields was the long-time head librarian for the Guildford Public Library, and retired last year after 32 years of service. She was still a familiar face, though, serving on the Library Executive Board, and also filling in when other staff members were ill or on vacation.

Miss Shields was the daughter of the late Henry and Elisa (Keating) Shields, of Rochester. She was predeceased by a brother, Andrew Shields of Baltimore, Maryland, and a sister, Verna Lindley of Binghamton. She leaves behind to mourn her passing a brother, Darius Shields of Chicago, seven nieces and nephews, and a great many friends. She will be missed by all who knew her.

A memorial service is planned, the date and location for which will be announced.

I stared at the newspaper, my hands shaking, for several minutes, reading the words over and over.

Dead. Both of them, within twenty-four hours of each other, and less than a week after they'd given me information about the legends surrounding Devil's Glen.

Alban Bishop was right. How long would it take before I was the next one in an obituary?

It was hard to set aside the feeling that I'd directly caused the death of Alban Bishop and Melvia Shields.

That they were not natural deaths, I had no doubt whatsoever. Both of them, in their own way, had tried to warn me. Bishop as much as said outright that he was being targeted because of his association with me. And I went ahead and talked to him again anyway.

In public, no less.

And Melvia Shields? I had only spoken to her once, in a mostly-empty library, and even that passing contact had turned her into a victim.

Now, I was drawing my only son into this knotted web of fear, letting him accompany me into the forest instead of saying, *No way in hell do I want you anywhere near that place.*

Dan was right. I was obsessed, and two people had now died because of my obsession.

I didn't mind risking my own life. I don't have that much to live for, and I don't mean it with any self-pity. I live alone, not even a pet to keep me company, in a rented house five miles from where I grew up. I've accomplished very little other than having a steady job for twenty years. Otherwise, I've been in stasis, as if I'm waiting for something or someone to shake me up and show me it's all worth it.

So the idea I might die trying to find out what happened to Brad and Cara didn't bother me. At least it would mean I ended my life working to accomplish something worthwhile, something more than job, eat, sleep, repeat.

Putting my only son at risk, though, was a different matter. Which is why I sent him a brief email, telling him about my second conversation with Alban Bishop and his and the librarian's deaths two days later, and that apparently the danger had not just been the old man's imaginings. *You can find their obituaries in the* Times, *if you're in doubt that I'm telling you the truth,* I wrote. I ended with, *I really think you shouldn't get involved with this, and I'm sorry I asked you to be.*

No response. I figured he was at work, but when dinnertime came and went and he hadn't answered, I thought he might have decided to take my advice about staying well out of it, and the easiest way to accomplish that was not having anything more to do with me.

This was why I was more than a little surprised when he drove up that evening. The scrunch of the tires on gravel brought me to the window, suddenly afraid of who it might be, but I recognized Dan's boxy, rust-colored Honda Element. I watched him in the fading light of evening as he eased his long, lean frame out of his car—carrying a cardboard box.

When he saw my expression upon opening the door, he said, "Thought you'd scared me off, didn't you?"

"I was kind of hoping I had. When I saw those two obituaries, I regretted calling you."

Dan shrugged. "I dunno, Dad. I looked at the obituaries myself, and I have to say they kind of freaked me out." He paused and gave me a crooked smile. "You didn't kill the old man and the librarian yourself, just to make a point?"

"I wouldn't do that..." I started, sputtering a little.

"Kidding, Dad. I'm kidding." He patted the air. "Relax. But I'll admit I'm curious, and a little afraid for you. Whatever's going on in those woods, I think there's a decent chance you—and Bishop—are right that there are people who don't want you to find out. That's why I brought this." He opened the top of the cardboard box, and pulled out a fancy-looking trail cam. "Motion-activated. I picked it up, intending to put it out on Riley Frederick's land to scope out the area for deer hunting, then never got around to it. I'll help you put this underneath the eaves of your house, kind of hidden, but pointing at the front steps. It'll also pan across the end of the driveway, so you'll be able to see if anyone crosses to go around the back of the house or tries to break in through one of the front windows."

"You're honestly worried about me, aren't you?"

"Yeah, I am, kind of." He looked vaguely embarrassed. "I just hope that hooking up a security camera isn't a case of Chekhov's Gun, though."

The puzzlement must have showed in my eyes. "He's the Russian guy from *Star Trek*, right?"

Dan smiled, but not unkindly. "Different Chekhov. Anton Chekhov, the playwright. He said that if a gun appears in a story, sooner or later it's going to go off."

"So if we put up the trail cam, sooner or later it's going to catch someone trying to kill me."

"Exactly."

"Sounds like you're not a doubter anymore."

He shrugged again. "Look, Dad, I don't know what's going on here any more than you do. But to believe Bishop and Shields both died of natural causes, a couple of days after the old man himself told you he was going to be killed because of talking to you, is too big a coincidence for me to swallow."

"Me too."

"It's possible. I'm hoping it *was* a coincidence. But I'm not going to wait until you get killed to decide to err on the side of caution. I'll help you set up this trail cam, and at least I'll sleep a little better knowing if someone comes skulking around, we'll have a shot at figuring out who it is." He gave me an even more sheepish look. "And

Dad...I brought an overnight bag. If you want—if you're okay with it—I'd feel more comfortable if I could stay overnight, at least for a couple of days until we can make some progress in figuring this all out."

"My bodyguard?"

To my surprise, he didn't laugh. "Something like that."

I acquiesced without putting up much of a fight. Truth be told, I was glad to have him there. Sleeping out in my secluded cottage, with the nearest house a quarter of a mile away, was becoming increasingly difficult, and the previous few evenings I'd found myself startling awake at the slightest nocturnal noise.

So he retrieved his bag from the car. I noticed he locked the car behind him, something I'd only rarely seen him do before. I guess he really was spooked by the whole thing. We spent the next hour installing the trail cam underneath the eaves of the house as he'd suggested, at the end dispelling the evening shadows using the beam from a high-wattage utility light on a long extension cord, hanging by its hook from the gutters.

Then we went back in the house. Locked those doors, too. Only then did Dan seem to relax, and we cracked open a couple of beers and deliberately steered the conversation away from Brad's disappearance and the deaths of Alban Bishop and Melvia Shields for the rest of the evening.

~

Chekhov's Gun didn't go off for three days.

Dan arranged with his boss that he was taking a week's vacation, and told me that on Saturday—at that point four days away—we were going to take a hike into Devil's Glen.

Having made the decision, and set a date, was almost a relief. It was like finding out the day and time you're going to have major surgery. It becomes more real, but at the same time, it's now a fixed point, and you can imagine what life will be like after it's accomplished. Or maybe it's just that this felt like a way to give a face to the fear. If you don't even know exactly what you're afraid of, your imagination has license to make it as terrifying as it wants. Our upcoming hike occupied all of my waking thoughts, and I had honestly forgotten the trail cam—and the direct threat it was meant to protect us against—until Thursday, at one in the morning, when I was awakened by a shout from the living room of, "Hey, what the *fuck* are you doing?"

I jumped out of bed and ran into the room. Dan had bedded down on the sofa, and now he was standing at the window, clad only in a pair of pajama pants, staring eye to eye with a gaunt, panicked-looking face that vanished into the darkness only seconds after I saw it. With another shout, Dan flung the front door open and took off in pursuit.

I followed as best I could, the sticks and driveway gravel painful under my bare soles. Ahead I could hear the sound of two pairs of running feet, then a cry and a thud. Despite the discomfort I ran as well, and in the vague, bleached light of a half-moon I saw Dan had tackled a tall, skinny man who was writhing like a snake in his attempt to get away. Dan had been a wrestler and a state qualifier in track in high school, so it was no wonder he'd been able to catch up with and tackle the man.

But he evidently had not factored in desperation. The scarecrow-like figure twisted around and flailed out with one bony fist, catching Dan just below his left eye. His grip loosened just enough for the man to wrench himself free. He bounced to his feet and took off at a sprint.

Dan got up to give pursuit, but only a few moments later we heard a car engine start, and the sound of wheels peeling out in gravel.

"Are you okay?"

He had turned and was loping back down the driveway, rubbing his cheekbone. "Yeah. Might have a good bruise tomorrow, but I'm fine. That fucker was stronger than he looked." We returned to the house, and Dan showed me the marks of a chisel where the man had tried to pry up the window.

"Jesus," I said under my breath.

"Let's see whether we can get a good look at our intruder." He went over to the garden shed, where we'd put away the stepladder earlier that evening, and climbed up to remove the trail cam from its housing.

"I didn't think we'd need it that quickly."

He opened the door for me. "I was hoping we wouldn't need it at all. But I won't be able to get any more sleep until we see what we got. Do you have a spare USB cable? If not, I have one in the car."

"I've got one."

After a few moments, we had my computer booted up and the trail cam hooked up. It had taken six still shots. The first two showed very little but darkness and blur—the camera's shutter must have been tripped by something innocuous like a leaf blowing on the wind or a bug flying by.

The other four, though, were of the intruder.

The images were in the ghostly grayscale of the infrared flash, looking like a photographic negative. It showed a rail-thin, raggedly-dressed man with unevenly-cut hair and a furtive expression. His wide eyes held a combination of desperation and fright. They showed him stepping up to the window, then worrying at the frame with a tool of some kind. In the final one his body had pulled back. The camera had evidently caught the moment Dan yelled at him. His face showed the raw fear of a cornered animal, and his frame seemed coiled like a spring, ready to bolt.

In the middle two images, his features were clear. Long, beaky nose, a weak chin, a prominent Adam's apple. Easily recognizable should I decide to take the matter to the police—or if I saw him again.

I had no doubt this man wasn't just a chance burglar. He'd targeted me specifically, probably just as he or someone he knew had targeted Mr. Bishop and Miss Shields, with more success.

The most chilling thing of all was that I had never seen this man in my life.

"Now what?"

The frustration and fear must have sounded in my voice, because when Dan spoke, it was in a determined, take-no-shit voice. "Now we figure out who this asshole is."

"How?"

"Didn't you tell me Bishop said there were people still living on the edge of the woods who were in cahoots with the ones that lived in the woods itself?"

"Yes. *Them on the Edge* and *Them Inside.*"

"So we go knocking on some doors."

~

The next day we drove to Guildford, taking Highway 226 out of the village into the hilly farmland in the western part of the county.

Then took a right onto Claver Road.

I'd only been out there a couple of times in the ten years since Brad and Cara disappeared. Both times I had come with the intent to see the spot where my brother's car had been found abandoned, half intending to go into the woods myself, and both times I'd gotten spooked as the road dwindled and the scrubby underbrush closed in on both sides. I'd found a place to turn around before the shoulders narrowed to nothing and headed back home, feeling shamed at my own cowardice.

Now, I told myself, we were after something different. We'd be heading to the end of the road soon enough. Today, we were going to find out about *Them on the Edge*—and see if we could find the man who had tried to break into my house the previous evening.

The last turnoff before Claver Road headed off to the vanishing point under the trees was Cain Creek Road, which according to county maps we'd perused before leaving, ran alongside the south edge of the green patch representing the "public land"—meaning Devil's Glen, but of course it wasn't marked as such—finally bending northward and connecting to Highway 18, which led away from the haunted trees and toward the bustling communities of Geneva and Canandaigua. But between Claver Road and the intersection with Highway 18, Cain Creek Road hugged the perimeter of the woods. I could think of no likelier place to find *Them on the Edge*.

The widely-spaced houses along that lonely stretch were all on the left side, away from the woods, and all were in varying states of dilapidation. A few had small, tilled fields behind them, with stands of sickly-looking cornstalks and anemic rows of beans, or weed-infested patches of vegetable garden hewn from the rocky soil. Very few had any concessions to aesthetics. One or two had pots of rangy, wilted flowers by the doorstep, and we saw one that had a set of rusted wind chimes hanging from a hook under the eaves, but other than that, it was all gray siding with flaked paint, cracked and grimy windows, overgrown gravel driveways, and bent and probably non-functional gutters.

"Hard to believe we're less than fifteen miles from Guildford," I said to Dan in a near whisper. There was something about that place that made you not want to speak loudly, hope your presence would go unnoticed, that you could pass by these dismal dwellings and return to the bright modern world without being seen.

"This kind of poverty is pretty common in upstate New York." Dan was driving, his posture relaxed, one hand on the wheel and the other elbow propped on the open window frame, but when he spoke his voice was solemn. "This county has an amazing number of people who don't have electricity and running water. You don't hear the blue-haired ladies of the Guildford Village Beautification Society talking about it, though, much less trying to do anything about it. If it's outside of their pristine little village, it doesn't concern them."

"I wonder if they even know it exists."

"Maybe not. But sometimes ignorance is willful. If you're ignorant of something, it absolves you of any responsibility for fixing it."

"I don't know what you *could* do to fix this."

He evidently had no ready answer to that, and we drove in silence for a few more minutes.

"Where do we start?" I gestured at a ramshackle cottage that looked at least marginally cleaner than some of the others we'd seen. "There's a light on inside that one. Someone's probably home."

Dan shrugged. "May as well start there, then." He pulled into the short driveway and braked to a halt. "Don't think it matters."

When he turned off the engine, the silence surged back over us like an ocean wave. This wasn't the quiet of a countryside summer, this was a near-complete absence of sound. In the far distance, I could hear the roar of a jet, just at the threshold of audibility, but nearer by there was nothing. No crickets, no birds, no automobile traffic, no human voices, only the occasional soft sigh of the breeze rustling the weedy fields.

The closing of the car doors sounded explosively loud, and it was no surprise when I saw a hand twitch aside the curtains of the window nearest the door. My heart was pounding, but I worked my face into a passable semblance of calm, went down the cracked concrete sidewalk and up the two steps to the front door, and knocked.

Almost instantly, the door opened a few inches. Inside I saw the suspicious face of a woman of about sixty. She was round-faced and heavy-set, her bulky frame clothed in a shapeless sack of a dress as dingy and drab as everything else about this place. Her thinning gray hair was tied into an untidy bun at the back of her neck, and she was barefoot. There was one incongruous thing about her—around her neck was a thin, shining silver chain, hanging from which was a small, flat piece of carved gray stone that she was fingering nervously. The surface of the stone was engraved with a series of thin lines in a spiral pattern, and had a hole in the middle.

But that exotic touch was all there was. Everything else about her and her home was old, worn, unadorned, the color of dust. Past her, a light fixture with a single glowing light bulb illuminated a living room with a shabby chair and a few other disreputable-looking pieces of furniture. The floor looked like it was unfinished wood planks, and hadn't been swept in years.

"Hi, I'm wondering if we could ask you a few questions." I tried to feign relaxation and good cheer.

"What do you want?" Her voice was heavy with suspicion.

"We're trying to find someone we think lives around here, Mrs....?"

"Mason."

"...Mrs. Mason," I finished. "It won't take much of your time."

51

"Who is it you're lookin' for?"

"Well, we don't know his name. But we have a photograph." I reached into my pocket and pulled out a printout of the trail cam photograph, unfolded it, and handed it to Mrs. Mason.

She squinted nearsightedly at it for a moment, then handed it back to me, her eyes narrowing into a glare. "Why'd'ya want to find him?"

"We just have a few questions for him."

"Huh." I could tell she didn't believe me. And, after all, the grayscale photo was clearly taken with a security camera of some sort, and it must have looked likely to her that whatever we wanted him for, it wasn't going to be something he was happy about.

Of course, from her manner, she probably was suspicious of everybody and everything.

"Do you recognize him?"

"Naw."

"Are you sure?"

She squinted up at me, and her nervous caressing of the stone pendant intensified. "I said naw, and I mean naw. I got no idea who he is."

I had no doubt the woman was lying. It didn't take an expert. If he was a stranger to her, wouldn't her first statement have been *I don't know him*, not *why do you want to find him?*

"Do you know who else we might ask?"

She shrugged her thick shoulders. "Ask anyone you like. How'd I know who knows him and who don't?"

"But don't you…" I began, but she shut the door in my face.

After a moment, I turned back down the sidewalk. I gave my son a frustrated shrug.

"Charming lady," Dan said as we climbed back into his car.

"She was lying, of course."

"That didn't take a polygraph machine." He started the engine. "At least that tells us we're in the right neighborhood."

I glanced back at the house, and Mrs. Mason was once again standing at the window, her body backlit by the single light bulb, glaring out at us with eyes filled with mistrust and wariness.

"Where next?" Dan asked.

"Pick a house, any house. Start with the one that looks least like we'll be greeted with a gun barrel."

"They all do."

"True. But like you said, if she recognized that guy, he must live nearby. Someone's gotta know who he is."

"The question is whether anyone will admit it."

A quarter of a mile further along—only two more houses' distance—we happened upon a slightly better-kept house with a front yard that had seen a mower at least once that year. A girl of about ten, wearing a dirty calico dress with a design of pink flowers, was sitting in a patch cleared of grass, and was building a tower out of wooden blocks.

We pulled over, but she didn't look up until Dan called from the window.

"Can I ask you a question?"

Her head jerked toward us with the swiftness of a wary animal scenting a predator. Her eyes held caution that bordered on fear, and it was clear if we made any sudden movements, she'd run. This was beyond the usual don't-talk-to-strange-men rule most children are rightly taught. This was an almost feral attitude of distrust, directed toward everything and everyone. The similarity to Mrs. Mason's expression was striking.

She didn't answer Dan's question, just continued to stare, her face still and unsmiling.

He gave her a smile intended to be reassuring. "I'm not going to hurt you. Look, I'm not even going to get out of the car. I'm trying to find a guy who I think lives around here, and I've got his picture." I handed him the photo printout, and he held it up for her to see.

She still hadn't risen, but from her position, perhaps twelve feet away, she could probably see it clearly enough.

"Do you know who he is?"

"Lem," she said in a clear voice. "That's Lem Stutes."

"Where does Lem Stutes live?"

Her head twitched to the left, but her eyes stayed fixed on us as if she were afraid to look away. "Down the road a piece."

"Do you know which is his house?"

"Course I know."

"Then which one?"

"'s got a big tree in front with a tire swing. And you'll see his car in the driveway. Old brown car with a cracked windshield."

"Ginny!" A woman's panicked voice called from the front door, now open a crack. "Who you talkin' to?"

"Man in a car wants to know where Lem Stutes lives," the girl called back, and still she didn't turn her head, but continued to stare at us.

The door flung open, and the woman—tall, thin, of indeterminate middle age, with a shock of bright red hair—came flying down the sidewalk, and her eyes held undisguised terror. She grabbed Ginny by her hand and yanked her to her feet. One of the girl's feet swung around, and her heel kicked down her block tower with a rattling crash. As the woman dragged Ginny back toward the house, I heard, "Don't you be talkin' to strangers, where's your head, girl? Ain't safe and you know it."

The front door slammed behind them, and the unnatural quiet flowed back over us, drowning us in silence. When Dan turned the key in the ignition, the engine sounded loud as a scream.

"This is just a charm-filled neighborhood," I said, as Dan pulled away.

"Did you notice?"

"Notice what?"

"Both the girl and her mother had a necklace like Mrs. Mason's. Oval gray stone on a thin silver chain. We were too far away to be sure, but I bet it had the same spiral pattern we saw earlier."

"Some kind of cult?"

"Could be. I doubt it's that somebody in the neighborhood picked up two dozen of them at Dollar General."

But at least now we had a name and a place for my mysterious would-be intruder.

The girl's directions were accurate enough. A few hundred yards down the road was a house with an unpainted wood façade, overshadowed by trees, its roof furred with moss. A huge sugar maple in the front yard had a worn tire swing, and in the driveway was a battered brown Buick Skylark resting on four bald tires. A long crack zigzagged its way across the front windshield.

We both got out and went to the front door. My knock was answered by a voice, once again female, but the door didn't open.

"Yeah?"

"We're looking for Lem Stutes."

"Ain't here."

"His car's in the driveway."

Long pause. "Don't mean he's here. He's got two legs, you know."

As I spoke, Dan caught my eye and nodded toward the front window. I kept her talking as he edged along the wall and peered into a grimy glass pane unencumbered by curtains or shutters.

He met my eyes, and gave an almost imperceptible nod.

"Then you need to tell Lem something when he comes back," I said.

"What's that?"

"I'm the guy whose house he tried to break into last night. We got a photo of him on the security camera."

I heard a hissing intake of breath from inside, and almost simultaneously the woman's voice said, "So what?"

That confirmed what I'd inferred from Dan's nod. There were two people inside that house, and I'd have bet cold hard cash one of them was Lem Stutes.

"So tell him that if he tries it again, I'm going to the police with the photograph. Maybe next time it won't be him, it'll be one of his friends, or one of the other folks who lives on the edge of Devil's Glen."

Another little gasp, this one sounding more angry than scared. Evidently the people near the forest didn't like that name.

"It doesn't matter to me who it is. I'll go to the police with this photo, and the photos of anyone else we catch on the security camera, which we're leaving on twenty-four-seven. Whatever reason he has to come after me, you might want to ask Lem if it's worth his getting arrested and having to explain himself to the police."

"I'll tell him." Her voice sounded sullen. "Can't guarantee he'll listen."

"Maybe he'll listen if you tell him we know about Alban Bishop and Melvia Shields, too."

There was a sudden commotion inside, and Dan took off at a sprint, yelling, "He's bolting!" He cornered the house and disappeared around the side.

I followed him at a much slower run, but got around to the rear of the house in time to see the back door explode open and a skinny scarecrow of a man pelt down the two steps into the back yard and tear across it, then inexplicably loop around the front toward the road.

I suddenly realized what he was doing.

The forest was that direction. Once he got across Cain Creek Road, he could lose us under the trees.

He was trying to escape into Devil's Glen.

But once again, Dan was too fast for him, and like last night, the man didn't get far before being tackled and pinned. This time, Dan was ready for him to fight back, and within moments had him immobilized, one arm twisted behind his back.

It was definitely the same man who'd tried to break in the previous evening. Scraggly, dirty blond hair sticking up like straw, gaunt face, bony arms, a prominent Adam's apple. In the light of day we could see his eyes, which were wide and staring, and a disconcerting pale blue.

Lem panted, his face in a rictus of pain, and twisted in Dan's grip. His expression held raw terror.

I didn't think we were the only thing he was afraid of, somehow.

Then I noticed something odd—he, too, had one of the necklaces with a gray stone. At closer proximity, like Mrs. Mason's, the design on the surface seemed to be some kind of pattern of spirals, and there was a hole in the center.

Did everyone in this neighborhood wear one of these?

"Why were you trying to break into my house?" I demanded, standing over him.

He didn't respond, just made desperate animal noises as he writhed, trying to escape.

"You ask yourself which you'd rather deal with. The police, or *Them Inside*."

His eyes flew open wide. But then—he laughed. It was a wild, nearly hysterical laugh that sounded as if it were mostly borne of fear. "You think that's gonna scare me?" His voice was high-pitched, creaky, but filled with scorn and defiance. "I'll take the police. Send 'em, then, tell 'em to do their worst."

"You're that afraid of *Them Inside*?"

"You should be, too, mister."

"More frightening than a charge of murder?"

All he did was laugh again.

Moved by a sudden impulse, I said, "Where's Cyndy Evans?"

His laugh was cut off like someone flipped a switch, and he gave a quick little intake of breath. "I didn't do nothin' to her."

"Then where is she?"

"I just...I just warned her. Said not to talk to you, that she'd better take a few days off from work. They said I could. They said I could just tell her to stay clear, that she didn't know nothin' worth..." He stopped, and licked his lips, and gave a salacious leer. "I'm glad. She's pretty."

There was a ratcheting click behind us, and a woman in a faded print dress stood there, aiming a shotgun at my head. Flyaway gray hair, her face a maze of wrinkles. One watery eye, the same pale blue as Lem's, sighted down the barrel, and her expression was fierce and unwavering.

She, too, wore one of the odd necklaces.

"You two get off my property," she snarled, "'fore I blow your head clean off. Don't think I won't."

The tableau was frozen for only a second or two, but it seemed like an eternity.

I nodded toward my son. "Dan, let him go."

Dan let go of Lem Stutes's arm and got up, dusting the knees of his pants off as he stood.

Lem gave a squawk, leapt to his feet, and fled back toward the house. A moment later, we heard the back door slam.

"Now git." The woman hadn't moved.

"You tell your son to stay away from me and my property."

"You done told him yourself. If you said your piece, clear off. If you know what's good for you, stay right the hell away."

"If he knows what's good for him, he'll do the same."

And like her son, she laughed, but she didn't lower the shotgun. "You talk tough. You better know what you're about, or ain't gonna be Lem come for you one of these nights."

"Who are you talking about? Who'll come for me?"

"If you don't know, you'll find out soon enough."

"Why doesn't it come for you?" Dan asked suddenly. "Because those necklaces protect you?"

Her eyebrows shot upward, and she lowered the gun slightly. The fierceness had evaporated, turned into fear, in the blink of an eye. "You don't know what you're gettin' into," she said, her voice hoarse.

"I know enough," I said. "Just remember what I told you. If he and the rest of you stay away, I won't have any reason to bother you again."

We didn't wait for her to respond, but turned and headed back toward the car. We had only gone a few steps when we heard her voice call out from behind us.

"You got no call to be stirring things up." She sounded desperate. "You gonna bring down the evil on all of our heads. They don't take kindly to meddlin'. You're gonna end up dead, just like the others. You and your friend both."

It was exactly what Alban Bishop had told me. *I'll be waiting to see you and your son's names in the newspaper.*

I turned toward her. "I wouldn't be meddling if they hadn't been responsible for my only brother's disappearance."

She was still holding the gun, but the barrel was pointed toward the ground. Her mouth was hanging open, and I could hear the sound of her breathing. She seemed to be in the last extremities of terror. "You meddlin' ain't gonna bring him back."

"Maybe not. But that's not the only reason to try to find *Them Inside.*"

"Yeah?"

"Yeah." I met her eyes steadily. She looked away first. "There's revenge."

VI

On the way home, Dan said, "You know, Dad, you kicked ass. I didn't know you had it in you."

I chuckled. "There's some spirit in the old guy left."

"I guess."

"You didn't do so bad yourself. You haven't forgotten the moves you learned on the wrestling team in high school."

"It stays with you." His face became serious. "Do you think you've just made the danger worse, though? Hell, if you're right, they *killed* Mr. Bishop and Miss Shields. We don't know why Lem Stutes was trying to break into your house, but Jesus. If they didn't have a reason for wanting you out of the way before, they do now."

"What's so goddamn important about keeping these secrets?"

"Because they could be the key to solving a ten-year-old double murder."

I didn't answer for a moment, just watched the scrubby trees and dismal houses on Cain Creek Road slip past. "You don't know they're dead."

"C'mon, Dad." His voice was gentle, but firm. "It's been ten *years*. If they're not dead, where are they? You said you didn't believe they'd just taken off for parts unknown. If they went into those woods, and no one has seen them in all that time..."

"Maybe they're still alive, too."

"Like Alban Bishop's long-lost kin."

I shrugged. "If there's a chance they're still alive, even a tiny chance, I have to keep looking."

He turned right on Claver Road, heading back toward Highway 226 and the village of Guildford. "What did you think of those talismans? Every person we saw today was wearing one of them."

The change of subject was deliberate, but I let it go. "I don't know. The ones I got a close look at all seemed to be identical. Could you make out the symbol engraved on the stone?"

Dan shook his head. "Not well enough I could draw it, or anything. It was a bunch of looped curves with a hole in the middle, that's the best I can do." He stopped, frowning thoughtfully. "It reminded me of drawings I've seen of fractals."

"I've heard of those, but don't know I could tell you what they are."

"They're an odd mathematical construct. It's a drawing that looks more or less the same on any scale. If you magnify a piece of it, it's identical to the whole. The pattern extends all the way down, and it results in some really bizarre properties, like shapes with finite area and infinite perimeter."

"I don't see how that's possible. So you could paint the interior, but couldn't paint the edge?"

He laughed. "Yeah. But don't ask me to explain it any further. In any case, there's no way a carving on a stone could capture the detail of a true fractal, but the pattern I saw looked like something called a *strange attractor* one of my math professors showed us. Spirals surrounding a gap in the middle."

"Hard to imagine someone like the Stuteses and Mrs. Mason and the weird little girl and her mother knowing anything about exotic mathematics."

"I don't imagine they do. But using a talisman doesn't mean you necessarily understand why it works."

"I didn't think you were superstitious."

"I'm not. But it's like when someone asked Niels Bohr why a famous physicist like him had a horseshoe on the wall for good luck. Bohr responded, 'Because a horseshoe brings you good luck whether you believe in it or not.'"

I chuckled. "That's like the people who go to church on Sunday because they figure if they're wrong, they've only lost a few Sunday mornings, but if God exists and they *don't* go, they're fucked."

"Always best to hedge your bets."

There was a pause.

"Do you think I should be worried about all the dire warnings about not messing with *Them Inside*?"

He frowned thoughtfully for a few moments. "Only if you think there's something supernatural going on here."

"You just said you aren't superstitious."

"I'm still not." He gave a quick grin, there and gone in an instant. "But think about it. What could they do? If we're saying what we've heard is at least substantially true, it's pretty apparent that for whatever reason *Them Inside* don't come out of the forest, and rely on *Them on the Edge* to carry out their instructions and keep them provided with food and other necessities. So unless there is some kind of supernatural force that can leave the woods and come after us, which I flat-out don't believe, it means all we have to worry about is the likes of Lem Stutes. And I'll put the two of us up against Lem Stutes, both in terms of brains and brawn."

"He or one of his buddies have already killed two people."

"That's still a surmise, although given how Lem Stutes and his mother reacted to hearing those names, I think there's a good chance you're right. But both Bishop and Shields were elderly. And even Bishop, who sounds like he knew something was up, may not have been anticipating how or when they would come after him. Lem's little escapade last night, and how he reacted today, took away the advantage of surprise. If they try something like that again, we'll be ready for them."

~

I have to admit I went to bed that night feeling more confident than I had since my first conversation with Alban Bishop.

Dan's reassurances that we were perfectly capable of handling whatever Lem Stutes and his cronies threw our way had the effect of quelling my anxiety, and I said good night to Dan—he planned to sleep on the couch again—retired to my own room, and for once was asleep within minutes.

I was awakened at about one in the morning by a noise like a high wind. I squinted over at the clock on my nightstand, and tried to remember whether the weather forecast had predicted a storm. I got up and pulled aside my curtains to peer out into the darkness of my back yard. It sounded like the tree branches were whipping in a gale, and as I stood there, a shower of leaves and broken twigs clattered against the glass.

I quickly donned my bathrobe and ran into the living room. Dan was already stirring, sitting up on the couch blinking groggily.

"What the fuck is that?" he said, reaching up to rub his eyes.

"Sounds like a hurricane."

As if in answer, there was a crash as a larger tree branch hit the roof, making the entire house shudder.

I went to the front door and pulled it open. It only opened with considerable effort, as if there were some kind of suction holding it closed. A gust of warm air struck my face, carrying with it leaves, dust, and other debris that swirled around my legs and settled onto the living room rug.

It also carried an acrid odor, a rough, sour smell like spoiled milk catching in my throat and making me cough. I slammed the door shut.

Dan's eyes met mine, and he looked terrified.

"We've got to get out of here."

"If it's a storm, we're safer inside…"

"It's not a storm. Listen." He held up one hand.

Above the howling of the wind there was another sound, a high-pitched screech almost beyond the range of hearing. But it wasn't a mechanical noise. I knew, in the first moments I was aware of it, this was an organic noise, made by a mouth and vocal apparatus nothing like a human's.

Because in that screech I could hear words.

It sounded like no language I had ever heard, and I could not even begin to try to transcribe it. But there was no doubt in my mind that what we were hearing was some inhuman creature speaking, chanting an incantation whose every tone dripped evil.

And it was getting closer.

I grabbed my wallet and keys from the counter and a pair of shoes from near the door. Dan was hurriedly pulling on a shirt as I once again yanked the door open. The acrid smell flooded into the room, and behind me I heard Dan gagging. We pushed our way outside against the rush of the foul-smelling wind, and somehow were able to stagger our way to my car, get in, and start the engine.

I was halfway down the driveway when there was an earsplitting crash. Despite our desperation to get away from whatever it was coming toward us, I couldn't stop myself from swiveling around and looking behind me.

The roof of my house had been caved in as if from the punch of a giant fist. Around the edges of the hole there was a bluish, phosphorescent glow, and in that weird light the wood framing seemed almost to have melted.

There was a rushing, swirling noise, as if the force that had crushed my house like a matchbox was gathering itself up, and with a roar it lifted upward into the sky.

I stopped the car and got out. I heard Dan screaming, "Dad, what the *fuck* are you doing?" but I turned and looked upward.

I caught a second's glimpse, no more, of something swirling, transparent, and glassy rippling across the stars, making them shimmer as if they were underwater. Then it slipped away in the direction of a bright blue star directly overhead, and vanished.

~

Police, ambulance, and fire trucks came and went. We were both questioned about what had happened, what we'd seen, what we might have been doing that precipitated the destruction of my house. The police clearly thought we'd been cooking meth or something of the sort, an impression the lingering sour odor did nothing to dispel, but evidently a cursory examination of what was left of the structure gave them no evidence warranting our arrest.

We assured the paramedics we'd been the only ones in the house at the time and were both unhurt, although Dan had a small cut on his arm where he'd been struck by some piece of flying debris while we fled. The firemen stuck around longer, trying to make certain there was nothing that could explode and cause further damage—propane, natural gas, fuel oil—and when I told them I'd had electric heat and didn't even own a barbecue grill, they left, too.

It was nearly sunrise before everyone had cleared out. I drove us to Dan's apartment in silence. His car was relatively unscathed, but his keys were in his pants pocket, currently somewhere under piles of broken two-by-fours and roof shingles. He loaned me some clothes—he's broader across the chest than I am, but we're close to the same size otherwise—and we went to a nearby café for some coffee and a light breakfast.

"Still not superstitious?" I said, eyeing him over my mug.

He gave me a raised eyebrow. "I don't know if I have any choice."

"You didn't see what I saw at the end. If I'd had any doubts, those blew them away." I described the eddying swirl, like a clear curtain rippling in the wind and finally disappearing up into the night sky.

"Jesus, Dad. That's terrifying."

"Thank you for not doubting what I saw."

"C'mon. I think something pulverizing your house kind of trumps any objection I could make."

The call to my boss to let him know I probably wouldn't be in that day was received considerably more poorly than the previous two.

"Your house…blew up?" The incredulity was obvious, as was the subtext of, *How big an idiot do you think I am?*

"Look, Joe, I'll send you pictures. We're heading back out there soon. If you don't believe me…"

Heavy sigh. "Yeah, yeah, I believe you."

"I'd much rather be at work than sifting through debris and seeing if I have any worldly goods left."

"Okay." He still sounded doubtful, but at least he wasn't arguing anymore. "Let me know if there's anything I can do to help. If you need a place to stay, I'm sure Carol and I could put you up for a few days."

"Thanks, but I'll be staying with my son." I looked over at Dan, and he smiled and shrugged.

We paid for our breakfast and headed back out into morning weekday bustle. Once again, I was struck by the ordinariness of it all, while only a few miles away, we'd just been through something very much like a scene from a horror movie.

"How are you handling all this, Dad?" Dan glanced over at me, and there was concern in his eyes.

"Shook up. Scared. But honestly? Mostly I'm mad. You know? Whatever or whoever is behind this, they took my brother from me, and more or less killed Grandma and Grandpa in the process. Anyone in his right mind would want an explanation, but now they're doing everything up to and including murder to stop me from finding out what the explanation might be. And now, they destroyed my fucking house." I gave an angry gesture with one hand. "Yeah, I'm mad enough that I don't give a rat's ass how scared I am. I'm going to find out who is responsible, and why, if it's the last thing I do."

"Judging by what's happened so far, it might well be." His tone was sepulchral, at odds with his usual easy-going cheer.

"But you still want to help?"

There was a long pause during which he looked out of the window, a distant expression in his eyes. Finally he turned toward me and sighed. "If you'd asked me a few days ago, I'd have said I was only helping you in order to get you to let all this go."

"Cooperating so I'd shut up about it?"

"I wouldn't have put it that way."

"No, I get it. But now something's changed?"

He nodded. "I didn't think you were lying, or deluded, or whatever, but all the talk about evil cults in the woods sounded so preposterous. I still honestly thought Uncle Brad and his girlfriend got killed by some lunatic and buried in the woods—no weird demon-worshipers necessary. Either that, or they took off for reasons of their own."

I opened my mouth to respond, but he held up one hand.

"I'm aware you don't think the last bit is possible given what you know about Uncle Brad's personality. I get that. But people do weird things sometimes, and I still thought it was more likely than the two of them being abducted by people who are still out there, still conducting rites in their temple or whatever. Even after I heard what happened to Alban Bishop and Melvia Shields, it was easy to write it off as two old people dying of natural causes."

"On the same day?"

"I know, I know. You just don't want to believe it could be true. You flail around looking for some possible explanation until there's no way you can do that anymore."

"So now…?"

"Watching something invisible smash the roof of your house in makes it kind of hard to believe in a reasonable, natural explanation for it all."

"So what explanation are you going for?"

"I'm withholding judgment for the moment, pending further information."

"Spoken like a scientist."

"I don't know any other way to speak."

We pulled into my driveway a few minutes later. The woodland surrounding what was left of my house was peaceful, filled with the small noises of animals and birds, and the rustling of the warm breeze in the leaves. In the midst of it all, though, was the wreckage of my house, crushed like an eggshell.

The front wall was still substantially intact, and I opened the door and walked through it into a pile of broken lumber and the remains of furniture, carpeting, and appliances. The edges of the gap, and much of the crushed debris, appeared to have partially melted, and were coated with a translucent whitish slime that had dripped into glossy puddles on the floor.

"Looks like a giant alien ejaculated all over your house," Dan said.

I was just in the process of scooping some of it up with one hand, and I gave him a wry eye. "My house was knocked down by alien jizz?"

"Must have been a hell of an orgasm."

I tentatively sniffed the glop on my fingertips, and got a whiff of the acrid sour-milk odor that had been so overwhelming the previous night.

"Smells rancid," I said.

"Maybe the alien needs to see a urologist."

I scraped the residue from my hand and wiped it dry on my pant leg.

"Sorry," I told Dan, when he looked askance at my smearing the gunk on jeans that belonged to him. "I hope it comes out in the wash."

"Jizz usually does."

We made our way to what had been my bedroom. The dresser had provided some protection from the falling roof joists, and I was able to salvage a good bit of my clothing. Dan helped me haul to the car everything I could find that was still in reasonably good condition. This turned out to be more than I expected. A few of my things were destroyed—pretty much everything I had hanging on the walls, most of my books, the stereo, the dining room table and chairs—but we piled as much as we could of the intact things into my car and Dan's, which had amazingly sustained no damage at all. Underneath a couple of two-by-fours we found Dan's jeans, left where he'd shucked them as he got undressed for bed, and—more importantly—his car keys in the pocket.

Afterward, we stood in the driveway. I felt a strange reluctance to leave.

"I wonder if this is what Lem Stutes's mother meant by *ain't gonna be Lem come for you one of these nights."*

Dan nodded. "Looks like it."

"That doesn't get us any closer to figuring out what exactly 'it' is."

"No. But it does tell us the people out there on Cain Creek Road were afraid for a reason."

"And are cooperating with *Them Inside* for a reason."

"Right." He stretched and yawned. "I'm beat. Between the comedown from the adrenaline rush, and getting only a couple of hours of sleep, I'm ready for a nap."

"You and me both."

"Let's head back to my apartment. There's nothing more we can do here without heavy equipment to lift some of the big chunks of the roof. More than likely anything under there is smashed to pieces anyhow."

"I get to sleep on your couch now?"

He grinned at me. "Turnabout's fair play."

~

The rest of the day was occupied with gathering the camping equipment we'd need for the foray into the woods the day after tomorrow. Dan had a lot of gear—he was an experienced back-country camper—and he even had extra sets of things like eating utensils, water bottles, and flashlights from times he'd gone hiking with less well-equipped friends. A quick trip to Eastern Mountain Sports garnered me a backpack and sleeping bag, which I'd had before the previous evening. But they'd been in my front coat closet—the area of the house that had sustained the most damage—and now they lay under a good ton of debris.

"How long do you think we'll be in those woods?" I asked him as he pulled together packages of camp food on his kitchen counter, mostly of the lightweight, easily-packed variety.

Dan shrugged. "That's up to you. I took a week's vacation, so I need to be back by a week from Monday. Other than that, I've got no time restrictions."

"If I don't show up for work next week, Joe's gonna kill me. Or fire me. Or both, one right after the other. I've lost track of the number of days I've been late or absent in the last few weeks."

"Can you try to explain to him what's going on?"

I snorted. "Joe Overby? Have you met him?"

"Yeah, I remember talking to him once or twice. I guess you're right."

"He's a good enough boss, but is about as unimaginative as they come. Convincing you about all this was a cakewalk compared to him."

"You sent him photos of your house, though, right?" Dan tossed a couple of packages of dried fruit and freeze-dried soup into the growing pile.

"Yeah. His response was, 'Looks like your natural gas line exploded.' I told him I didn't have a natural gas line, my house was all electric. He wrote back, 'Oh. Hell of thing, then.'"

"No curiosity about what actually happened?"

"None. It's filed under 'hell of a thing,' and that's enough for him."

"So we've got to make this a short trip."

"If it's possible."

"Well, the woods we'll be exploring just aren't that big. My guess is if after two or three days we haven't found anything, there's nothing there to find."

"At which point we give up."

"At which point there's really no other choice."

"After last night, I have to say our likelihood of finding nothing is getting smaller and smaller."

Dan gave me a thoughtful look. "The open question is whether we'll be glad we found it when we do."

~

I went to work on Friday—made a passing attempt at convincing Joe Overby I hadn't been inventing some weird story the previous day to take a day's impromptu vacation—and was met by a verbal shrug.

"Okay," he said, in a flat, incurious tone. "Like I said, let me know if you need anything."

I was there at work, I hadn't called on him to help despite his offer, and that was that. No longer something he had to worry about, so it effectively didn't exist.

I debated telling him I might not be in on Monday, and decided to keep silent. No sense in pushing my luck by bringing it up again.

And, like Dan said, if we were in there for more than a day or two, either it'd mean we found something—which would make any amount of explaining myself to Joe worth the trouble—or we'd have disappeared, same as Brad and Cara, the victims perhaps of whatever it was that attacked my house.

I got home Friday to find Dan broiling a couple of porterhouse steaks. The smell was mouthwatering, and there were already two glasses of red wine poured on the dinner table.

"Nice choice for a last meal."

Dan pulled the broiler pan with the sizzling steaks out of the oven and glanced over at me with a smile. "I was saving these for a special occasion. I don't have a girlfriend at the moment, so this seemed as good as any."

"Better than the camp food on the menu for the next couple of days."

"It is." He put down a plate in front of me, and one for himself, and got a bowl of steamed broccoli out of the microwave. He sat down, lifted his glass, and said, "Cheers. To a successful expedition."

I clinked his glass, and took a sip. The wine was rich, heavy, dark as blood. "To success. Whatever that might mean."

VII

Saturday morning dawned clear and calm. The pleasant warmth of the end of August was still with us, but already some of the trees were showing the first hints of yellow and orange as the quick upstate New York summer drew to its close. Goldenrod and purple asters, the harbingers of autumn, were in full bloom in the fields as we drove toward Devil's Glen and whatever lay in wait for us there.

"You afraid?" I asked, as I saw the crooked sign saying *Claver Road* and turned right, toward the belt of trees showing as a vague dark line in the distance.

"I haven't pissed myself yet," Dan said without smiling. "I count that as a win."

"Still not too late to back out."

"Hell no. Dad, they destroyed your house. What are you going to do, call the police? It was pretty clear they weren't interested unless you'd blown it up while pretending you were Walter White. What would you tell them, some woman and her son who look like they were rejected as extras in *Deliverance* on the basis of being too inbred told you the Powers of Darkness were after you?"

"You have a way of making everything sound absolutely idiotic."

"Well, it's how the cops would see it, don't you think? If you told them about Lem Stutes, even showed them his photo, they'd ask, 'And you think this guy is the one who smashed your house in?' How would you answer that?"

"You have a point."

"So far as I can see, we want this taken care of, we take care of it ourselves."

We crossed Cain Creek Road, and I looked up toward where the first of the houses of *Them on the Edge* sat, dismal and squalid, half expecting to see a whole crowd of them standing there with pitchforks. But there was no one there.

Dan's car bumped its way down the road, the potholed asphalt giving way to rutted dirt, finally narrowing in so much there was barely room to get through without the blackberry and willow branches scraping both sides. At that point he stopped, put it in park, and turned off the engine. We were once again struck by the absolute, overwhelming silence.

We got out, unloaded our gear, only speaking in whispers. I felt conspicuous, a loud, solid, brightly-colored being in a land of vague and watchful wraiths. The trees lay ahead, only a hundred yards farther, and beneath them impenetrable shadows so dark even on this sunny day they looked like they were filled with some opaque blackness more real and more powerful than the light.

I knew if I stood there looking at them any longer, I'd lose my nerve. Dan looked scared but resolute. We shouldered our packs, and he locked the car doors.

Then we turned our faces toward the darkness that awaited us.

To our credit, neither of us hesitated.

But immediately as we crossed the threshold, it felt like we had stepped back in time by millions of years. Behind us lay at least the withered vestiges of a road, and a way back into civilization. Ahead were trees, rotting logs, and lichen-encrusted rocks that looked as if they had been there since before the first human walked the Earth. Underfoot were the spongy remains of thousands of years of fallen leaves, decayed into mold, and around us damp air redolent with the smell of loam and charged with an intense wariness, felt as a pressure that made our ears ring and left us breathless.

We didn't talk. It seemed unwise. We walked forward, Dan in the lead, and our footfalls sounded overwhelmingly loud, advertising our presence to whoever, or whatever, waited within.

But two hours' walk brought no changes. Twice we waded across narrow streams, cold clear water chattering among gray stones. Dan cautioned me, unnecessarily, against drinking it.

"I wouldn't drink stream water without boiling it first," I whispered.

"I wouldn't drink this water even if it was boiled."

My expression must have looked perplexed.

He took a deep breath, wincing as he did so. The place seemed to be fighting us for every lungful of air. "I just remember the River Lethe in my college lit class. One swallow of its water, and you forget who you are, sit down by its side, and never rise again."

Instead, we both took a sip from our water bottles. We'd have to make it last if we weren't going to use creek water when needed.

Several times Dan used his compass to correct our bearings and keep us walking more or less in a straight line. It's a good thing he did. There were no landmarks, nothing for the mind to latch onto if you needed to remember your position. Trees, stones, fallen branches, ferns so huge they looked prehistoric. I would hardly have been surprised if a dinosaur had lumbered out of the shadows toward us— but we hadn't seen nor heard a single animal since we'd started walking.

Four hours in, we took a break, slipping off our packs, stretching sore muscles, and peeling away sweaty t-shirts from our skin. It was cool under the trees, but the dampness was cloying. We ate a light lunch, all I really had the stomach for. Both of us took a quick pee— not even stepping out of sight, merely turning our backs for propriety's sake.

Neither of us wanted to be out of visual range of the other, not for a moment.

"How far have we come?" I whispered, as we shouldered our packs and prepared to continue.

"According to the USGS survey map of the area, it's about fifteen miles north-to-south and eight miles east-to-west, although the boundary is kind of irregular. We've been heading pretty close to due north, as well as we can given the terrain, and not honestly pushing ourselves, pace-wise." He consulted the GPS tracking band on his wrist. "According to this we've gone about seven miles, but it's not getting a great signal here because of the trees. My guess is we're getting near the geographic center of the woods."

"No evil cult members or monsters."

He didn't smile, merely said, "Not yet."

I was reminded of the terrifying passage from the book Alban Bishop had sent me, the one titled *What Lives in the Forest?*

If, even after reading this, you decide to go into those woods looking for those who dwell there and the evil they serve, do not ask yourself how you will find them in those trackless acres of forest. Depend upon it: they will find you. And afterward, you will wish you had fettered your curiosity and remained in safe and secure ignorance.

But I didn't bring that up. Speaking it aloud, here in these dark trees, would be to call it into being.

Two hours later, we were moving more slowly, not only because of fatigue and the oppressive, all-engulfing silence, but because the terrain had become more uneven. Directly across our path were deep gullies, the banks made up of cracked and rotten shale, dripping wet and overgrown with ferns and moss. It was hard to find a safe way down even for Dan, experienced mountaineer though he was, and more than once a seemingly solid handhold pulled out from the side in a shower of dirt and flakes of rock. We were each time saved from a nasty fall by a combination of quick reflexes and dumb luck, but I couldn't help but feel our good fortune wouldn't last forever.

At the bottom of the gullies were clear, tumbling streams, chattering over algae-slicked slabs that made for treacherous footing. Hemmed into those narrow clefts, it was almost as dark as night, and each time we made our way across using flashlights even though it was only a little before three in the afternoon. One of them had an opening in the farther rock face, half as high as a man, which looked like it extended back into the hillside. A creek only a few inches deep bubbled across our path, but that was easily forded. Maybe this cave was the hiding place of the brother of the "half-breed" informant Zachariah Larkin quoted in *An Account of the Doings by People in the Hill Country, and the Prodigies that Followed.* No way to tell, of course. What was more important was that here and now, the terrain was slowing us down considerably.

After crossing the third one, we took a rest to reevaluate our plan.

"We could strike off east, the direction the streams are flowing," Dan said, munching on a rather squashed peanut-butter-and-jelly sandwich he'd retrieved from his pack. "The forest is narrower east-to-west than it is north-to-south. But we're not really *trying* to get out of the forest, at least not yet, so I'm not sure that's what we should do."

"I didn't really have a plan. Just go into the woods and see what we can find."

"So far, all we've found is trees. No animal life at all, have you noticed? Not even any mosquitoes. It isn't like I miss them or anything, but it's bizarre. Even the bugs avoid this place."

"It really was kind of a ridiculous idea that two people could comb an eighty-thousand acre forest. Hell, a few dozen policemen tried it after Brad and Cara disappeared, and *they* didn't find anything."

"Didn't you tell me Alban Bishop said some of the policemen had found something, but wouldn't say what it was? But whatever it was scared them enough to swear off ever coming anywhere near here again?"

"That's what he *said*. But you know how it goes. That's the part of his story that seemed the most likely to me to be exaggeration or an outright fabrication. It had the feeling of a campfire story, you know? 'And when they got home, they opened the car door, and *there was a hook hanging from the handle of the door.*'"

Dan laughed, but his laugh sounded a little breathless in the heavy, still air. "Yeah, I've heard that one, too. But I have to say, it's a lot easier to believe those kinds of stories here than it is when you're sitting in your own living room."

"We're suggestible creatures, aren't we?"

In the end we decided to keep going in the general direction we'd been heading, but had only gone another couple of hundred yards when we came upon a cliffside springing up from the forest floor like a wall. It was overhung, and flaked shale and debris lay in mounds around its foot. It was clear getting up this without climbing gear would be somewhere between dangerous and impossible.

"Okay, plan B," Dan said, peering up at the top of the cliff hanging a good forty feet over our heads.

It looked as if the barrier was lower toward our left—west—so in the end we skirted against the wall, our feet crunching on the piles of fallen rock, hoping eventually we'd find a place where it was possible to climb it.

My spirits were at the lowest I could remember. The whole enterprise seemed to be a foolish and pointless waste of time. As long as we still had the possibility of going into Devil's Glen, seeing for ourselves what was there, I could be buoyed up by the chance we'd find something to put my mind finally at rest. But to trek across the place for hours and find nothing was such an anticlimax that I felt the hopelessness I'd experienced in the weeks following Brad's disappearance return tenfold.

This was it, then. I wouldn't find any answers, because there were no answers to find.

I didn't say any of this to Dan, but I could tell he was picking up on at least some of my despair. He became more solicitous, giving me a hand across difficult ground and saying things like, "The cliff is definitely getting lower, I think it'll be manageable in a little farther" and "We still have a lot of hours of light left before we need to pitch camp."

In fact, I thought it was just another attempt at encouragement when he pointed to the cliff and said, "I think that's a path."

I squinted into the deepening shadows, following with my eyes where he was pointing. My assumption was he was simply talking about a way up the wall, perhaps natural hand and footholds.

Then I realized what he'd said was literally correct. It was a path, with rough-hewn steps, hugging the cliff face.

No doubt about it. This was no natural feature. It was the work of human hands.

Our eyes met, and I saw raw fear in my son's face. Whatever it was we were trying to find, this was the first sign we'd had that it actually existed. We silently went to the bottom of the steps and began to ascend.

They may have been made deliberately, but they were fashioned out of the native stone—fragile and rotting shale—and we both clutched the rock wall as we made our hesitant way toward the top. What good it would have done if one of the steps had collapsed is uncertain, but at least having our hands in contact with the cliffside gave us the illusion of safety. We reached the top and scrambled up, panting, onto a higher vantage point than any we'd had. There was also more light up here, and we could actually see a bit of the sky, now covered by a sheet of gray clouds. We looked out over the tops of trees stretching southward as far as we could see. Somewhere in that direction was Claver Road and the way back to the village, but from where we were, it looked like the forest went on forever, encircling the entire world.

We were facing outward, back the way we came, thinking about who'd made those steps, for what purpose, and where we'd go from here, when a voice spoke from behind us. It was hoarse, laden with emotion, almost disbelieving.

"I knew it. I knew you'd come eventually."

We both whirled around, our gasps cutting through the silence like a razor blade.

For a moment, I had the impression of looking into a mirror, but one that erased the ravages of age. A lean and muscular frame, more powerful than mine. Thin lips parted in a genuine smile, revealing perfect white teeth. A scruff of beard, but his skin was smooth, not even crow's feet or laugh lines at the corner of the eyes.

I could have been looking at a photograph of myself from ten years earlier.

The only real difference was a ragged scar running from the right corner of his mouth across the side of his face, curving above his cheek and disappearing under his hairline. That was new.

My twin brother. Bradley James Ellicott.

I tried to speak, but no words came out.

"My dear brother." He stepped forward and threw his arms around me in a warm hug, and his voice cracked. "My dear brother. Welcome to Ulthoa."

VIII

The hug broke, and Brad stepped back, looking at Dan and me, his eyes glistening with tears.

"Dan," he said. "You look good. You were in middle school last time I saw you."

"Uncle Brad…" Dan stopped, glancing at me as if looking for help.

I just gave him a shrug. I was as dumbfounded as he was. All the other outcomes I had considered seemed more likely than the one I found myself facing—my brother, meeting us in the woods as if he'd been waiting for us to show up.

"Brad…" My voice was a croak, and it was hard to push the words out of my throat. "Where have you been all this time?"

He gave me a faint smile. "Here."

"But…why didn't you leave? You could have walked out and in a day been back." I didn't add that anger was rapidly overcoming my astonishment. How could he have done this to me, being here in the woods for ten years, well and healthy, and not tried to contact me? How could he have done this to our parents?

"Oh, you can't *leave*. It isn't allowed."

"Isn't allowed by whom?"

His expression became wary, and even though his mouth was still smiling, his eyes betrayed fear. "You'll see. But they have...they have ways of discouraging you from trying to leave."

"What ways?" Dan said. There was an edge of anger to his voice, too.

Brad sighed, as if it were a topic he didn't like discussing. He lifted his thin t-shirt. In the middle of his chest, right between his nipples, was a huge, furrowed, star-shaped scar.

"Is that..." I began, then stopped, horrified.

"The results of defiance. Yes. I tried to escape once, you see. They made sure I wouldn't try it again." He dropped his shirt and tugged the hem back down, then reached up, his fingertips tracing the scar on his cheek. "I nearly died. I've no doubt that's what the intent was. Having your face ripped open, and coming very close to having your heart blown from your chest, has a way of leaving you determined never to let it happen again."

"Who did that to you?"

He shook his head. "Let's not talk about this. You must understand it's an unpleasant memory. I only tell you about it so you'll be unlikely to suffer the same consequences. I couldn't bear watching that happen."

"Wait," Dan said suddenly. "Where's Cara?"

Now Brad's smile disappeared completely. "We should get back to the encampment. It'll be getting dark soon. I'd rather not have to find our way in the complete darkness."

"She's dead, isn't she, Uncle Brad?"

Brad shot a fierce look at Dan. "You'll get your answers, but not until we're safely back at the encampment."

"And what if we turn around and walk away? I've got a GPS. We can find our way out."

"Oh, I wouldn't do that if I were you." His light, conversational tone made his words sound much more sinister. "I really, really wouldn't. Night's falling soon. That's when...that's when we got caught. Trust me when I tell you, however good an outdoorsman you are, at night you are at a serious disadvantage. If you tried to walk out the way you came, you wouldn't get a mile before you got captured. Even running wouldn't do you any good. They can see far better in the dark than you can." He paused, swallowed. "They knew about your presence before you'd been in the forest five minutes. Believe me, you're safer with me."

"Come along peaceably and no one will get hurt," Dan said, his voice filled with barely-contained fury.

But Brad smiled again. "Exactly."

I quickly considered what choice we had other than to obey. I had no doubt the substance of his threat was the truth, even if there was a lot he wasn't telling us. I knew Brad better than anyone else, and I could tell when he was lying.

Plus, the scars on his chest told their own story.

"So how many people live in Devil's Glen?"

A quick scowl passed across Brad's face, there and gone in a moment. "Brother," he said gently, "the first thing you must learn is we do not call it that. If you must speak of our dwelling, you will call it Ulthoa. But best not to speak of it at all."

I nodded. But in my mind was the defiant conviction it would remain Devil's Glen, whatever rule they had about it. The name seemed appropriate.

"We should go. Your arrival is anticipated, and there will be a cabin ready for you, with two clean mattresses. Probably not as comfortable as you're used to, but you'll adjust to it."

"It looks like you've had to get used to a lot of things," Dan said in a dark tone.

If Brad took offense, he didn't show it. "Indeed I have. And so will the two of you."

I shook my head. I felt compelled to keep trying to reach him, to gain access to the brother I had known. At the same point, a feeling of despair rose in me that he was gone, gone forever, even though his body was still animated and sat before me on a rock outcrop as if it were the most natural thing in the world. "It looks like you took to all of this fairly readily."

"You think so?"

"The Brad Ellicott I knew would have said 'fuck you' to being told what to do and what to say."

"I began that way. You saw the results."

"But now…" I gestured around me. "All of this is just…your world, now?"

"It is. I belong here, and when we reach the encampment, you will see that I am as much a member of the community as any. You asked how many people we have here. I think we number between twenty-five and thirty."

"All descendants of the people who settled here two hundred years ago?"

His eyes narrowed a little, but he said, "Yes."

"And you're happy?"

Again, there was a short pause, and the thought *the next thing he says is going to be a lie* passed through my mind.

"I'm happy enough. My needs are provided for. We have sufficient food and water without my having to work for it. No daily grind, nine-to-five jobs in the woods. We all get along, we all cooperate. There are few tensions between us. Even our other needs are taken care of. There is no marriage. If you and another person desire it, you have sex. If tomorrow the two of you desire someone else, and all are agreeable, it happens. There is no stigma on it, it's looked upon as simply another need to fulfill. Those whose predilection is their own gender meet that need, too, with others of like mind, and it is not considered abnormal or sinful as so many did in the outside world."

"But people have no desire for long-term relationships?" Dan asked.

"If two people desire to be monogamous, it is their choice. But it's not considered any better or any worse than other desires. We are human beings who have bodies with needs. Sex, and everything that goes with it, is simply a need to be met however you see fit." He smiled.

"And there's no risk of disease. Not even a risk of pregnancy. For reasons I don't understand completely, pregnancies here are extremely uncommon. You can enjoy sex completely guilt and risk-free. Wouldn't that have been nice to have when we were younger and hornier?"

Something about Brad's voice—the patient, uninflected monotone—was beginning to grind on my nerves. Before he had been emotional, passionate, fiery. Now, all of the spark seemed to have been ground out of him, leaving him a dry husk, passive and acquiescent. That he could even talk about sex and have it sound as boring as doing your taxes was alarming.

This was not the brother I'd grown up with, even if he looked like he had barely changed in the ten years since I last saw him.

"And it's all worth what you've given up?" Dan asked.

The question seemed to displease Brad for some reason, but the momentary frown was quickly swallowed up by his previous placid expression. "What have I given up? Participation in the outside world? How many people would give that up if they could? Having to worry endlessly about money, all the rules and laws and petty obligations of modern society. Who is in love with that? Here, there are only a handful of strict rules. If you follow them, the benefits become obvious immediately. The tradeoff is not unfavorable, really."

There was a note in this as if he were trying to convince himself as much as he was us.

"You said you were going to tell us what happened to Cara," I said.

"Yes." Again, a slight wince of discomfort at her name. He looked downward for a moment and didn't speak.

"Do you still have questions about this place?"

"About a million," Dan said. "But it didn't sound like you wanted to answer any of them."

My brother sighed. "There are certain things that by custom we do not discuss. But the same is true of the outside world, isn't it? Every culture has its taboos and its sensitive topics. Here there are different ones, that's all. You just have to learn what those are, and you'll get along fine."

"What about Cara?"

"What about her?"

"You said you'd tell us about her later. How about now?"

A long pause, and I wondered if he'd respond. Finally he said, "All right. I suppose it's understandable you want to know. But it's not a pleasant story, I'll warn you."

"None of this is pleasant."

"I hope you'll come to revise your opinion in time. For now, I understand your fear and anger. I felt angry and afraid myself, when I had only lived here a short time. That passes."

"You've told us that," I said. "Give it long enough, we'll drink the Kool-Aid and afterward we'll be like all the other happy little drones. How about you tell us what we want to know?"

Another harsh sigh. "Very well. I suppose it was inevitable. And in any case, it will answer some of your other questions as well, and put to rest your curiosity. I'll tell you what I can. Then we'll see if afterward you think my decision not to fight them was the right one."

PART II:

THE INSTRUMENTS OF DARKNESS

Ten years earlier

Brad Ellicott's consciousness rose slowly, like a bubble in still water, when Cara Marshall rolled over in bed and slipped her arm around his waist.

He gave a little moan of pleasure, but didn't open his eyes.

"You sure you want to do this?"

"Do what?" Brad stretched and yawned, his toes curling under.

"Go camping this weekend. I like being in a nice comfortable bed."

Still without opening his eyes, he smiled. "You getting soft?"

She ran her hands down his body. "Maybe. I notice you're not."

He chuckled. "Happens to guys in the morning."

"Doesn't take much at any time of day, as far as I've noticed." She nestled up closer to him. "I still like camping. But right now, the idea of exchanging this for a sleeping bag on the hard ground doesn't sound very appealing."

"It's only for a couple of days. And I'll still be there."

She gave him a quick kiss on the neck. "That's good. Okay, you talked me into it. What's so attractive about this place, anyhow?"

Brad yawned again. "I've heard it's spooky. The locals claim it's haunted. That's according to Rich, and he grew up in Guildford. I guess it's got quite a reputation."

"You and your ghosts and ghouls."

He rolled toward her. "I get off way harder when I know the spirits are watching."

"Do the spirits ever visit your apartment?"

"Let's find out."

Cara's laugh was cut off as his mouth found hers, and for a time there was no more talking.

Afterward, Cara dozed, curled up next to him, and Brad lay there, pondering.

There was something to what she'd said earlier. To be honest, Brad was wearying of camping. He was thirty-five, and the ground was less kind to his body than it had been when he was twenty. He remembered trips into the Adirondacks where he'd sleep like the dead, wake up with the sun, get out of his tent and take off at a dead sprint for the lake, stark naked, and dive headfirst into the chilly water. The transition had been gradual—poorer nights' sleep, waking up more often to pee and having a harder time getting back to sleep afterward, aches and pains from sleeping on hard ground or even from carrying a pack whose weight he would have laughed at five years earlier.

There was no doubt about it. Middle age loomed on the horizon.

But what Rich Stendahl had told him about these woods was intriguing, there was no doubt about that.

"I heard of a couple of kids when I was in high school who got dared to go into the woods at the end of Claver Road. Neither one of them would ever tell anyone what they'd seen, and one of them spent weeks afterward in a psychiatric hospital."

Brad had laughed. "That sounds like one of those 'friend of a friend swears it's true' kind of stories."

Rich shrugged. "One of the kids I knew slightly. He was two grades above me. He was the one who ended up in the hospital, so I know that part's true."

"There are a lot of reasons why teenagers end up in psychiatric care."

"You sound afraid." Rich grinned at him. "Big tough mountaineer, and you're scared to go into the woods a half-hour's drive from where you live."

"I didn't say I was scared." Truthfully, the comment stung a little. There was something about the place's reputation that was uncanny, but he couldn't put his finger on how it was different from haunted house stories he'd scoffed at. "Fine, dude. I'll talk to Cara tonight. If she's game, we'll head up there this weekend."

"Bringing your girlfriend along for protection?"

Brad grinned. "That's not why I'm bringing my girlfriend along."

That got a laugh, and ended the conversation.

Cara had acquiesced, enthusiastically at first.

"Sounds like fun," she said over dinner, the day he brought it up. "I didn't know there was a stretch of old growth forest that close by."

"I guess it's state land. That's what Rich said, anyhow."

She leaned forward, her chin resting on her palm. "It's been a while since we've gone camping. I'll need to check what shape my gear's in."

Brad looked at his girlfriend, thinking—as he so often did—how lucky he was to have found her. She was gorgeous by anyone's standards. Dark brown hair falling in waves to her shoulders, sparkling brown eyes, a smile that betrayed a real sense of mischief. When they'd first become a couple, more than one of his buddies had wondered aloud what on earth she saw in him, and truth be told, he wondered the same thing.

Since then, his appreciation for her had done nothing but deepen. She shared his love of hiking, historical documentaries, jazz, and Thai food. She was amazing in bed. Her quirky sense of humor and wry attitude toward life were so similar to his that sometimes they came close to completing each other's sentences.

So Cara had always been game for anything he proposed. It was a surprise that she was voicing misgivings about the upcoming camping trip. He debated prodding her for more details—surely it couldn't just be worry about the discomfort of carrying a pack and sleeping on the ground—but decided to let it be.

It was only Wednesday, so they had at least a couple of days for her doubts to calm.

Or not. If that was what happened, he'd probably let himself be talked out of it in favor of staying home and chilling that weekend.

He wondered momentarily why he, too, was reluctant, and whether he was the one who preferred to avoid the woods with the odd reputation.

But then he chided himself for being suggestible, and put that out of his mind as well.

After work, Brad went over to his parents' house—Cara had the yearly open house at the elementary school where she taught, and he'd received a dinner invitation when his mother found out he'd be on his own at dinner.

"Mom," he said with a laugh, "I'm thirty-five and have spent most of my adult life single. You think I can't cook for myself?"

Nancy Ellicott responded in a completely serious tone. "Be honest, you were just going to eat cold ravioli out of a can, weren't you?"

"No. I was probably also going to have a beer."

She snorted. "That's it. I'm making pot roast, and you're going to come over for dinner. You've lost weight."

That was a battle of long standing, so he chose not to address that part of her argument.

"Okay, pot roast it is. I can't resist."

"I know. You always did love a nice roast with potatoes and gravy."

"The way you cook it, of course. I'd be crazy not to."

So he went over to his mom and dad's house, a rambling old farm house in the little village of Lamont, at six in the evening, and was greeted at the door by the savory smell of beef cooking in the crock pot, the Ellicotts' hyperactive golden lab Barney, and Brad's dad, already holding two open bottles of beer.

Ron Ellicott handed Brad one of the bottles, and they clinked them together. "Your mother told me you were upset about missing your bottle of beer at dinner, so I thought I'd make sure it was taken care of."

Brad rolled his eyes. "I did *not* say any such thing."

Ron laughed. "I know. Nancy just worries about you for some reason."

"Not about my brother?"

Brad regretted blurting it out. He and his twin had never had much in the way of sibling rivalry, but there was something in their mother's attitude toward them that had been off for as long as he could remember. It probably started when he was six and had an accident while riding his bike that sent him to the hospital with a severe concussion. The doctor had apparently mentioned that there could be permanent brain damage, and had made Nancy feel like an incompetent parent for allowing him to ride a bicycle in the first place.

She internalized the criticism all too well. Even after he made a full recovery, she always hesitated whenever he wanted to do something risky. She seemed to trust his brother more, consider him more mature and capable, while Brad was always in need of a hand, always wanting for something, always less mature and more dependent.

So Brad felt driven to prove he was capable and independent, while his brother seemed to glide along, unaware of the disparity. It was a frustratingly one-sided problem.

But the evening went along pleasantly enough. The roast and sides were delicious, and dessert—a fragrant apple pie right from the oven—was mouthwatering. Afterward, a second bottle of beer for both Brad and his father were opened and consumed, and conversation drifted lazily from topic to topic.

"Are you and Cara going to be around this weekend?" Ron asked. "I'm working on the basement renovation project, and could use some help from anyone willing to wield a paint roller. We'll treat you to another dinner as payment."

Brad grinned. "We'd be happy to, but we're going to be off camping for the weekend."

"Oh? Where? You heading up into the Adirondacks again?"

"No, closer to home. There's this weird stretch of woods out west of Guildford. Rich at work more or less dared me to spend the night in it. He said it's haunted. So, you know, once the dare was issued, it was do it or turn in my Guy Card."

He expected that to get a laugh, but when he looked up, both of his parents were staring at him with a frozen expression.

"What?"

Nancy glanced at her husband, her head moving in a quick, jerky, almost panicked movement, but didn't say anything.

"Where exactly are you talking about?" From Ron's tone, it seemed as if he were having a hard time modulating his voice.

Brad frowned. What the hell had just happened? "It's just this stretch of forest, maybe fifteen miles west of the village. I don't have the directions memorized, but it's at the end of a road, um…"

"Claver Road," Nancy filled in. The words were thin, strained.

"You know about it?"

Ron nodded. "Your friend was right about the place having a bad reputation. I guess the younger generation kind of forgot, but when I was growing up, everyone in the county knew about those woods."

"Knew what about them?" Once again, his eyes moved from one of his parents to the other. He'd done far more dangerous hikes—mountaineering, real back-country camping where you were a hundred miles from the nearest town and might go two weeks and never see another human being, where accidents were not an inconvenience but a matter of life and death.

Even Nancy had finally resigned herself to her son's choice of a pastime—although it didn't seem to alter her perception of Brad as the weaker brother—and her cautions when he announced the previous summer that he was spending his three weeks of vacation in the High Cascades had an air of resignation to the inevitable.

Now, he was going to be within a few hours' walk of a village, and she was freaking out.

The silence stretched out. The only sound was the ticking of a clock in the next room.

"Well?"

When Ron spoke, it was with obvious reluctance. "You really don't know why that place has a bad reputation?"

Brad shook his head. "Ghosts? I dunno."

"It's not ghosts." Ron cleared his throat. "I don't know too much about the details. But when I was a teenager, it was...I don't know. You remember the movie *Deliverance*?"

"About the guys who get captured by these crazy inbred hillbillies?"

"Yes. Something like that. Only worse."

"Worse? That movie was fucked up."

Normally Nancy didn't appreciate swearing, but she let the word go past her with barely a flinch.

"Yeah. Worse. Look, I'm not playing cagey here. If I knew more details, I'd tell you."

Another quick jerk of the head from his mother, and her eyes registered alarm. Brad suddenly had an absolute conviction that his father was lying—they both knew more.

But why on earth would they not admit it and explain further, if they wanted him to take their warning seriously?

"I don't know what you expect me to do with all this," Brad said.

"Don't go." Nancy blurted the words out, speaking far more loudly than usual. She was holding her cloth napkin in her hand, and had nearly twisted it into a knot.

"I'm not cancelling a camping trip just because of some vague warnings. If it's dangerous, why haven't we heard of incidents? It's not like there have been people attacked or kidnapped or whatever, at least not that I've heard."

"Exactly," Nancy snapped out.

Brad's ire rose. There it was again. He was young, inexperienced, incapable of handling things. He had no doubt if it were his brother having this conversation with their parents, they'd tell him, "Be careful, but have fun," and that would be the end of it.

The thought doubled his determination not to let them scare him into staying home. That had happened far too often in his life. Don't take the risk, don't join the team, don't go for broke. Play it safe.

You can't handle anything more.

"I'm not staying home if you can't tell me why I should." He kept his voice steady with an effort. "This conversation is going nowhere, and it's obvious you're not going to give me any details, so let's change the subject. I'll come by next week and tell you about all of the evil throwbacks and their deformed children I saw while we were hiking."

Nancy winced as if he'd struck her, but said nothing.

"There's nothing we can do to talk you out of it?" Ron said.

"No."

The older man's lips tightened, and he gave a harsh sigh. "All right, then. We'll leave it in God's hands."

The rest of the evening passed in uncomfortable small talk, and by eight Brad excused himself. Cara would be home by now, he told them, and would be waiting for him. It wasn't the truth—open house went till nine o'clock—but he felt like he had to get out of his parents' house before he said something he'd live to regret.

If he hadn't already.

On the drive back to his apartment in Colville, he debated telling Cara about the conversation. Maybe present it in a humorous light— *you won't believe what my parents tried to tell me about the forest we're going to this weekend*—but somehow he wasn't able to work up enough energy to make it convincing.

In the end, he said nothing about it. When Cara asked him how dinner with his parents had gone, he smiled and said, "Fine," and hoped it sounded sincere.

But she was tired herself from her long day at work, and if she picked up any uneasiness from him, she didn't mention it. They chatted for a while about nothing and then went to bed, and that was that.

~

Saturday morning dawned bright and hot. Brad was able to put aside the cloud of misgivings he'd been under since the unexpectedly disturbing conversation with his parents, but it had taken a significant effort. He gave a brief summary to his coworker, Rich, and asked if there was anything to their worries, if he should reconsider the camping trip.

Rich laughed. "Yeah, okay, there are some redneck types out there. I'm guessing there are a fair number of meth labs, too. But there's nothing to all the rumors, that's what I think. People afraid of their own shadows. But hell, if your mom doesn't want you to go…"

The subtext of *stay home, then, if you want to be a damn coward* was as clear as if he'd spoken it aloud.

Brad forced a laugh himself, hoping Rich would take it as meaning he'd been half kidding all along about having any second thoughts. "No, I'm going. You said the magic three words."

"Which are?"

"I dare you."

Rich smacked him on the upper arm. "Bring along a hunting knife, or whatever. Dude, okay, I'm pretty sure there's nothing to it other than a dark forest and people's overactive imaginations. But hell, if something were to happen to you and Cara, I'd never forgive myself."

"I always bring along a knife camping. So far, I've only had to use it to field dress a rabbit or two. I'm not worried."

"Good. I don't think there are rabbits in those woods, though." He frowned, and the mirth disappeared from his face. "You know, that is one weird thing I've heard. Those kids I went to school with—the one who ended up in the psych ward and his friend—I remember hearing they said there were no animals. Like, *none*. No birds, no squirrels, no bugs, nothing."

"The *no bugs* thing sounds fine to me."

"I know, but don't you think it's a little strange?"

"Now who's trying to talk me out of it?"

Rich gave him a quick frown, and then relaxed into a smile. "No, dude, I'm not. I don't know why I remembered that all of a sudden. It was probably not true anyhow. I'm guessing they just made it up to give it...um..."

"Atmosphere."

"Right."

"Okay, so trip's on. I'll bring my hunting knife to fend off the creepy forest dwellers." Brad grinned. "I'll tell you all about 'em Monday."

"If you find a wild cave girl, bring her back for me."

He snorted laughter.

Brad had told Cara neither of his conversation with his parents, nor the weird turn his exchange with Rich had taken. She seemed to have put aside her own misgivings, and was cheerful enough as they were throwing their gear into the car.

No sense upsetting her, now that they were on their way there.

They drove up the highway from Colville to Guildford and took a left on Highway 226. The pretty little village was lost to view after they made the first bend, and the ribbon of asphalt snaked its way between cornfields and bean fields, over bridges crossing little spring-fed creeks too small to have names. The sprawling old building housing the large-animal vet's office was the last building for miles other than the occasional barn, and they went into a series of rises and falls, each climb a little more than the one before, as they ascended gradually into the hilly western part of the county.

A right onto Claver Road. Brad was acutely aware of how the sides closed in on them, as if they were driving into a funnel. First open scrubland on either hand, and the road had wide shoulders with a deep ditch on either side. Then the ditch filled in, clogging with brambles and branches, finally disappearing altogether. The shoulders narrowed. Asphalt was replaced by potholed dirt. The scrubland grew into a wiry tangle of small trees, and in the distance they saw a dark smudge that marked the beginning of the real forest.

Cara looked at the underbrush slipping by, close enough to touch through her open window. "Okay, this place is kind of creeping me out."

"I haven't even stopped the car yet."

"I know." Her gaze was distant, unfocused. "Do you think there's anything to the possibility that these woods are haunted?"

"I guess it's possible."

She turned toward him. "What would you do if you ran into a ghost?"

He shrugged, and forced a smile he didn't feel. The fact that practical, capable Cara was being freaked out by the atmosphere of the place was unsettling. It was one thing that his hyper-protective mother was worried.

It was another to see that reaction in a woman who had accompanied him on hikes into bear country, spent nights in a tent during thunderstorms, and once had given him a hand up out of a slot canyon in Arizona moments before he would likely have been washed away by a flash flood.

Now she was apprehensive about a patch of woods only thirty miles from their home.

Brad debated asking her if she wanted to turn around, bag the trip, but took a deep breath and set the possibility aside. The thought of showing up to work Monday and telling Rich Stendahl they'd gotten almost all the way there then backed out—no, that wasn't gonna happen.

So he kept driving.

There was only a short distance farther he could go without scraping the paint from the doors, though. Before the branches closed in enough to prevent them from exiting, Brad braked to a halt and killed the engine, and the silence flowed over them like water.

"Rich was right," Brad whispered, as they exited and began to pull their packs and gear from the back seat.

"About what?"

"There aren't any animals around. He said he'd heard that about these woods. No critters. Not even birds."

Cara gave a little shiver and an embarrassed grin. "We're both afraid to raise our voices, did you notice? Who do we think will overhear?"

"I have no idea."

She put her hand on his arm. "Look, you know we don't have to do this, right?"

"Are you getting bad feelings?"

"Yes. But we've been in more dangerous places than this. And I know…I know facing fears and not backing down is important to you."

Had she sensed the attitude from his parents, and especially, how it differed from their treatment of his brother? He'd never opened up to her about that, but she was extraordinarily perceptive.

"Yeah. I guess it is."

She took a deep breath, loud in the intense quiet of the place. "Okay. Then let's do it."

Brad locked his car up, and they shouldered their packs and turned their faces toward the forest, where the road dwindled into first a set of parallel wheel ruts and finally an overgrown trail before vanishing into the shadows beneath the branches.

They didn't speak as they went into the trees, Brad leading. The silence was like pressure against their ears, pushing at them from all sides. He had a sudden certainty they were being watched, although nothing in their field of view—not a leaf, not a branch—moved.

It was an effort to force his feet forward, but he kept walking, mostly out of a dogged determination not to let his nerves get the better of him. Cara's footsteps behind him, boot soles on dry leaves, were muffled, as if her feet were wrapped in cotton.

He gave only one quick glance over his shoulder. His girlfriend's eyes were wide, and her movements were tense, like the coiled posture of a rabbit when it knows a fox is near, every muscle ready to spring and carry it away from deadly danger.

Still they kept walking.

The feeling intensified all through the morning, and they stopped for a quick lunch next to a little crystal-clear creek tumbling over flat slabs of slate. Knotted, gnarled tree roots, exposed on the banks, plunged into the rocky soil on the edge, their splayed fingers clutching the ground, seeking out the plentiful moisture.

Brad felt a strange reluctance to touch the creek's surface, even though it was as limpid as tap water. The idea of filling their water bottles from it, even if they planned to boil it later, was repellent enough to make his stomach clench with sudden nausea. If they were going to keep going in the same direction, they'd have to cross, which would mean wading barefoot—the water was only a foot deep at the most, but sufficient to fill their boots if they left them on—and that was bad enough.

But to drink it?

Not just no, but fuck no.

As he unlaced his boots and pulled off socks, he tried to laugh at his own peculiar rush of fear toward this innocuous little brook, but his brain rebelled.

However irrational it was, he was absolutely convinced there was something wrong with the creek.

Hell, there was something wrong with the entire *woods*.

Trying not to show any hesitation, Brad rolled up the legs of his lightweight hiking pants, and put his foot in. The water, ice-cold, swirled around his ankles and between his toes. The sensation was like being caressed by a slimy, chilly hand, and he looked down, expecting to see something—trailing stems of water plants, maybe some leeches or insect larvae, *something* to explain the repellent sensation.

Nothing.

He crossed the creek as quickly, and with as long a stride, as possible. When he sat on the ground to pull socks and boots back on, he saw Cara's nose wrinkle and her mouth twist in an expression of unmistakable nausea.

Once again, it wasn't just him. But what could possibly be the cause of their reaction was not apparent. Under any other circumstances, the little creek would have been a pretty spot to sit for a while, but now all he could think of was getting away, finding a place where he wouldn't hear the bubbling and splashing of the water tumbling over the stones.

So they kept hiking.

By evening, Brad's wristband GPS placed them near the center of the woods. They'd covered almost eleven miles without pushing themselves particularly hard.

"Let's find a flat place, and pitch the tent. I'm ready to pack it in for the evening."

Cara took no convincing. But the usual chatter and laughter following a long day's hike never really happened. The tent was set up, gear unpacked, and dinner consumed mostly in silence, and by the time the shadows had deepened to full darkness, they retired to their sleeping bags.

Neither of them were in the mood to make love, which by itself was odd. There was something about the place that effectively doused ardor. But at least sleep was quick in coming, as the soporific quiet swallowed them up, drowning them in oblivion.

~

What exactly awakened Brad, at some unknown point in the middle of the night, he was unsure. When he opened his eyes, his entire body suddenly tense, there was still no sound, but it felt as if their little tent was surrounded, the focal point of dozens of pairs of watchful eyes. Moving as quietly as he could, he reached toward the spot beside his head where he'd placed his hunting knife as they were preparing for bed, and unsheathed it. The faint *swick* sound of steel on leather sounded loud in the stillness.

There was a sudden vibration, like a shudder, from outside of the tent.

They knew he was awake, and they knew he was armed.

Whoever *they* were.

The question was, what to do about it. He could wait, motionless, and see if they attacked, or go out into the night to find out what was out there. An unaccustomed anger rose in him, borne of the tension that had been rising in him all day. This was supposed to be a nice, easy hike. Whatever had turned it into an unnerving walk into the fear-shrouded darkness was right there, waiting for him, ready to show its face at last.

He'd be damned if he'd let them sit there and scare him into immobility.

He slipped his naked body as quietly as he could from the sleeping bag. Cara seemed as if she were still asleep. At least, she hadn't moved. He hoped that if she did wake, she'd assume he was going outside to take a piss and not pick up on his alarm, and on the unseen threat circling their little tent.

He unzipped the flap, pulled himself upright, took a step with one bare foot out onto the leaf-strewn forest floor—and was immediately seized by hands, human hands, cold though they were. Some clutched his upper arms, others his shoulders, and one long arm slipped around his waist.

He struggled, lashing out blindly with the knife. More than once it struck a target, and he heard a strangled yell and a string of what sounded like imprecations, although they were not intelligible, perhaps not even English. A moment later he heard Cara's voice from behind him, "Brad? What's happened...?" Then she too, was grabbed. He could hear her fighting like a wildcat, struggling to free herself.

But even with a knife, he was still captive. And she was unarmed.

The worst was his attackers' invisibility. The darkness was complete. Their assailants, however, could obviously see. Their grasping hands were unhesitating and accurate. His wrist was pinned, and the knife—slick with someone else's blood—wrenched from his hand.

"Who the hell are you?" he choked out. It felt like an effort to force air out of his lungs, to make any sound at all.

"Stop struggling," came a voice. An obviously human voice, steady and calm, as if what was happening were perfectly ordinary.

"You attack us in the middle of the night and you expect us not to struggle?"

A hint of annoyance came into the voice. "You trespass in our dwelling place, and you expect not to be challenged?"

"How about 'can you please leave?' instead? Who knows, we might even have acquiesced."

"It's too late for that. It was too late once you entered the edges of Ulthoa."

"Ulthoa?"

The voice turned away a little, as if it had spoken to him all it would. "Clear every trace of their belongings. Bring it all with you. Three of you attend to the ones who are hurt, then follow us back."

Brad was propelled through the woods, stumbling forward, expecting at any moment to run into a tree or fall into a gully. But the hands guiding him were accurate, and other than the discomfort of walking barefoot on sticks and stones, and the general unease at being captive and naked, it was an easy walk.

Within ten minutes, they reached a spot that felt more open, the air a little freer. There was a murmuring of voices around him, and he sensed perhaps a dozen people nearby.

A deep male voice said, "You got them both? The woman, too?"

"Yes."

Brad recognized the answering voice as the one who had spoken to him earlier.

"We were unprepared for the fact that he had a weapon. At least two, possibly more, of us were injured. I do not know how severely."

A long pause. "Lock them up. At dawn we will find out how severe the injuries are, and then determine what should be done with them."

"Done with us?" Cara's panicked voice came from somewhere nearby. "What do you mean, 'done with us?'"

"You have deliberately come into a place where what happens is not under your control. If you make such a choice, do not expect to be consulted on your own fate. Do you understand me?"

Neither of them answered, but the man continued as if they had affirmed.

"Very well. You will learn our rules soon enough."

"Should we allow them access to their belongings?" came the first voice.

"Once you have gone through them and made sure there was nothing else there that could be used as a weapon, or in freeing themselves. Other than that, I see no harm in it."

101

The unseen hands, that had never loosened their grip on him since he was first captured, pushed him through the darkness. A rustling noise behind him convinced him that Cara and her captors must be following.

"A step up," said a voice near his ear.

With caution, he lifted his foot, and felt underneath the sole what was unmistakably a wooden step.

There was the sound of a door opening, and he was shoved into an enclosed space of uncertain dimensions. Cara followed.

Then the door closed, and there was the sound of a bolt being thrown—from the outside.

All that came afterward was silence.

II

They dressed silently in the dark. Then, driven by a desire to know more about their surroundings, they felt their way around what appeared to be a cabin. Finally they found a low cot that barely fit them both. They climbed in, and Cara nestled up beside him. He could feel her body trembling, and knew she was crying, but there was little to say. So he simply held her and let her cry, and eventually they both passed into an uneasy doze.

The sound of the bolt being thrown back woke Brad, and he squinted as the door opened, allowing the cold gray light of dawn into the little room. He looked around him. It was a small windowless cabin, something more like a storage shed than a habitation. Standing silhouetted in the doorway was a tall, thin man wearing old-fashioned clothes—a shirt made out of coarsely-woven cloth, a pair of loose pants tied at the waist with a thin belt, a nondescript pair of leather shoes.

"Come," he said. "They're waiting for you."

Brad got stiffly to his feet, gave Cara a hand up, and followed the man out. They were immediately flanked by two stronger-looking men, whose eyes were narrow with suspicion.

Taking no chances on their trying to escape again, apparently.

They walked amongst a set of larger cabins, obviously dwelling places. They were all made of logs, and the wood-shingle roofs were moss-covered. The camouflage was effective. Even from a hundred yards off, in the shadows of the woods, they would be completely invisible.

Behind the cluster of cabins was a much larger structure which, even though constructed of stone, had a strangely organic appearance. It looked as if it had grown out of the bedrock, like it was part of the geology. Something about its gray, lichen-encrusted walls seemed almost alive.

Sitting on a chair in the entryway of this larger building was a stern-looking man of perhaps forty-five years, gaunt but powerful, whose dark eyes looked down on Brad and Cara with a disapproving stare. There was no preamble, no greeting.

"Your struggle to escape last night resulted in the injury of three of our people."

"Weren't you expecting us to struggle?" Brad shouted up at him, but his anger was like waves breaking on a cliffside. The man's expression did not change, and in fact he gave no evidence that he had even heard what Brad said.

"You entered Ulthoa without permission. The result is you will not leave again. We will accept you into our community once we are assured that you will not further break rules, nor attempt to escape and return to your world."

"Ever?" Brad shouted.

"You can't just…kidnap us!" Cara said.

He turned his unsmiling gaze upon her. "Oh, but we can. You were the ones who came into our place unbidden. If we were to let you leave, you would tell others. We cannot chance that. So here you will stay."

"We'll escape as soon as your back is turned." Brad threw defiance at him, trying anything to get the man to react.

No response in his still, stony confidence. "You will die, then. My people are woods-crafty. You would not get a mile before being captured. My instructions would be to slay you on sight."

"So we're just supposed to stay here?"

"Yes."

Brad's mind was racing, trying to come up with something, anything, that could change the course of this. "There are people who know where Cara and I are. If we don't show back up on Monday, there will be policemen combing these woods looking for them. My twin brother is one of them. He'd never give up."

One of the man's grizzled eyebrows rose a little. "You are a twin?"

Why this was of interest, Brad wasn't sure. "Yes."

"Identical?"

"Yes."

The man regarded Brad with a slight frown. "Fascinating." Whatever it was that had intrigued him passed, and he resumed his impassive demeanor. "But as for any who attempt to find you, including your twin brother, let them come. If any get separated, they will meet the same fate as you. If there are groups too big for us to capture, we have ways of evading sight. Don't try to frighten me. I assure you there is nothing you could say that will alter this situation in the slightest." He paused. "You will remain captive here until you have resigned yourself to it. Once there is no longer any possibility you will foolishly attempt to run, you will be formally accepted as one of us."

Brad heard Cara whimpering, but he couldn't take his eyes off the leader, whose face seemed to be carved from marble. Beyond the reach of human emotion.

"No," he managed to croak out. "You can't. Look, Cara didn't do anything. I talked her into coming along. She doesn't deserve this. At least let her go."

The man's dark eyes regarded him for a moment. "After she knows where we are, how to find us, how many we are, and that you are being held against your will? Don't speak nonsense. If there is a chance that your brother, or others you know, might try to find you, that chance would become a virtual certainty were we to let her go with the knowledge she has. A ridiculous suggestion. She shares your fate."

Something snapped in Brad at that moment. The unfairness of it all, especially that Cara, sparkling, cheerful Cara, would spend the rest of her life imprisoned in this dark forest, overwhelmed him. There were two people flanking each of them, but their grips on his upper arm had loosened when he showed no sign of fighting. With a sudden burst, he pulled free of them and sprinted toward the leader, still seated in his stone chair.

Up the three stone steps. He heard Cara scream, and a commotion behind him, but he didn't turn, determined to tackle the leader, pin him to the ground. What he hoped to do afterward, what it might accomplish, he had no idea. But the animal desire to attack his captors, to strike back, was overpowering.

The leader's face showed alarm, his eyes widening, and his long, bony hands came up in an attempt to shield himself. But then—not from the leader himself, but from somewhere in the dark recesses of the temple behind him—there came a surge of energy rising in a cresting wave, carrying with it a sour, rancid odor.

It was cold, like the heart of interstellar space, a fraction of a degree above absolute zero. But embedded in it was an awareness, an intelligence, and all of its malignancy was focused on Brad.

He heard Cara shriek, "Brad, stop! Don't! They'll..." just before the energy peaked and exploded outward toward him. The burst hit him in mid-chest, and he was picked up and thrown backward like a ragdoll. The last thing he felt was his skin freezing solid and his heart rapping out a staccato rhythm as it attempted to continue beating, to keep blood flowing through frozen veins and frost-hardened tissue.

Then his body hit something solid. There was a shower of fireworks in his skull, and everything went dark.

~

He had no way to tell how long it took him to regain consciousness, but finally it did return, at first feebly and in short bursts interspersed by blessed periods of black, dreamless coma. Eventually he recognized the passage of time, but even then his awareness was torn as his body tried to decide whether to live or die.

Even in his barely conscious state, he realized that his life was hanging by a slender thread, hovering over the abyss. He wasn't sure if he desired death or not, whether it might be easier just to let go and drop into the darkness beyond. The thought carried with it no emotional weight. It simply was.

But at some point, he decided to live.

The next two weeks were a confused haze of pain and delirium. He was given food but was unable to take more than a mouthful, and the first time he gagged and threw that small amount up.

For a long time—he had no idea how long—it was difficult to tell what was real and what was a dream.

He was up and wandering. Naked, aching, and breathless from what felt like a giant bruised hole torn in the middle of his chest. The side of his face hurt, and his exploring fingers gently probed what felt like a deep gash on his cheek. The twigs and rocks were sharp underneath his bare feet as he padded through the encampment. The people there looked his way—then looked right through him, as if he were a ghost, a shade that slipped across their field of view and was gone and forgotten. He wandered down to the stone temple again. The chair where the man had sat was empty, and he went up the three stairs to the rough gray platform and looked into the dark interior.

Echoes struck his ears. Cara's scream of horror when she realized he was running up the stairs to his own death. His own hollow gasp as he was hit, like a man being gut-punched. Then others, shouts and imprecations and howls of dismay that seemed to ring back for years, for decades, for centuries. Drawn by it despite his fear he walked past the chair and into the vestibule of the temple. The interior had no windows or torches, but he could see—the walls glowed with a surreal phosphorescence that gave everything a bluish cast. He looked down at his own body, and his skin looked livid in the eldritch glow except for the ridged and puckered wound on his torso, a wound that wasn't even bleeding, as if it had been cauterized as soon as it was delivered.

As far as the rest of him, he looked dead.

The vestibule opened into a larger space, lit with the same eerie half-light. The place was bigger than it seemed from the outside. His nostrils were struck by a smell, an acrid odor like spoiled milk. His gorge rose, but there was nothing in his stomach to bring up, and he forced his feet to keep moving, willing back the nausea.

Ahead was a stone staircase leading down into the ground. Its steps were polished smooth in the center by the passage of uncounted pairs of feet. How old would this place have to be to show such wear? Not a hundred, or even two hundred years. This place clearly antedated the European settlers in the area, who came in during the late eighteenth century.

This place might even have been here before the Native American tribes who were dispossessed by the white man's invasion.

But who, then, built it?

He walked down the stairs. The air was chilly and damp against his bare skin. The smell got worse the further down he went. Ten steps, twenty, thirty, and he lost count.

Finally his feet struck a solid platform as the staircase ended, and ahead of him in the same ghostly glow he saw an even larger space, hewn from the bedrock. At that rear of this room another and larger hole led farther down. At this point his fear mastered him, as a sense of horror swelled and crested over his mind.

He suddenly realized he was not alone.

Something down there was aware of him. Something sinister, but with great intelligence and purpose. He knew it to be the same force that had injured, nearly killed him. It was moving toward him. He could feel not only its eager mind reaching toward his, but a flow of air was pouring from the hole in the floor in the far edge of the room, cold as ice and laden with the odor of sickness and death.

Then he saw it, and did not know what he was seeing.

It gushed from the opening like smoke, streaming in tendrils toward where he stood, small and helpless and naked. That it would kill him when it reached him he had no doubt whatsoever, but his feet were fixed to the floor, and he was unable to move to save himself. The cloud rose up, now more solid, like a translucent shimmer blurring the walls behind it, and in the air he saw a face…

Brad screamed.

For a moment, he was in two places at once—standing in the temple, waiting for the icy blow to fall upon him and destroy him, and lying on his back, thrashing on a cloth-covered straw mattress soaked with sweat.

Then he was there in the little cabin, weeping with pain and fever, until blissful unconsciousness took his mind beyond where either could reach.

The days passed. Still he teetered between life and death. Someone—Cara?—came in periodically with a cool wet cloth to clean the wound on his chest, giving him some hope of escaping an infection, which even in his barely lucid state he realized would kill him outright.

Then one day he woke, weak and still hurting, but at least with a clear mind. He had been moved to a different cabin, one less like a storage locker—or prison cell. Pale sunlight, attenuated from the passage through tree branches, filtered in through a small window.

He tried to sit up, thought better of it, and lay back down with a moan.

A female voice near him said, "How are you feeling?"

"Probably better than I look," he croaked out. He turned his head, wincing as the movement pulled on the healing gash on his cheek. Sitting in attendance was a thin woman wearing a nondescript dress and a head scarf. The fact that he was being watched by a strange woman while lying in bed stark naked was distressing, but in his condition there was nothing he could do about it.

"You will have a scar," she said, looking at his damaged chest with a curious expression.

"No kidding."

The sarcasm seemed to pass her by. "You have barely eaten in the two weeks since you were injured. You should take some food."

He nodded. The mention of food made him realize his hunger, which was sudden, huge, and overwhelming.

The soup she provided was bland but filling. It was hard to tell in the dim light of the cabin, but may have been split pea or something like it. He ate it gratefully, downed a cup of water, and lay back and rested his head on his pillow.

"You've been caring for me this whole time?"

"I and others." She paused. "My name is Bethiah."

"Where's my girlfriend? Cara?"

For the first time, the woman's expression changed, and she seemed wary. "I do not know if I should say. I was not told how to answer that."

A clutch of ice-cold fear seized Brad's heart. If she were okay, they surely wouldn't have any hesitation in telling him so. "What happened to her? What did you people do?"

Bethiah's mouth tightened, then she appeared to come to a decision. "It was not our doing. She...she took her own life."

The shock of that, stated so bluntly, was so sickening that he almost vomited up the soup he'd just eaten, but he forced his gut to hold on to it. "When?"

"It was two days after you were injured. There was a time...it appeared virtually certain you would not survive. You were burning with fever and raving in your delirium, and your heart was pounding in your chest so fast we feared it would burst from your ribs. The damage seemed too great for any to recover from. She was in despair, believing you were dying and she would be left here without you, and with no hope of returning to your people. She alternately wept and railed against us."

"Did they hurt her...?" He could hear the horror in his own voice.

She shook her head. "Nothing was done to her. Nothing would have been done to *you* had you not tried to attack the Patriarch." There was stern disapproval in her voice, but in a moment she went on with a milder tone. "Seeing you hurt, and then believing you would die, overthrew her mind. The day she became convinced you would not survive your injuries, a change came over her behavior. She became resolute, as if she'd made some kind of decision. The Patriarch said it would be prudent to watch her, as she seemed ready to do something rash. And as evening was falling that day, she bolted, attempting to escape the forest."

"She didn't make it," he gasped out.

"She made a fine effort. Had we not been watching her, she might have succeeded. But in the dim light, and with her lack of knowledge of the forest, she came upon a deep gorge suddenly. We were closing in on her, and she knew she was trapped. When she was certain there was no escape, she waited until our people were close. She met their gaze steadily, then she smiled, closed her eyes, and threw herself into the gorge."

His frame was so exhausted that he could barely sob, but the tears flowed from his eyes and soaked his pillow.

"Our people know a safe path down into the gorge. We went to see if, by some miracle, she still lived. But her body was broken on the rocks. She must have died instantly."

The moment hung suspended. Brad was finally able to choke out, "I don't believe you. Where is she?"

"We buried her body. When you are well enough to walk, I could show you the spot if it would bring you solace."

"Solace...?" This was so far from what he needed that at first he didn't even understand the word. He pictured Cara's shining brown eyes, sweet smile, remembered the touch of her fingertips on his skin. Impossible to believe she was just...gone. And now he was the one who was facing being left alone with these people, with no hope of ever getting home.

"Has no one come looking for us?"

She nodded. "At the end of last week, there were perhaps twenty men wearing dark uniforms who were investigating the forest. They were too many to ambush, and also appeared to be armed with guns, so we were instructed to let them pass through, but to lead them deep into the woods where…" She stopped, frowning. "I have not been given knowledge of what I may tell you and what I may not."

"You're saying they didn't see you."

"It is unlikely. Our people know these woods like they know the terrain of their own bodies. If they want to remain unseen, they remain unseen. As far as knowing you are here, I cannot be sure. I would guess they suspect you'd been here, but as they were unable to find any trace of you, they were forced to give up and return empty-handed."

"Why would they give up if they know I'm here?"

"I do not know the answer to that. Even if they know you might have passed through the forest, there would be nothing to tell them where you are now. Without any evidence of where you'd gone, you could be anywhere. Perhaps they think you left the forest for reasons of your own, and might now be far away from here."

"Leaving my car behind?"

She shrugged.

"My brother…"

She shook her head again. "We were given specific instructions to watch for your brother, and to capture and bring him back here if it were possible. He would have been seen had he attempted to enter, so we conclude that he did not try."

"So that's it, then." The very words struck despair into his heart. "I'm stuck here forever."

The woman gazed at him, not without compassion. "That was your fate from the moment you set foot into the woods."

~

It was another week before he could dress comfortably. The wound finally began to seep, as if the damage had healed enough to allow normal tissue to replace what had been flash-frozen. Then it peeled, and his chest itched horribly, but he was able to stand and pull on clothes without being in agony, and get up to take care of his bodily needs and to eat and drink. A week after that he went to the communal table at dinner, and was greeted with dozens of curious eyes, but no one spoke to him. In fact, conversation was hushed when he was around, as if he were still not trusted, as if they expected him to bolt, to try to escape the forest and betray them at his earliest opportunity.

Truthfully, he wasn't sure he would have done that even if he hadn't been aware of being watched continuously. He was still weak from his ordeal and from spending three weeks barely eating. But even if he'd been completely healed and had regained his previous strength, the threat of what would happen if he were caught trying to escape was enough to stop him.

There was no way in hell he was going to risk that kind of injury again. Not for anything. Their threat to kill him if he tried to escape was apparently nothing short of the literal truth. Alone—running through the woods without any way of knowing where he was going, what obstacles lay ahead, even where to hide if he needed cover—no, that was certain doom, either from the hands of these people or from whatever it was that had attacked him in the temple.

There was the choice that Cara made. Suicide on her own terms rather than being recaptured.

But he also realized what that implied. He was going nowhere. Which meant spending the rest of his life in these godforsaken woods. Never seeing his friends or family again.

The only other option was death. And having so recently pulled himself back from the brink, he was still clinging too tenaciously to the feeling of life returning to his own body simply to embrace the risk of his own demise, or to end his existence by his own hand as Cara had done.

Perhaps at some point he'd be strong enough to take the chance of running. At the moment, all he could do was eat, try to avoid meeting the staring pairs of eyes, and sneak back to his cabin and escape into the oblivion of sleep.

III

The days slid by, shortening as winter approached. The odd glances Brad got during his first meal with the people of Ulthoa diminished over time. Apparently he was, on some level, being accepted.

Ignored, however, was probably a better word. Being avoided because he was a novelty and an oddity was honestly no better than going unnoticed. If he spoke to someone, they responded courteously enough, but no one ever initiated conversation with him. It was a remarkably dreary existence. There was no music, no dancing, no books, not even much conversation. As time passed, the restive energy of being continuously on guard, surrounded by danger and uncertainty, died down into passivity and boredom, where one day and the next were so similar that they were indistinguishable.

With the closing in of winter, the priority was gathering firewood before the snows started. To Brad's surprise, he was allowed to go out into the forest with the others, and the caution not to go too far or get separated from the group seemed almost perfunctory.

He did try to strike up a conversation one morning with a lean, sinewy young man named Ethan who was helping him to saw a fallen branch into pieces light enough to carry.

"Aren't you people bored?"

"How do you mean?"

"Stuck here in a woodland in the middle of nowhere. Just chores every day, day in, day out, year after year."

The young man shrugged. "It is the way it is. It is not my place to question it." He frowned. "Is it so much worse than your own life of work and noise and rushing about? It is different, that's all."

"But don't you even want to know what it's like?" He tried to make the question sound offhand. "What stops you from leaving?"

Ethan looked at him questioningly. "We're not permitted to do so."

"I know that's what you're told. And I'm not trying to stir things up, it's simple curiosity. There's only one leader, and even if he's got henchmen to do whatever he asked, there's enough of you that if you wanted to get out, you could find a way to do it. Don't you want to see what's out in the world, instead of spending your entire life here in the woods?"

"What I want has nothing to do with it."

"Why not?"

"My life is here."

"You could have a life somewhere else."

Ethan's eyes narrowed, and he gazed at Brad in silence for a few seconds. "You think that?"

"Of course. Why couldn't you?"

"You'll just have to trust me when I say that's impossible."

More emphasis on the follow-or-else command from the leader. Ethan stared at him for a few moments as if daring him to ask more, but Brad realized the fruitlessness of pursuing the topic, at least with him.

It was only after he returned to the encampment that evening that he paused to consider the young man's choice of words. Not *inadvisable* or *bad idea* or *unlikely to succeed*—Ethan had said it was *impossible*. But Brad had too little information to know if that was mere hyperbole or if there was something else behind it.

The evening passed with a quiet dinner and the usual retirement to their cabins when it got too dark to see. Brad was still in the cabin he'd occupied since his awakening to find that he'd somehow survived his injury. Even though many people shared cabins, he was still alone, which suited him fine. He no longer instantly mistrusted the inhabitants, as he had in the first few weeks, but having a refuge where he could get some solitude was welcome after a day spent with the silent, somber men and women of Ulthoa.

He had just dropped off to sleep that evening when he heard a faint creak as the door to his cabin opened. There was no lock—the only place he'd seen one was the bolt on the outside of the tiny cabin in which he and Cara had been confined their first night—and truthfully, no one seemed to own anything that would be coveted by the others, so security against robbery was unnecessary. As far as locking him in at night, they were evidently confident that their veiled threats about what would follow from any attempts to escape had worked.

Truthfully, they had.

In his experience, a visitor at night was unprecedented. He squinted into the darkness, but could only make out a vague shadow among other shadows, and recoiled a little when someone sat down on the edge of his bed.

"Don't be afraid," a voice said. "It's Bethiah."

"Why are you here?"

She didn't respond, but pulled down the sheet covering his body and put her hand on his bare shoulder.

"I thought...I thought you might want some companionship at night."

"Companionship?"

"Someone to make your time here more pleasant."

So this is what passed for seduction here. He almost laughed. "You mean you want me to make love to you?"

She didn't answer for a moment, but if his bluntness upset her, she gave no sign. "Don't you wish it as well? You have been alone for two months. You must have needs."

"Well, yeah, but..." He cleared his throat. "Don't you think the others will object if we sleep together? I'm not one of you."

She ran her hand down his arm in a gesture he supposed was meant to be enticing, but in reality gave him a shudder of revulsion. "But you *are* one of us," she whispered, leaning in close to him.

"Look..." he began, then stopped.

"Do I displease you? Would you prefer another?"

She said this in a flat, emotionless voice, as if she were asking him if he preferred coffee or tea with his breakfast.

"It's not that. I just...I just..." He paused. "Can you stop touching me, please?"

She pulled her hand back with some reluctance.

"I'm used to when I...when I have sex with someone, it's not that I meet a strange woman and say, 'Hey, how about it?'"

"But I am not a stranger. I cared for you while you were recovering from your injuries. I saw your naked body. It was why I thought—"

"So because you got a glimpse of my junk, you thought you owned it?" Brad was rapidly growing angry. He'd always thought of himself as having a strong sex drive, and in the years before he connected with Cara, he hadn't objected to a no-strings-attached hookup with a willing woman. But this?

There was something really, really wrong here. And whatever it was made sex completely out of the question. In this frame of mind he doubted he could get it up enough to have sex with her anyway. This was revolting to him on a fundamental, physical level. It wasn't that Bethiah was unappealing—she was, in an unadorned way, attractive enough—but the idea of coupling with her made his gorge rise.

"I do not think I own you." For the first time, her voice registered hurt. "I thought you might want me, that some physical comfort might be enjoyable for you. I'm sorry I judged wrongly." She stood up suddenly and moved toward the door.

"Bethiah…" he started.

She stopped and turned.

"It's not that it's you. I'm not rejecting you specifically. It's just that…I'm not ready for this, with you or with anyone."

She made a small noise of assent, and left the cabin as quietly as she'd entered.

Brad took a deep breath and pulled the sheet up to cover himself, even though the air was still comfortably warm.

Like the conversation earlier with Ethan, he was certain there was something behind this other than what it seemed on the surface. It wasn't just that Bethiah felt sorry for him and figured she'd give him some relief, or that she was horny herself and thought she could entice him into a quick lay. Either of those seemed flat-out impossible given what he'd observed of her before this.

But what else might have incited her to seek him out was anyone's guess.

~

It was shortly after breakfast that a middle-aged woman whose name he couldn't recall came up to Brad with the air of someone carrying an important message.

"The Patriarch wishes to speak with you."

A shudder ran through his body. At mealtimes he'd seen the leader—he wasn't at the point of calling him "the Patriarch" yet, that would be to admit he'd joined the cult—but had not spoken with him since the ill-fated meeting that left his body broken almost beyond repair. In fact, he couldn't even remember making eye contact with the man. Although he had no intent of trying to attack him again, a thrill of fear vibrated its way up his backbone.

"What does the leader want with me?"

The woman shrugged in a disinterested sort of way. "He does not tell me his reasons, only what he wishes me to do."

"Another useful little drone, then."

She shrugged again.

What would it take to get these people to react?

118

Did they even have emotions? He'd seen no evidence of it.

As far as finding out what the leader wanted, apparently there was only one way.

"All right. Where is he?"

"I will take you." She gave him a come-hither gesture and walked away without looking back. Obedience, apparently, was assumed.

Brad expected to be led back to the temple, but instead she went the other way, toward a cabin on the periphery of the settlement. She tapped on the door.

"Yes?"

"It's Jerusha. I have brought him, as you requested."

"Excellent. Let him enter." She pushed the door open for Brad, but made no move to come in herself.

Brad stepped up into the dimly-lit interior. He expected it to be sumptuous, or at least more luxurious than the one he lived in, given the leader's status, but to his surprise it was as simple and unadorned as his own.

"You wanted me?" Brad looked at the leader, seated in a rickety-looking wooden chair in front of a small desk. The man raised his gaunt face, the dark eyes regarding Brad with curiosity.

"Yes. I wished to ask you why you refused Bethiah's offer last night."

Brad stared at him in surprise. "News travels fast."

One corner of the man's mouth turned upward. "The couplings of the people here are none of my concern as long as they are consensual. I don't keep track of who spends the night with whom. I only know about this because I am the one who asked Bethiah to go to you."

This was such an unexpected turn that Brad could think of nothing to say in response.

"You will no doubt want to know why, if my previous statement about not caring about who makes love to whom was correct, I would take it upon myself to pair the two of you."

"That thought had crossed my mind."

The leader nodded. "It was for more than one reason. One is that I was concerned that you were still setting yourself apart from the rest of us. You have formed no friendships, and as far as I've seen no one really knows you. I thought that a physical connection would bring you closer to our community."

Brad just stared.

"Second, I am fully aware that the sexual drive is part of the human condition. You are a young and vigorous man, and your needs should be met in more ways than solitary pleasure, over and over."

"I'm okay with jerking off when I need to, thanks." Brad felt the same revulsion rising in him that he'd experienced when Bethiah touched him. Despite the leader's calm voice and neutral expression, he had the sense of drowning in something foul. He could almost feel its slimy touch against his skin even though there was nothing there but the cool, damp air of the cabin.

If the man was aware of Brad's visceral reaction, he gave no evidence of it. "Perhaps," he said, and shrugged. "All of us use that option from time to time if no other way is available. If I have not made this clear enough, we do not engage in moralizing about sex here. It is simply another need to be met, no more wicked or illicit than eating or drinking or sleeping."

"That must be fun for all of you."

Again, if the leader caught the sarcasm, he didn't show it. "It makes a frequent cause of conflict between people far less likely, and renders the whole activity less secretive and shameful." He paused. "But there is another reason I asked Bethiah to go to you, one that may not be as apparent." He stopped, looked down as if composing his thoughts, and then continued. "You may have noticed that there are no children here."

"Yeah, I noticed. And if you're doing as much shagging as you implied, that's pretty weird."

Another flash of a smile, there and gone in an instant. "I have not heard it called that, but I take your meaning. And yes, it is indeed odd. We do not fully understand the reason, but it seems that…our presence here, although it gives us much in return, has one significant negative consequence. It has rendered us infertile."

"Really?" There was no need to feign shock. Whatever he'd been expecting the leader to say, it wasn't that.

"We do not know if it is only the men who are affected, only the women, or both. You can see there would be no way to determine that. We know that the women have continued in their monthly cycles and that the men still respond the same way and produce normal amounts of semen. Nothing seems odd by comparison to the sexual response all humans have. But despite the lack of restrictions on intercourse, there has not been a conception here for…for a good many years."

Brad frowned. The youngest person he'd seen in the encampment was probably Ethan, who looked to be between twenty and twenty-five years old. That meant if the leader was telling the truth, there had been ordinary amounts of sex going on in the intervening years, and not a single pregnancy.

"You can see why this is a concern."

That was when the light dawned. "So you wanted me…you wanted me to fuck Bethiah so you could see if maybe I could make her pregnant."

"It was my hope. Bethiah was at the point in her cycle when conception would have been likely had everything been working normally. I thought that if it was only the men who were infertile, perhaps you might not have been affected yet. Bethiah was agreeable to this, and in fact finds you very attractive. She had no objections."

Brad fought down an urge to laugh. "So you were trying to use me as a…as some kind of stallion?"

The man shrugged again. Nothing seemed to upset his equanimity. "Only if you were also willing to play that role."

"It'd have been nice if she'd told me that's why she came."

"As I said, it wasn't simply that. She is honestly attracted to you, and likes you a great deal." He sighed. "We had hoped…when you and your woman arrived, we thought perhaps the two of you might be the start of a new generation here. But the unfortunate events that followed your arrival made that impossible. I very much regret the circumstances of that meeting, and want you to know it was never my intention for either of you to be harmed physically. I blame myself for the outcome."

"Doesn't do Cara much good."

"No. No, it does not. But you must realize that regardless of my regrets, my principal duty is to this settlement and the people here. I can see that you are upset by the idea of being 'used,' as you put it, to impregnate one or more of the women here. I understand that, although I hope that at some point you will be willing to at least allow us to conduct the experiment. What do you have to lose by it?"

"Other than my self-respect?"

The leader chuckled. "Come now. Are you honestly trying to tell me that every time you have had carnal relations with a woman, it has been for true love?"

Well, that was a direct hit. "All right, I get what you're saying, but...Jesus. You don't think this is a little...unnatural?"

"I cannot answer that because none of us knows why the infertility has occurred. It could be the water, the air, or any of a number of other things. We are certain it isn't the food, as our food is provided from outside."

"The people who provide it could have added something to the food that has that effect."

He made a scoffing noise. "Not only would they have no reason to do so, they do not have the intellectual capacity to accomplish such a thing."

"Nice."

"I mean no disrespect to them, as we depend upon them, but it is simply a statement of fact. In any case, the infertility could originate in any of a variety of sources. We know neither its origin nor its full effects at this point, nor how quickly it manifests in a newcomer. You see now why it is troubling to us."

Brad regarded him for a moment. "That's fucked up."

Another quick smile. "I understand your meaning, although you use that word for a great many purposes that have nothing to do with one another."

"It's versatile." He took a deep breath. "So Ethan is the youngest person here?"

"Ethan?"

"He's the youngest-looking person I've seen. He's what, twenty-two or twenty-three years old? So there have been no births since then?"

A look of understanding came into the old man's eyes, but with it, a guarded, canny expression. "So you are wondering how long this infertility has troubled us."

"I think I can make a fair guess."

The leader nodded, his brow furrowing. "Since Ethan's birth we...we have had two other births. The infants were born sickly, and neither survived."

"Whose children were they?"

"The children outlived their mother. She died in childbirth."

Brad had the sudden and absolute certainty that this was a lie. But what was he lying about? Perhaps they'd sacrificed the babies in that hideous temple. Maybe the mother, too. But why would they sacrifice children, their only hope for long-term survival of the community?

Something didn't make sense here.

"So you really want me to have sex with as many women as I can manage, and see what happens."

"A crude way of putting it. But correct in its essence. Understand, however, there is no compulsion here. The only firm rules here in Ulthoa are the prohibition against leaving, and that there is to be no violence against each other. Other than that, we operate by the same rule the pagans followed of old—if it hurts none, do what thou wilt."

"What if what I wilt is to stay celibate and tell you to take your human breeding program and shove it up your ass?"

There was barely a twitch of the old man's lips. Brad fought down the desire to keep pushing him, to be ruder and ruder, and see where the threshold was. How much it would take to get him to respond in kind. He'd shown alarm when Brad had attacked him, but was that because he feared Brad would hurt him—or because he knew Brad was about to be hurt or killed by the power he'd unleashed in the temple?

After a long pause during which the leader studied his face closely, he said, "Then you sleep alone, and take care of your needs by yourself."

"And everything continues as before? No penalties for disobeying?"

"It is not disobedience, because it was not a command."

"What is that thing in the temple? The thing that attacked me on my first morning here?"

The out-of-the-blue question also had no impact. In fact, it almost seemed as if the old man had been waiting for the subject to come up.

"You will find that out. But not now. Once you are fully integrated into our community, you will learn about the power in the temple."

"What if I want to know now? What if I go investigate myself?"

"That would be singularly unwise."

"So there *are* more than two rules."

Annoyance flickered across the leader's face. Maybe Brad was finally raising his emotions. Perhaps there was a crack in that armor, an ingress into the man's arrogant confidence.

"I did not say it was against the rules. You are free to go into the temple whenever you wish. However, you are unlikely to come out alive. Therefore such an action is not prohibited, it is only foolish. If you told me you were going to climb to the top of a tall maple tree and jump off, you would probably die, but not because it is against any sort of rules, only that it is dangerous. The natural world is full of such inherent risks. Surely you realize that."

"I don't think that shadow creature in the temple has anything to do with the natural world."

"Oh? Then what do you think it is?"

"I don't know. Not yet. When I find out, I think I'll know a great deal more about you people and why you behave as you do."

"That," the leader observed, "is the first thing you've said that is unequivocally true."

IV

The grip of winter tightened down on the little community, and everyone but Brad seemed hardly to notice.

The cabins were snug, each with its own fireplace, so he was warm enough at night. Any time he was outdoors, however, he was chilled to the bone. It had been the height of summer when he was captured, and he had no cold-weather gear in his pack. The people of Ulthoa provided him with a rough-woven jacket and thicker pants, but it wasn't nearly enough. He was aware of the necessity to conserve resources, but he went through firewood faster than anyone else in the encampment.

After his strange interaction with the leader, everything slid back to the previous monotonous pace. He caught Bethiah looking at him with longing more than once. It seemed the leader's comment that she actually liked him for himself and not just his potential as a sperm donor was correct.

But every time he met her eyes, she looked away.

~

In the following weeks, the shortening of the days indicated they must be approaching the solstice. Something was afoot in the encampment, something more than the dreary rotation through chores and meals and sleep. It was impossible to tell if it was fear or excitement or some combination, but it had a galvanic effect on the entire group.

Brad was curious enough that he decided to ask someone what was going on. The worst that could happen was a refusal to answer. After some deliberation, he decided to ask Bethiah. She was already predisposed toward him, and would be more likely to give him an honest answer because of it.

Of course, she might interpret his speaking to her as his acquiescence to her amorous intentions.

Well, there was nothing he could do about that. If it came down to it, he could always refuse her again.

He caught her after lunch, on a day when flurries were spiraling down between the bare gray tree branches, dusting everything and everyone and muffling all sounds. He touched Bethiah's sleeve after helping clean up the lunch dishes.

She turned, frowning, and didn't say anything, the puzzlement clear in her eyes.

"Can we talk?"

"Of course."

"Not here."

She nodded, and followed him across the camp and back to his cabin. Again, there was the possibility of her misconstruing his intentions, but he didn't want to be overheard questioning her, so his cabin was the obvious place.

It was also warm.

When he closed the door behind them, she turned toward him, the question still in her expression.

"There's something I need to ask you."

"Ask it."

"What is going on in the encampment? People seem...different. I'm not sure if they're apprehensive or excited. But something is up, or something's going to happen, and I want to know what it is."

Her brows drew together, and she tucked a loose strand of her dark brown hair under the edge of the gray scarf that covered her head. He noticed for the first time that the scarf she wore had some faded but intricate embroidery along the edge—the first sign he'd see of adornment in the clothing worn by the people here. She regarded him in silence for long enough that he thought she wasn't going to answer.

Finally she said, "It is the Ceremony of Rededication."

"Rededication? To what? To the leader?"

She shook her head, and the strand of hair came loose again. "No. To the temple. The leader is merely the conduit. He speaks for us, but he is in need of the reconnection as much as the rest of us are. Without it, we would not survive."

"When is this happening?"

"The solstice. Five days from now."

"And this ceremony—what exactly happens?"

Now her reluctance was obvious. She bunched the corner of one sleeve in her hand, and said nothing.

"If I'm going to be there anyway, what harm is there in telling me what to expect?"

"I do not know if I should say. It is not my place. And this...this will be your first. You will be before the temple as a novice."

He recalled the vaporous creature he'd seen twice now—although he was still uncertain whether one time had been a dream—and shuddered.

There was no doubt in his mind who they were dedicating themselves to.

He tried to keep his voice level, as if he wasn't concerned. "Don't you recall your first time, what it was like?"

She gave a quick, nervous shrug. "It was so long ago. I don't remember it, hardly at all."

He forced a laugh. "You don't, like, sacrifice someone on the altar of the temple, or anything?"

Another short, sharp shake of the head. "Of course not."

"Then why are you afraid?"

Her eyes flickered up to his and then away. He'd hit it directly. It was fear, not excitement or anticipation.

"I am more afraid for you than I am for myself. I have been through this every winter solstice for years. It is...not easy. But I know I can endure it. But as a novice, I fear for what you will experience." She swallowed. "I fear for your life."

"I've already been through a lot, I suspect I can make it through this."

"What happened to you the day you arrived nearly killed you."

"And you think this will be as bad?"

She shrugged.

"I'll be all right. If the rest of you can take it, I can."

He hoped his voice sounded more confident than he felt.

Her mouth twitched upward in a faint trace of a smile. "I hope so. I hope you believe that I wish you only well."

"I know that, Bethiah."

She met his eyes and did not look away this time. "I should return to my duties. They will wonder where I went."

Brad nodded.

She went to the door, opened it a crack and peered out. A shiver passed through her thin frame, and she crossed her arms, tucking her hands into the folds of her skirt to protect them from the cold. Then she left, her footsteps making no sound on the snow-covered stairs.

Brad sat on the edge of his bed. Rededication. A ceremony involving the temple, and almost certainly, the monstrous entity that dwelt in its depths.

No blood sacrifice. She had assured him of it, and he didn't think she was lying.

But if there were no sacrifice involved, why did she fear for his life?

~

Three nights afterward, he was awakened by the same stealthy noise that had disturbed his sleep before.

Someone quietly opening the door of his cabin and walking toward him carrying a lit lantern. The floorboards creaked slightly with each step.

"What…" he began, but stopped when the person shushed him with a hissing intake of breath.

"Quietly," came the voice in a whisper. "It is Bethiah."

"I don't want to…" he began, but she clutched his arm with a desperate strength.

"No." Another breath, which she let out slowly, obviously trying to calm herself. "I am here to help you escape."

"But you can't…"

Again she interrupted. "I cannot let you go through the Ceremony. It is hard enough on us initiates. I tried to plead with the Patriarch to let you remain safely in your cabin all through that night, but he said no, that if you were to finally become one of us, this was the only way. That was when I realized that I could not allow this to happen."

A shudder rippled through his frame.

"I care for you. I know you don't feel the same for me…" Bethiah's voice was mournful.

"I'm sorry if I hurt you."

"It is of no consequence. Such feelings cannot be produced on demand. But my care for you is not feigned, and my desire for you not simply from the Patriarch's attempt to see me bear a child. So I determined…after we spoke three days ago, I determined that I would see you safely away from this place."

"What about the risk?"

"I can accept the risk if you can."

Hope rose in his chest, hope that he thought was permanently expunged. If he succeeded, he would see his parents again, see his brother and his friends. He felt once again the loss of Cara as a physical pang of grief, that she would never have this opportunity.

But if there was a chance, he had to take it.

"It has to be tonight," she said. "There is a snowstorm beginning. All will be in their cabins, so the chance of being seen is slim. It makes our escape less likely to be thwarted. At the same time, it increases the risk of our becoming lost, or being killed outright by the cold."

"Are you willing to do this?"

"If you are, I am. I know the way to the boundary with the outside, down to where Them on the Edge leave our food and supplies. I can guide you." She stopped. "Will you let me come with you afterward? After we escape from the perimeter of the forest? I do not know what they will do to me if I return alone and they find that I have helped you." She shivered. "Such a betrayal, they might have me executed. I do not know."

"You can come with me."

What she would do upon emergence into a world she had never seen before and knew nothing about, Brad didn't know. They'd have to figure that out when the time came. After all, refugees were faced with the same sort of situation, and many of them adjusted well enough. In any case, if she was willing to risk not only her place in the community but her life to help him, he could do no less for her.

"Then dress quickly, in the warmest clothes you have. But travel light. It is two hours to the edge of the forest, but it is rough terrain, and the snow will hinder us. Leave behind whatever you can."

He slid from beneath the blanket and quickly pulled on his clothes, the rough jacket and pants he had been given when the winter descended in earnest. Already his body was cooling, and he was still in the relative warmth of the cabin. The wind was making the shutters rattle.

It would not be a pleasant hike. But even to have a chance at returning to his previous life was better than giving up and accepting what he had here. Bethiah herself was dressed as always —a long dress of some rough cloth, a scarf over her head holding back her long brown hair, a light jacket that seemed inadequate for a crisp fall day, much less a snowstorm. She was at least wearing heavy leather boots that looked like they had thick padding, but that was her only concession to the weather.

He, on the other hand, was shivering before even going outside.

Once he was dressed, Bethiah went to the door, as she had three days earlier, opening it quietly and peering out. What little light there was scattered from swirls of falling snowflakes, confounding the eyes. A sudden misgiving arose in him. His body had never fully recovered from his injuries. Was he strong enough to make such a hike, in these conditions?

But Bethiah was already outside. To admit to her that he didn't have the courage to make the attempt was such a jab to his pride that he couldn't bring himself to say it.

They quietly threaded their way between the dark cabins. As she had said, there were no guards posted, no one out and about. Once they were amongst the trees, over rough ground and slick stones, she took his hand to steady him. What he'd been told the night he arrived—that the people of Ulthoa were woods-crafty and could see like owls in the dark—was apparently nothing more than the plain truth. Bethiah led him along unerringly, finding their way through twisted roots and clutching branches, always taking the surest path.

But the cold was taking its toll. He was shivering uncontrollably, and a half-hour into the forest he could no longer feel his hands or feet. He stumbled more than once, finally catching his toe on an unseen rock outcrop and doing an unceremonious face-plant into the snow.

She pulled him back to his feet with surprising strength. He expected her to ask if he was okay, but all she said was, "Come on. We can't delay."

He wanted to respond with annoyance that he hadn't fallen deliberately, but his teeth were chattering so hard he couldn't form the words.

After another twenty minutes, he was becoming delirious. There was no choice but to keep walking. He was uncertain whether he'd walked for one hour or ten, or if he'd never been anywhere else but trudging calf-deep in drifts, on rock surfaces he could no longer feel, surrounded by the ebony shadows of tree trunks and a gauzy lace curtain of falling snow. Bethiah was still holding his hand, but he only knew it when he looked down.

It was some indefinite amount of time later that he became

gradually aware of a lightening in the air in front of him, a sense of a release of oppression. Far off in the distance he saw something he thought at first must be an optical illusion—points of yellowish light that moved and danced above the snowdrifts. They had reached the edge of the forest. Those dots of light were flashlights. Real, solid, modern flashlights.

They had not only escaped, but there were people there waiting for them. How that had happened he was uncertain, but his heart gave a quick flutter, a combination of excitement and relief.

They stepped out from under the eaves of the trees.

Two noises struck him, nearly simultaneously. The first was a cry of "Over there! There they are!" from the holders of the flashlights. The beams angled wildly for a moment then swung around in their direction. The second sound was a strangled gasp from Bethiah.

He turned toward her, smiling to assuage her fears.

Bethiah was staring, but not at him. The golden light of the flashlight beams caught the side of her face, and her pale eyes were staring into the middle distance as if she were seeing something no one else could. Her mouth was frozen in a rictus of terror.

He grasped her sleeve. "Bethiah? It's okay…"

She croaked out words that were barely audible. They sounded dry, dusty, as if they'd been trapped in her body for centuries. "I would have…I would have gone with you. I would have saved you if I could. I'm sorry. I didn't believe it was true. I didn't…"

As he watched, her skin seemed to tighten, and her narrow face became gaunt. The color washed out of her cheeks, leaving her a ghastly white, like wax. Her hand in his clenched down so hard that the pain reached him even through the numbness.

Then her eyes frosted over. Cracks formed in the corners, around her mouth, widened, pulling apart like rotted leather. Her knees buckled and she fell onto her back.

"Bethiah!" Brad knelt next to her.

But she was obviously already dead. As he watched, the withering progressed, her face turning skeletal and then collapsing away into gray powder. Finally what was left of her hand released his, and it too crumbled into nothing.

In moments, all that was left was a plain dress, jacket, scarf, and boots, lying in the snow. Of the woman who had worn them the only traces were caught up by the wind and scattered like ash.

By this time the flashlight-bearers were near him. He heard one of them say, "It got her. Like they said. They was right. But why didn't It get this fellow, here?"

"Dunno. But they'll want him back, I'll warrant."

"Maybe we should hide him. *Them Inside* can't harm us, not while we have the talismans."

"No, but don't mean It can't come after us, smash our houses, destroy everything we have. You want to risk it for this stranger?"

"No. I suppose not."

Brad looked down at the remains of the woman who had tried to aid his escape. He tried to rise, to utter something that might induce these people to help him, but could do neither. Strong hands caught him under the arms and hoisted him upright.

That was the last thing he knew for quite some time.

~

When he regained consciousness, his awareness took in where he was and what he felt, but it was with a clinical detachment, as if he were reading about it in a book. He knew the pain and fear would come later, but at the moment they couldn't reach him.

First was that he was lying on his back in his cabin in the encampment. A roaring fire was burning in the fireplace, and there were four people there, the leader seated in a chair beside the bed, and three others he barely knew standing in a semicircle behind him. Even in this simple setting the leader's rigid posture communicated authority.

Somehow, Brad was still alive. His hands and feet were still numb, but looking down he saw they were wrapped with cloth.

What part of his memory was real? Had he dreamed Bethiah attempting to help him escape, and her horrible death? What about the flashlight-wielding outsiders? None of it could grab his brain for long. The thoughts floated past like snowflakes on the wind he could still hear rattling the shutters.

The leader looked down at him, his dark eyes flashing with anger. "We told you not to try to escape."

"I…" He stopped, cleared his throat, and went on in a stronger voice. "It wasn't my idea. Bethiah came and said she'd show me the way out."

"And perished in the attempt. Bethiah was more foolish than I thought. She knew what the outcome would be."

"I didn't want her to die."

"Perhaps not. But that was the result."

"How did I get back here?"

"We have…friends who live outside the forest." There was the slightest hesitation on the word *friends*. "When we found you and Bethiah had gone, we sent word to them to watch for you. Fortunate they did, or you would have frozen to death."

"Sent word? How?"

The leader's lips tightened. "There is no need to discuss that. Your action, whether or not you were the one who initiated it, cost a life." He smoothed back his thinning gray hair with one hand, the first sign of nerves he'd shown. Evidently this was not a topic he wanted Brad to focus on. "Were it not so close to the Time of Rededication, that transgression would have to be paid for. It is long since we had to use the lash on someone for such sins, but in times past that would be the penalty."

Brad just stared at him.

"But in two days we will have the Ceremony, and you will be brought forward as a novice. It would not do to have you face that while recovering from being whipped. Consider yourself fortunate." He paused, and a faint smile twitched over his thin lips, there and gone in a flash. "Although afterwards, you may have wished you had stood for a flogging instead."

Brad swallowed hard. "What happens at this Ceremony?"

"You will become one of us. It is something that cannot be undone. You will endure much, as it is your first time, but the gifts it bestows are many. Perhaps then you will fully understand the gravity of the sin you have committed, and why it cost Bethiah her life."

"And if I refuse to go through your Ceremony?"

The leader gave him a frosty smile. "You act as if you have a choice."

V

B rad spent the next two days fighting down a rising sense of panic. He was right about the pain from his near-death in the snow coming full-on once the numbness wore off. The morning after his abortive escape attempt, his hands and feet were consumed with a throbbing ache that left him nearly unable to think. A woman—one of the ones who had accompanied the leader into the cabin the previous night—was tasked with feeding him until his hands had healed sufficiently that he could hold a utensil. She was tall and thin as Bethiah had been, but there was no gentleness in her pale, narrow face and hooded gray eyes. She tended to his needs with a silent, grim efficiency.

"What's your name?" he said to her, as she put together the dishes from his breakfast, which had tasted like plain oatmeal, not delicious but warming him through.

She paused in her movements, and locked eyes with him for a moment. "Asenath."

"Odd name."

She shrugged.

"Thank you for feeding me." He held up one wrapped hand. "Kind of hard to hold a spoon if you've got paws."

If he expected a smile, he was disappointed. "The Patriarch gave me this task," she responded, her face stony. Her voice sounded as if she were barely containing her loathing of him.

Brad felt impelled to press on. He wasn't used to being disliked, especially in what was apparently a deep and visceral way, and simultaneously he felt as if he wanted to win this strange woman over and wondered why he cared. "Why did Bethiah die? I had no idea that was going to happen, and I wouldn't have gone with her if I *had* known."

Asenath stared at him, her heavy-lidded eyes full of scorn. "Bethiah was my friend. She was a good person."

"I suppose that's why she wanted to help me."

"She should have known better. The Patriarch commanded us all not to let you talk us into helping you flee."

"I didn't talk her into it. She came up with that idea all on her own."

Asenath's face softened, just slightly. "It is something she would have done. She had a big heart, and always wept for weak and injured creatures."

He nodded, and the guilt over his rejection of her rose in his gut. He remembered the little hints of her spirit that he had hardly given thought to, like the faded embroidery on the edge of her scarf. Perhaps there was more to her than he'd realized, and she hadn't been the drone he'd taken her for.

Still, there was no way of knowing that now. "But you never answered my question. Why did she die?"

"I don't know if the Patriarch…"

He waved at her in impatience. "Look, in two days I'm going to be initiated into your cult, or whatever it is, whether I want to or not. I think I should at least know that much. Hell, if your leader had told me what would happen if she left the forest, I'd never have gone with her, I'd have talked her out of it. Bethiah would still be alive."

Still, she hesitated. "If you try to escape again…before the restriction is put on you, following the Ceremony…the penalty will fall upon me for having told you too much."

Brad lifted his cloth-wrapped feet, causing another jolt of pain to shoot up his legs. "You think I'd get very far like this? I'm not going to be running anywhere for several weeks, and it doesn't look like there's a way for me to avoid your Ceremony. Why not tell me?"

She regarded him in silence for a moment. "We are...forbidden to leave."

"I know that much."

"That which sustains us..." She lifted one hand and gestured vaguely in the direction of the stone temple. "It has lain that stricture upon us. If we leave the forest, it withdraws its life force from us. We have grown...dependent upon it. Once that has happened, the spirit is destroyed, and the body crumbles to dust."

"It was horrifying to watch. You've seen it happen?"

She shook her head. "It has only happened one other time that I know of, and that was years ago. But I have spoken to those who found the...the remains. Afterward."

"If you can't leave the forest, how did your leader send word to the ones who live outside it, that we were trying to escape?"

"We cannot leave. The being who sustains our lives—that which lives in the Temple—is under no such restriction. It can leave at will, although never for long. Were it to abandon us, we would all perish, just as a man would perish if he were deprived of water and food."

"Why do the people on the edge of the forest do what your leader and the thing in the Temple want? Why would people help this...this cult of yours?"

Her eyes narrowed suspiciously. "That was established years ago. *Them on the Edge* help us, bring us food, because we cannot leave the confines of the forest. The being in the Temple, that which sustains us—we also keep a rein on it by our devotion, and in return it protects us and them insofar as it can. I am told *Them on the Edge* do not trust it entirely, and wear talismans to repel its power, but as long as all do as they have agreed, no harm comes to any."

"Détente," Brad said quietly.

"What?"

"A balance of power. Help us, we won't hurt you...and vice versa."

She shrugged. "That is essentially correct."

There was silence for a moment. "Will you tell me about this Ceremony I'm going to be a part of?"

"What of it?"

"Your leader said that once I went through it, I'd wished I'd gotten a whipping instead. That sounds pretty horrible."

Asenath swallowed. "It is...difficult."

"Painful?"

She gave a quick nod. "Painful, yes. But even beyond the pain. It tests you. You must both acquiesce to its power, and also resist it, lest you lose yourself entirely."

"Another balance of power."

"Yes."

"Has anyone you know done that? Lost themselves?"

"None recently. Many years ago, I believe there were ones who could not withstand it, and lost their minds." She paused. "They are all dead now."

"But you still go through with it every year?"

"We have no choice. It's that, or have the being in the Temple withdraw from us. And you saw the result of that. The Ceremony is not pleasant, but it is far better than the alternative." She gave him an evaluative look. "You will survive it. You have twice faced worse in the past months, and survived both times."

"Even injured as I am?"

"Your bodily injuries will not be a problem. It is your spirit that must not quail. It is much like standing upright in a windstorm. You must bend, but not so much that you lose your footing and are blown away."

"That all sounds pretty vague. Can't you tell me any details about what I'm in for?"

Asenath's expression became canny. "I'm not certain it can be put into words. In any case, you will soon find out for yourself. Afterward you will understand why I say it is one of those things that once experienced, cannot be described."

~

The remaining time until the Ceremony passed all too fast.

Brad felt a primal terror rising in him, so powerful that he would have fled alone even though the cold was unabated, had his feet not been so painful he could barely walk. It was a temptation to get away from the encampment any way he could, even if it meant crawling through the snowdrifts until he flagged, fell unconscious, and died of hypothermia, alone in the frozen forest. Dying alone was not as terrifying as the thought of what might await him during the Ceremony.

The feeling of fear emanated directly from the stone temple. It was the same power he'd felt in the borderland experience between dream and waking, during which he'd gone down into the edifice itself and seen what lay below. He'd penetrated two levels down, but who knew how many more there were, what horrors lay beneath those gray stones? Whatever it was that dwelt there, the strength of it had grown, as if it were drawing energy from the lengthening nights. Even in his cabin he could feel it, like the heat from a raging bonfire that can scorch and blister your skin from a distance.

But this creature wasn't warm. It was cold, the black cold of interstellar space, only degrees above absolute zero. Wherever this thing had come from, it wasn't the warm, pliable, humid terrain of Earth. Its home was the darkness between the galaxies, the silence of a frozen vacuum.

What lay beneath the temple was the offspring of that void. If it wanted it could burn what it touched, burn it not with fire but with ice, tissue frozen solid in an instant. There would be no fighting back against it. A sparrow had as much chance of withstanding a blizzard.

It was no wonder that the Ceremony was held on the Winter Solstice.

~

One day and then another passed, and Brad's fear crescendoed as the thing's power did. He woke up on the morning of the shortest day of the year in a state of panic. The Ceremony was to be conducted at sunset, he'd found out, and the people of Ulthoa spent the day in what he would have interpreted as Christian prayer had he not known that the being they were praying to was light years from a beneficent god. No one spoke to him, and when Asenath brought his meals to him, she left them without saying a word, responding to his hushed question of "What's happening?" with only a short, sharp head shake.

When the light faded with the approach of sunset, two men came to escort Brad to the temple. Whether it was to help him walk on his injured feet or to prevent him from trying to run was uncertain. Perhaps both. But when they flanked him, and he felt two strong hands clutch his upper arms on either side, he felt as if he were being conducted to the headsman's block.

The chill of the snow bit through his thin shoes, making his frostbitten toes ache miserably. Twice he stumbled, and each time was caught by his silent guards and saved from a disastrous fall. The whole walk only took five minutes, but the pain and fear made it seem like a death march, as if he'd been trudging through the snow to his doom for hours upon hours.

The leader was once again seated in the stone chair in the portico of the temple, the dim light casting stark shadows across his face, accentuating his gaunt features. He was clad in a long, dark robe whose color was uncertain, but he was so still that he and the folds of cloth looked as if they were carved from granite. He was no longer an ordinary man. He was a wizard, a druid, a conduit of the power that lay behind him in the darkness, and its fierce energy beat against Brad's face like a gale.

The people of Ulthoa clustered around the base of the stairs, each face in some combination of elation, fear, and ecstasy. They were waiting, and it was clear they knew what was coming, even if Brad did not.

The leader spoke. His voice, although not loud, cut through the silence, and the assembled crowd standing at the foot of the stairs shuddered as if it had come on a high wind. The words struck Brad like a knife made of ice. He had thought his fear had reached its apogee, but now it arced even higher. If his two attendants had not been supporting him, he would have crumpled insensate to the ground.

"We are assembled to rededicate ourselves to that which sustains us. We ask your beneficence for another year. Come forth and lend us your power. Iä Azrok!"

The people as one responded, "Azroga kuroth bey." The voices had the dry monotony of churchgoers reciting prayers they long ago memorized and no longer understand.

"We are become the instruments of darkness, our wills are in your hand to use as you desire. Iä Azrok!"

"Azroga kuroth bey."

"As we have done of old, we offer ourselves to you, our lifeblood in exchange for your protection. Iä Azrok!"

"Azroga kuroth bey."

The prayer continued, call and response, each call louder than the one before. Dozens of chanted petitions to come to them, protect them, take what it needed from them, each followed by the words *Azroga kuroth bey* murmured in unison.

Behind the leader there was a force building, soaring toward a crescendo but still pent up like the water behind a dam. The hairs on the back of Brad's arms stood up. There was a sudden overwhelming rancid odor, like sour milk.

"Take us now, take us tomorrow, take us forever. Iä Azrok!"

The toneless refrain came once again in unison, "Azroga kuroth bey."

He began to struggle against his captors, certain in the knowledge that if he didn't free himself now, he would never leave this place again. Before, escaping from the forest seemed an impossibility. After this, it would be.

Now the leader was screaming, "Iä Azrok!" and his followers responding "Azroga kuroth bey," back and forth, faster and faster, a language older than English, perhaps older than human language itself. Brad's ears popped as if the air pressure around him was dropping fast, and reflexively he closed his eyes.

So it was that he felt, rather than saw, the force behind the leader rise up and discharge its power like lightning. There were cries as that power passed into each of the people standing before the temple, cries that seemed halfway between orgasm and agony.

Then the bolt hit him, and his thoughts were wiped clean.

He knew instantly that it was restructuring his body, touching each of his organs, perhaps even rewriting his DNA. It felt that fundamental. He writhed in the grasp of his captors, but even if they'd released him he couldn't have run. It was an exquisite edge of pain the likes of which he had never experienced. At the same time it was intensely pleasurable, and he wanted to prolong it even as he felt its power diminish, drawn into him down to the cellular level. He could hear his own heart pounding, and he wondered that it did not burst from his chest, killing him not from a withdrawal of the life force but from an excess of it.

No wonder Bethiah had crumbled to dust when she was taken away from this place.

With a startling suddenness, it was over. He looked around, and only then realized he'd fallen to his knees. Each of the people of Ulthoa had in some way collapsed, some to their knees, where they remained in postures of supplication, others sprawled on the ground. The leader had sunk back into his stone chair where he lay, his thin arms hanging loosely, his dark eyes staring into the middle distance, seemingly unaware of anything around him.

But something about the people was different. They looked more vital, more alive, despite being motionless, apparently so exhausted they were unable to stand. Even fallen in the snow, they radiated good health, and most of them had dazed half-smiles.

There was no pain in his frostbitten hands and feet. Clumsily he used one wrapped hand to remove the bandages from the other, and when the long cloth strips, stained with his blood, dropped into the snow, he saw only pink, undamaged skin. There was no sign of injury. He flexed his hand, and it responded smoothly, as if his injuries had never been.

He quickly peeled the bandages off the other hand, and it was the same. Slipping one hand under his shirt, however, he still felt the ridged scars in the middle of his chest and on the side of his face, where he had been struck by the being that had evidently now healed his frostbite. But there was no pain from them. Left there, perhaps, only as a reminder that the same power that could heal could also kill, making permanent the marks that it had itself placed upon him.

He looked up at one of his captors, only then realizing that the one to his right was Ethan, the young man he'd tried to pry for information while they were out collecting firewood. In the extremity of his terror, Brad had not even recognized him.

As he stared, Ethan opened his eyes and swiveled his head toward Brad. His cheeks were flushed with life, his eyes sparkling, almost glowing, in the dark. His broad chest rose and fell quickly, as if he had been running hard. He took a deep breath, let it out slowly, and gave Brad a broad grin. Then the young man caught him up in a powerful embrace.

"Brother." His voice sounded as if he were near tears. "We welcome you. You are now one of the people of Ulthoa. There is nothing more to fear. This is your home, now."

VI

Nothing in Brad's life had prepared him for the Ceremony and the days that followed.

The ritual he had witnessed, and ultimately become a part of, on the Winter Solstice reminded him on some superficial level of going to Catholic Church services as a child with his grandparents. The chanted prayers and the mumbled responses from the parishioners had the same cadence, and he could almost make himself believe that what he had endured was some strange, perverted survival of nineteenth-century religious rites.

But however his brain tried to reassure him, he knew that wasn't true.

Even though when he'd gone to Mass with his grandparents he'd been too young to understand much of what was going on, there was something ineffably comforting about it. Despite the grotesque and horrifying statue of Jesus bleeding out his life nailed to a cross, the church was a place of refuge. The dimly-lit sanctuary smelled of incense and candle wax, and there was an almost tangible sense of peace. So even if some of the imagery was gory and disturbing, there was no doubt that the deity the worshipers prayed to was a force of goodness and beneficence. The crucifix wasn't itself a symbol of evil—it was a symbol of what evil could do to righteousness, what righteousness should prepare itself for if it was serious about fighting the powers of darkness.

It wasn't celebrating pain and death. It was a warning.

Here, though? There was no doubt in Brad's mind that the being that lived in the temple was evil in its essence. He knew its name was Azrok—one of the strange words the leader and his followers had chanted over and over—and that it had come from the stars, falling here long before any humans were alive on Earth. He also knew that it couldn't leave the temple for long, because somehow its life force was bound up in the place, the same as the lives of the people who worshiped it. It would weaken progressively the further away it got, although it was not confined to the boundary of the forest the way its followers were, and even within the radius of its power it could wreak terrible damage on any innocents who got in its way.

So it was trapped on Earth, tied to this stone edifice, although why or by whom he did not know. Azrok conferred knowledge on its initiates, but not unlimited knowledge. There were things it didn't want its worshipers to know—or perhaps, did not know itself.

The realization that the being in the temple was evil didn't affect Brad on an emotional level. It was purely an abstract mental construct. On a physical level, his body craved renewed union with it, to recapture the overpowering sensations he'd experienced only days before. The closest parallel was in times he'd been desperately horny, unable to think about anything but finding relief for the discomfort in his groin. The moment he was pierced by the energy emanating from the temple was itself close to the release of orgasm, and afterward he slipped a hand down the front of his pants and was a little surprised to find he hadn't actually ejaculated. Now he craved a repeat of that release, and the knowledge that he would have to wait a year to experience it again was almost painful.

He also knew he had been changed physically by it. He not only was healed of his frostbite, but of the scar on his forehead he'd gotten from the bicycle accident when he was six, a scar whose size belied how severe the injury had actually been. The little white dent above his right eye was clean gone, and when he asked Asenath to take a close look and see if there was any sign of his injury, she'd squinted at his forehead, examining him closely. "There is nothing but smooth, unblemished skin. You see now why you should never have fought us? Healing is only one of the many gifts we receive. You will no doubt find others." She touched the scar on his cheek and gave him a superior smile. "But you were left with the ones the power itself gave you. Those you will wear forever, as a sign of the price of defiance."

Azrok could kill him with a mere touch. He knew that now. But far from repelling him, it simply increased his attraction. He wanted what it was doing to him, drawing his puny will into its own, and giving him a strength far beyond what he'd had.

Strength to do what? He was not sure yet. That he had only begun to tap into it, he was certain. By the time it was done with him the old Brad Ellicott would be gone forever, transformed into something with only a glancing point of contact with humanity, a mere tool in the hand of the thing in the temple.

A phrase the Patriarch had chanted came back to him. *We are become the instruments of darkness.* And he responded, *Take me. Turn me into the moving finger of your will. I understand now.*

The power obliged. It reached out to him from the depths of its home beneath the temple, flowing toward him like a tsunami, irresistible and devastating.

He welcomed that transformation, opened himself to it, and felt the burning cold of its energy pouring into his chest, flooding his heart and guts and brain, riding the wave of ecstasy as far as it would take him.

~

It was clear the day after the Ceremony that the geometry of Brad's relationship with the people of Ulthoa had changed. What had seemed dour reticence he now realized was mere caution, not to speak freely in front of someone not completely integrated. Now, he was impressed by the warmth and friendliness with which he was treated. Some barrier had been breached, and the guarded treatment he'd received was apparently a thing of the past.

Part of it, of course, was that he felt like something had changed in him. He had been pulled in, reluctantly at first, but once he accepted that he was a part of the community, his lingering fear and anxiety, never far distant since he and Cara had been captured months before, were gone. It was the sensation of struggling against an immovable object—once the struggle was abandoned, his muscles relaxed, comfort and peace seeping through him.

And when a woman named Tamar came to him a week after the Ceremony and asked if he wanted to spend the night with her, he had acquiesced without any hesitation. He had a momentary pang about having spurned Bethiah, but after all, she had been disobedient to the Patriarch's commands, and had paid the price. Perhaps it was better he hadn't let himself get too attached to her.

After he and Tamar were done making love, he slipped into a peaceful half doze, letting his mind wander. She was curled up next to him, one arm around his waist, breathing slowly. Asleep?

"Tamar," he whispered.

"Yes?" Not asleep after all, apparently. Her voice was clear, with none of the slurred quality of someone just wakened.

"How old do you think the Patriarch is?"

Her body twitched against his, and the arm clasping him tightened, then relaxed slowly.

"Why do you wish to know?"

He shrugged. "Mere curiosity, I guess. How long has he led Ulthoa?"

"As far back as I can recall."

Brad chuckled. "Really? You must be exaggerating. You can't be older than forty, and by the look of him, he's not that much older. He's been running the place since he was a child?"

"You don't understand."

"No, I don't. That's why I asked."

There was a long pause, and Brad wondered if she was going to answer at all—and simultaneously wondered why she was so reluctant. Was he or was he not one of them, and entitled to the same knowledge the rest of them had?

Finally she said, "The Patriarch is...he is older than he looks."

"Really? How much older?"

"I believe you should ask him that."

He frowned. "Well, how old are *you*? Surely that's not a big secret, is it?"

This time, no response.

"Tamar?"

"Yes?"

"Why won't you answer my question? I don't have any weird hangups about two people of different ages having sex. I'm thirty-five, but if you're sixty or something—hell, I hope I look as good as you do when I'm sixty."

He thought that would get at least a murmur of laughter, but there was still silence in the cabin.

"Tamar?"

She gave a long sigh. "I am trying to figure out how best to respond to you."

"You could say something like, 'Brad, I'm fifty years old,' and I'd say, 'Oh, okay,' and that'd be that."

She gave a little shake of the head. "That's not it." Another sigh. "Search in yourself. Feel in your body. You sense the difference since before the Ceremony, yes?"

"Of course."

"Describe it."

"I feel more...more alive. My energy is better. I don't need as much sleep." He paused. "And I'm hornier, too. It's like I've returned to being twenty years old. You want to go again?"

"Perhaps. But don't let yourself be distracted. Look inward, and you will find the answers you seek."

Was she hinting at what she seemed to be? It seemed to him

suddenly that the answer had been there, before his eyes, for months, and he had been willfully blind. The vigor coursing through his veins was undeniable, as was the healing of his frostbite and the scar from his childhood accident.

"Are we…" He paused, swallowed. The word sounded almost too ridiculous to say aloud. "Are we immortal?"

"Not immortal. You saw what happened to Bethiah."

That was clearly evasion. He scowled. "Well, if we stay within the confines of the forest, then."

"Still the answer is no. We can be killed, or die from misfortune, injuries too severe for our bodies to endure."

"But other than that?"

"Other than that…" She cleared her throat. "Perhaps the best way to say it is that we do not know what the upper bound of our lives will be."

"Azrok…the being in the temple…can do that?"

"You know he can. You have seen what miracles of healing he has worked upon your own body. If you still disbelieve, it is only your stubbornness in clinging to what you had in the outside world."

"I'm not clinging. It's just a lot to take in."

She nodded. "That is true. I spoke unkindly, and ask your forgiveness."

"No problem."

"In any case, it is time for you to speak to the Patriarch tomorrow about these things. You are one of us now. It is not right that you still have unresolved questions." She slipped her hand down his belly, then lower still. "But enough talk. There seem to be other matters more urgent."

And that ended conversation for the night.

~

The next morning, after the communal breakfast was done, Asenath came up to Brad and said the Patriarch wanted to see him.

Even her chilly attitude toward him seemed to have thawed slightly, although it was clear she still hadn't completely forgiven him for his role in Bethiah's death.

"What about?" Brad asked her.

One thin eyebrow lifted. "It is up to him to tell you that."

"I'm not in trouble, am I?" He gave her a little smile, hoping futilely for one in response.

The eyebrow lifted further. "Is there a reason you should be?"

He shook his head, said, "Thanks for letting me know," stood, and turned toward the Patriarch's cabin as he had the previous time he was summoned. This time, however, he was not accompanied by the message-bearer.

Apparently his obedience was assumed.

He tapped on the door, and at the murmured response, "Come," he opened the door.

As before, the Patriarch was seated at a small wooden desk waiting for him.

"I am told you have questions about our ages, and how long we live."

"Once again, news travels fast."

This elicited only a twitch of the corner of his mouth. "Tamar sought me out before breakfast, saying that the question was worrying at you. She was right to bring the information to me. Now that you are one of us, you deserve an answer to that."

"Was I right, then? Is the being in the temple making us immortal?"

"Not in its most literal sense." The Patriarch picked up a writing tool of some sort—in the dim light it was impossible to tell exactly what it was—and rolled it between his fingers in a meditative fashion. "Violence can certainly kill us. Accidental injuries as well. Disease? That is at present unknown, as no sicknesses have struck us in long memory. Whether that is because we do not fall ill, or because we have been fortunate enough not to come into contact with a contagion, is uncertain."

"Tamar said that other than those kinds of things, though, we don't die."

"That appears to be correct."

"How old are you?"

Another fleeting smile. "This worries you?"

"It's germane to the discussion, don't you think?"

"Oh, certainly, it is that. I suppose the question is reasonable enough. Very well." He looked upward, as if searching for information only half-remembered. "I was born in April of the year 1775. I do not know which day, as in those times keeping records of such things was not considered of critical importance. Be that as it may, I can tell you that if I am correct about which year it currently is, I am near two-hundred-and-fifty years of age."

Despite his half-expecting such an answer, given what he'd experienced and his cryptic conversation with Tamar, hearing it spoken aloud in such a plain fashion was like a punch in the gut.

"And all...all the others...?"

"Most are younger. I believe the youngest is my son, Ethan. He was born around the year 1810. He and the rest of us were dedicated to Azrok in the first Ceremony, in the year 1830." The Patriarch's dark eyes gazed intently at Brad's. "He has hardly aged since that time."

The thought *I'm glad I said I had no problem fucking an older woman to Tamar last night* flitted through his head, and he had to squelch a desperate, hysterical laugh.

"So you all...you're the same ones that..."

"The same ones who settled here in Ulthoa, almost two hundred years ago? With only a few losses to accidental death, we are the same people, and I have been their leader during that entire time." He paused. "My name is Enoch Bishop."

PART III:

THE MARK OF CAIN

My brain was spinning.

I couldn't disbelieve what my brother had said. It squared too well with what others had told me, and what I had read in Alban Bishop's books. But I also couldn't stop part of my brain from labeling the entire story sheer lunacy.

But...the new scars. And the missing *old* scar on his forehead. And the patient, calm fashion in which he told the story, so at odds with the vibrant man Brad had been. Of all of the ways I thought this search might end, this was one I hadn't even considered. Dan was staring at me, wide-eyed, undoubtedly waiting to see how I'd respond. He didn't know my brother as well as I did, but he clearly recognized that something was wrong, something beyond the bizarre experiences he had recounted.

"The experience changed you." My voice betrayed how tentative I felt.

He smiled. "How could it not?"

"You truly never tried to escape again?" Of all of it, that was the part that amazed me the most. The Brad Ellicott I knew would have torn the bars of a cage with his fingernails rather than allow himself to stay imprisoned.

He shrugged. "I can't know what would happen to me. I asked the Patriarch if Bethiah died the way she did because she was so old, or simply because when she set foot outside the forest, the power withdrew from her. What would happen to someone newly-dedicated? Would I merely lose the energy that had been pumped into me, and that has been renewed every December since? Return to what I had been? Or would I crumble to dust the way Bethiah did? He did not know."

"Said he didn't."

"Be fair. How would he? All of the people of Ulthoa were first dedicated two hundred years ago. There have been no new people from that time till this, with the exception of myself, and now...you and Dan." He gave us both a beaming smile, as if he expected us to be excited by the prospect.

"If you think I'm going to stand there and let myself get baptized into your cult, you can go fuck yourself," Dan growled.

Nothing seemed to affect Brad's equanimity. Dan's words broke from him like an ocean wave from a cliff. "You'll come to see it my way with time. You have everything to lose, and nothing to gain, from defiance."

"Bullshit," Dan said in a near-whisper, but by this time Brad's eyes were already back on me.

"So, brother, it seems like you knew some of this already. You've done your research."

"I knew about Enoch Bishop and his family, and the Dunstans and Craigs. I'm guessing those three families are the ones who live here?"

"Yes."

I gave him a long stare. "Can I ask you a blunt question?"

"Of course."

"How do you know the leader isn't lying about who he is? One

155

of Enoch Bishop's descendants, not Enoch himself?"

"It was corroborated by others in the settlement."

"The people in Jonestown would have corroborated the claim that Jim Jones was the reincarnation of Jesus."

For the first time, the annoyance showed. His lips tightened. "It's not the same thing."

"You admitted yourself when you first got here you thought it was a cult. Cara was so repelled by it she committed suicide rather than join. Now you're...you're one of the true believers. And this thing in the temple you people worship, what did you call it?"

"Azrok." He spoke in hushed, almost reverent tones.

"Azrok. That's the same thing that destroyed my house, you know that? It was trying to kill me and Dan both. This is the god you've sold your soul to?"

"I didn't sell my soul."

"Your leader, whoever he is—he sent that thing to kill me. I don't have any doubt that he's also responsible for the deaths of two others whose only sin was giving me information. How do you defend that?"

"You don't understand." Brad shook his head. "You don't understand."

I felt the rage rising in my chest. I wanted to strike him. This wasn't my brother. It looked like him, sounded like him, even moved like him, but the creature who sat on a rock outcropping across from me was nothing more than a flawed copy of the boy I'd grown up with and the man I knew. "You're fucking well right I don't understand. I don't understand how you've accepted any of this."

"Wait until you meet the others. Wait until you've had a chance to speak with the Patriarch. I won't say all of your questions will be answered, just as mine were not. That will have to wait until you and Dan are dedicated this year on the Winter Solstice. Like me, you will have to be patient for it all to make sense. But trust me that it will. When you undergo dedication, you will see that everything I've said is nothing more than that plain truth. Your stubborn clinging to your kneejerk emotional reactions will be destroyed utterly."

My kneejerk emotional reaction to get myself and Dan out of here, and steamroll over anyone who tried to stop us, was going to take a good bit of destroying, but I didn't say that. "We'll see."

His face relaxed slightly. "Come with me, and you'll see that I haven't lied to you. It will all be explained if you just don't fight it."

"Come with you?" I laughed. "Why should we come with you? I was hoping you'd come with us. I see now that was a forlorn hope from the beginning. But if you think we're just going to follow along behind you, you're out of your mind. Don't fight it, my ass. You haven't seen the beginning of how we're going to fight, against both you and your leader. Against the entire cult if need be."

Brad gave a deep sigh. "I was hoping that your love for me would have been enough, but I suppose that was a forlorn hope as well." Another sigh, and when he continued, his words sounded tired, perfunctory, as if they were part of a speech he'd memorized and hoped he'd never have to recite. "There are people from Ulthoa all around us right now, watching everything we do. In fact, your movements have been monitored from the moment you set foot in the forest. The people who guard the Edge let us know you were here. After that, you were simple enough to track. We see and hear much better than you do, and know these woods so well we could move through them in total darkness. If you don't follow me, you'll be captured and dragged. It is your choice which you'd prefer."

"So jump off the cliff or be thrown?" Dan snarled.

"If you choose to see it that way."

I was suddenly overcome with guilt over having brought Dan along. Had I listened to him, we wouldn't be here right now, surrounded by Brad's cult member friends—I had no doubt that part, at least, of what he had told us was true—but instead I'd followed my own obsession and gotten him ensnared too. "I'm so sorry, Dan, I…"

He cut me off. "Dad, if you'll remember, I'm the one who said you needed to get your mind settled by going into the forest. I volunteered to come with you. I'm a big boy, I make my own decisions. Don't beat yourself up over this." His eyes narrowed, and he glanced over at Brad. "Besides, I'm not giving up yet. I meant what I said. If you think I'm going to join your cult, you and your pals better prepare yourselves for a hell of a fight."

Brad shrugged, and a faint smile touched his lips. For some reason, that smile chilled me to the bone. Again, I was struck by the certainty that this wasn't Brad at all. His body and mind were being used as a mouthpiece by something not only evil, but inhuman. His tale of this creature in the temple coming from somewhere in the cold wastelands of interstellar space was all too plausible. What he was saying seemed to come from light years away.

"You're only two men," Brad said. "Two against two dozen, and that's not counting the power that gives us life, which will defend us if you become violent." He yanked his shirt up again, exposing the scar in the middle of his chest. "You think I don't understand the price of defiance? I almost died because I had the same attitudes you have. How much easier it would have been to acquiesce, relax and accept everything the day I got here. To make the transition painlessly rather than going through the agony of healing from a wound I didn't need to suffer, only to find out in the end that what the dedication gave me was far better than anything I had to give up?"

"That includes giving up yourself?"

"Yes." He stood, and now his expression was alert, as if he'd heard someone calling his name in the distance. "It is time. We have talked long enough. We need to return to the encampment. I remind you again not to attempt to bolt. There are men and women who will watch you the entire way, and who are faster and stronger than you are. If you run, you'll be caught, and you won't be dealt with gently."

We rose as well, and I gave Dan a tiny shake of the head. I knew how impulsive he could be, and I didn't think Brad's threats were idle.

There would be time to plan our escape later.

There was no sound during our walk to the settlement other than our feet crunching in the leaf litter. There still were no sounds of birds or small animals. The wood seemed devoid of life except for the ominous, brooding shapes of the trees, now fading into darkness as dusk approached.

We came on the settlement suddenly. It was as he'd described it—nearly invisible until you were in the midst of it. The cabins were small and moss-covered, and their positions chosen to block visibility. On the other side of the settlement was a hulking shape that could be mistaken for a rock outcrop, but which I surmised was the temple wherein resided the being that had stolen my brother's soul.

Without warning, we were surrounded by people. Some had come up behind us, and I guessed those were the ones who had been positioned in the woods to make certain Dan and I didn't try to get away. They were all thin, the failing light drawing deep shadows on their faces, making them look nearly skeletal. All were clothed in simple, drab garb, the women's heads covered with scarves, the men's with hats. From the look of them they could have walked out of a nineteenth-century farm village, and almost against my will I found myself believing the leader's claim that he was two-hundred-and-fifty years old.

None of them, however, looked as if they were older than fifty, and the majority had the faces and physiques of people in the prime of life. Their thinness, most likely from years of living on short commons, and the still, wary expression in their eyes gave them an otherworldly look. Like with my brother, I had the unsettling impression of people who were only mimicking humanity, but whose wills and motivations came from somewhere unimaginably distant.

One of the oldest—or oldest-looking—people stepped forward. He was a tall man with intense dark eyes, and he looked at us with suspicion. With no preamble at all, he said, "So you are the twin brother." He swiveled his head toward Dan. "And this, I presume, is your son."

"That's right."

"I am the leader of this encampment. I trust that your brother has already spoken to you about the expectations for your behavior."

I could hear Dan grumbling behind me, but he held his tongue. "He said we weren't to fight back or try to escape."

"Yes. There are other rules, of course, but those will do for now."

"Your name is Enoch Bishop?"

"Yes. Did he tell you that, or did you discover that name through your research?" A mocking smile flitted about his thin lips, and I knew at that moment he was far more aware of what I had been doing over the previous weeks than I was comfortable with.

"He told me. But I knew your name before. You are mentioned in more than one book, you know."

"All highly flattering accounts, I am sure." He gave a small wave of the hand. "Jerusha, Korah, get our guests food." His eyes flickered toward Brad. "Show them to the cabin we have prepared for them."

Brad and two of the people who were watching gave obsequious little bows.

"You will dine in your cabin tonight, but tomorrow morning you may join us for our breakfast. You may as well begin familiarizing yourselves with our customs right away. I am certain your brother emphasized this point, but in case it was unclear, do not attempt to flee during the night. Your cabin will be guarded. Even if you succeeded in breaking free and escaping into the woods, we have the advantage of better night vision and a familiarity with the terrain. Your chance of reaching the edge of the forest is zero. You should resign yourselves now to remaining here."

"We'll see about that," Dan muttered under his breath.

"Yes, your uncle started out with that same attitude." Bishop's thin lips curled upward in a smile. "He changed. So will you. So will both of you."

~

Dan and I were allowed to share a cabin, which I found curious. Apparently they were confident that the threats they'd made would dissuade us from plotting to escape.

They searched our packs to make certain we didn't carry weapons. They confiscated Dan's hunting knife, but other than that, we were left our belongings, and alone for the night.

As we readied ourselves for sleep in the two rickety, uncomfortable-looking beds, Dan said, "Do they really think we're going to give up?"

"Seems that way."

Dan pulled his shirt off. "Uncle Brad certainly seems to have drunk the Kool-Aid."

"I don't know." I pulled down the thin blanket and sat on the edge of the bed. "Did you really think that was Brad talking?"

Dan looked at me as if I'd lost my mind. And, to be honest, spoken aloud it sounded pretty ridiculous. "What does that even mean?"

"That thing in the temple. Azrok. Didn't Brad make it sound like demonic possession?"

"Sounded more like soft-core porn to me."

I laughed. "Well, yeah, he admitted as much. That ceremony sounded like half religious ritual, half orgy. But for possession to work, the demon has to give the host something, right? That's the way it's usually portrayed. Power, wealth, pleasure, long life, whatever."

"Didn't know you believed in demons, Dad."

"I didn't. Before now. But I don't have any doubt that this thing Brad described is real. And it sounds more like a demon than anything else I can think of."

"You think it's speaking through Brad? Using him as a mouthpiece?"

"That's exactly the word I thought of. I don't think it's literally true. I think there's some of Brad still there. I kept getting little flashes of him. When he was telling us about Bethiah's death, I got the impression that was my brother, feeling grief over someone he actually had cared about. But so much of it sounded like someone who'd been brainwashed, who was speaking the cult's talking points without any of his original self coming through. Like he was puzzled that we didn't both just say 'Hallelujah, praise Azrok' and come over to his team."

Dan slid underneath the blanket, and lay on his back, fingers laced, hands cupped behind his head. "Maybe that's the key."

"What is?"

"Their confidence. Their fatal flaw. They can't even conceive that we might win. All this *we see better than you in the dark* and *we know these woods like the backs of our hands* and *our pet monster in the temple will hunt you down and kill you.* The way they said it—Brad included—sounded almost perfunctory, like they were thinking, 'We just need to scare 'em a little. Put the fear of God in 'em, and they'll cave completely.'"

"How do we use that against them, though?"

"Do something completely unexpected. I don't suppose they'll believe us if we act like we've quietly accepted our fate, at least not right away. I'll be damned if I'll stay here long enough to convince them. We need to come up with a plan, soon. Not just what Brad did—run off into the forest during a snowstorm."

"Sounds like that was Bethiah's idea."

"If he was telling the truth." Dan paused. "Doesn't matter, really. But I want to come up with something they won't anticipate."

"I don't know, they seem to have all the avenues covered."

"There's got to be something." He looked over at me. "You know we won't be able to take Brad with us."

"As brainwashed as he is, that's probably true." I could hear the anger in my own voice.

"We can't even give him an inkling of it."

"Fucking cult."

"I know it must be hard, Dad. Your twin brother. You were probably used to trusting him with anything."

"Pretty much."

"You're going to have to get yourself to believe that you're not talking to the man you knew. I don't know if you're right about demonic possession, or if he's just swallowed what this cult is telling him for some reason, but I have no doubt that if he thought we were going to escape, he'd give us away in a heartbeat. Did you see how he bowed down to that leader guy when he was told to show us our cabin? I kept expecting him to kiss the man's ring and say, 'Your wish is my command,' or whatever."

"You don't think he could be convinced otherwise?"

Dan gave me a long look. "Honestly? No. Or not without some intensive psychotherapy and deconditioning. Certainly nothing we could do."

"It kills me to find him and realize that we still can't help him."

"I know." Dan took a long, deep breath. "Keep in mind, though, that if he did leave the forest he might die like Bethiah did. He said even the leader didn't know whether that was the case. If that's true, you couldn't rescue him even if you could somehow get him loose from the brainwashing. He could die."

"The old Brad would have preferred that to being trapped in a cult."

"Probably true. But in his current state, the only way we'd get him out is if we tied him up and carried him. And he still might crumble into dust."

I winced, and Dan must have seen it, because he continued in a more subdued tone.

"I'm sorry, Dad, I truly am. I can't imagine what this is like for you. I was only thirteen when Uncle Brad and his girlfriend vanished. My memories of him are pretty vague. He was just the 'fun guy who looks just like Dad,' who'd fool around with me at family get-togethers, tell me dirty jokes when he thought Grandma and Grandpa weren't listening, try to get me to laugh during the grace before meals. I didn't honestly think about him that much outside of that." He paused. "And then, one day, he was gone."

"I hate myself for not looking for him right away. Maybe at that point it wouldn't have been too late."

"You can't know that. From what I've seen of these people, the more likely outcome is that you'd have been captured along with him."

I didn't have any good answer to that.

"Anyhow, Dad, we can't spend our time trying to figure out what would have happened, or you beating yourself up because you didn't save your twin brother. What we need to do now is put our minds to how we're going to get the fuck out of this place."

I clenched my teeth, and had to take a deep breath before responding. "You're right, of course. Escape is the first priority. After that, we can figure out what, if anything, we can do for Brad."

I didn't say anything more, and within a few minutes I heard his breathing slow as he fell asleep. But my mind was roiling with fear, frustration, and anger, and far into the night I was still imagining coming back, armed, and killing every one of those cult lunatics who had stolen my brother away, caused his girlfriend's suicide, and sent our parents into a spiral of depression that ultimately contributed to their deaths, too.

Azrok? Let Azrok, whatever it was, do its worst. Because if it thought I was going to bow down to it and forget what it had done to my family, it was dead wrong. I had no clear picture of what I could do to defeat it, but I would die before I would give up on my brother.

I t was around two in the morning when I was awakened by Dan
saying, "Dad?"

I couldn't see a damn thing, but it sounded like his voice was
coming from the direction of his bed. Bad dreams?

No, he was too old for that. It was hard for me not to think of
him as a little kid, especially considering how young he was when Anna
and I split up, and how little I'd seen of him since then. But his voice
was alert, intense, as if he had been lying awake pondering.

I forced my groggy brain into semi-alertness. "What is it?"

He spoke quietly, his voice barely audible. "I think I have a plan
to escape."

"Now?"

He chuckled. "No. It's pitch dark. I'm not stumbling around at
night in unfamiliar terrain. That leader dude was right about that much,
they know this place a hell of a lot better than we do. We wouldn't
stand a chance." His blankets rustled as he turned in bed.

"So what's your plan?"

"It hinges on what they're expecting us to do. Put yourself in the
leader's shoes. You've got two prisoners who have blundered in from

165

outside, given them dire warnings that their asses will be turned into meatloaf if they try to escape. The prisoners act all tough and defiant, so you're confident they'll try it anyway. What do you think they'll try?"

"Not sure. I'm still focusing on my ass being turned into meatloaf."

Dan chuckled in the darkness. "Metaphorical meatloaf. But seriously. What's your best guess?"

I smiled. I could recall his doing this since he was a very young child—after figuring out how something worked, instead of telling me outright what he'd learned, asking leading questions so I could have the fun of discovering it for myself. He'd been a scientist pretty much from the cradle.

"Okay, well, they're pretty sure we don't know our way around, which isn't wrong. So what I'd expect is that we'd take off the way we came—at least that much is familiar." I stopped, considering. "Probably at night, when there's less of a chance of being seen, and making as straight a beeline for the edge as possible."

"Exactly." There was a long pause. "So we have to take them by surprise. I don't think playing along would help—you know, going all, 'I've seen the light, your cult looks so interesting, we want to join right away.' Uncle Brad would see through that immediately—he knows you, and I doubt all the brainwashing they've done has taken that away. So they'd see through it immediately if we tried to pretend we'd had a change of heart, and double up on the security. The other usual stuff you see in movies about prisoners trying to escape—one of them feigns being sick, or lures one of the guards inside and knocks him down, or anything like that—they'll be expecting that kind of shit."

"So what?"

"So we don't raise their suspicions by suddenly playing nice. Stay in character, act as if we're stuck here, but we hate it and them. Then— do something totally unexpected. When is the least likely time you'd think someone being held captive would try to escape?"

I gave a soft sigh. His didactic style of discussion was wearing a little thin, especially given that it was two a.m. "When everyone is watching them."

"So that's when we do it. Broad daylight. Maybe during mealtime. They must sit down to eat, and I'm guessing the guard will relax a little if we're chowing down, too. We suddenly bolt. I'll bet cold cash it would take them some time to respond and give chase."

"Yeah, but after that, they take off after us. One minute later, we get captured. The Great Escape is over."

I thought my doubts might have quelled his enthusiasm, but I should have known better. As an academic, he had no problem with people questioning his ideas—he was usually a step ahead anyway.

"That's just the beginning. We take off in some random direction. That won't be considered odd, they'll think we don't have our bearings, we don't know the direction we're aiming for. Or possibly that we just don't care, that any direction would do because the woods are small enough that we'll hit civilization eventually no matter where we strike off. So next—in their place, what's the least likely thing we would do?"

"Come back to camp. They'll expect us to try to put as many miles between us and the camp as we can, as fast as we can."

"Right. So as soon as we're out of sight, we double back. We could even hide out in our own cabin—talk about least likely places for us to go!—although it'd probably be better to go somewhere there's better cover and where there's less chance of being cornered. Maybe somewhere near the temple, where there are rock outcrops and bushes."

That thought made me shudder. "I don't want to go anywhere near that temple entrance, not after what happened to Brad. Did you see that scar? Damn."

"Yeah. I didn't say *in* it, I said *near* it. That's the most overgrown area around here, as far as I saw. But we wouldn't stay long. Wait until the search team is *ahead* of us, and with luck, going the wrong way. We head back the way we came, for unexpected thing number three."

"Which is?"

His voice rose with excitement. I guessed we were nearing the punchline. "Like I said, the most likely expectation is that we'd head for the edge as fast as we can. But you remember on the way in, that cave I saw?"

"You noticed that too?"

"Dad, I'm a geologist. If there's one thing I notice, it's rocks."

"I suppose so. Don't know if I mentioned it, but one of the books I read—one of the ones Alban Bishop gave me before he died—mentioned a cave where someone hid out for three days after being chased by these loonies."

"Oh." His voice sounded disappointed. "Well, if they've already captured someone hiding there, they already know about it and might check it out. Hmm."

"No, according to the book, the guy got away. Apparently, he was so freaked out he died not long afterward, but hiding in the cave worked."

"Okay." The excitement returned to Dan's voice. "So even if they know about it, which seems likely if they're telling the truth about how well they know these woods, it may not occur to them. The opening was small enough that it doesn't really capture the attention, and they'd probably expect we'd run right past it without noticing. We duck into the cave, go back as far as it's safe, and hang out."

"How long?"

"I'd give it at least a day. Long enough for them to give up searching, or at least for the majority of them to head back to the camp. I've got a pocket flashlight that we should take along, so we don't fall into a pit in the cave and break our necks."

"First, metaphorical meatloaf, then breaking our necks in a cave. You're really making me feel optimistic about this."

Another chuckle from Dan. "I'm taking steps to make sure that stuff *doesn't* happen."

"Okay, so we hide out in the cave. If I remember right, we made it from the edge to where the cave is in maybe three hours, loping along and taking it fairly easy. If we haul ass we can do it in half the time or better, especially since we're gonna leave the packs here."

"Right. It's the only option. Trying to outrun these creeps wearing a full pack? I'm in good shape, but not that good. We can replace the clothes and camping stuff."

His excitement was contagious, not to mention the relief of having an actual plan to focus on. "Absolutely. Well, it's mostly your gear anyway, so what do I care?"

Now he snorted laughter.

I rolled over onto my side, and propped my head in my hand. "So stay in the cave till we're sure the coast is clear. Probably overnight. Maybe leave as soon as it's light enough to see. From there make as straight a line as we can toward the edge."

"That's what I'm thinking."

"You sure you know how to retrace our steps? I want to get in the car as soon as we can. I'm still doubtful we can outrun them, at least not for long."

"I'm pretty sure. I did orienteering when I was in high school and college, so I'm good at finding my way around. Hit the car, peel out, get the fuck outta Dodge."

"Sounds good to me."

There was a long pause. "There's one other thing, Dad."

"What?"

"If anyone tries to stop us...we need to kill him."

I didn't answer. Hearing my own son speak like this was deeply shocking, even though I knew why he was saying it, and knew he was right.

"I took some martial arts when I was in college. Never got great at it, but I still remember the teacher talking about using it for self-defense. He said, 'Even many people who are black belts end up in trouble when they're attacked for real. When you spar, it's against your friends. We tell you to put a hundred percent into it, but no one ever does. So if you are in an actual combat situation, where your life is at risk, it is easy to hold back as you do when you are sparring here. And so you are beaten, possibly killed.' He gave us this intense look, and added, 'If you are attacked in earnest, you must try your hardest to disarm or disable your opponent, as far as you are able without hurting him. But in the back of your mind you should always be aware of the possibility that to defend yourself, you may have to kill. If you are not ready to accept that risk, your first response to being attacked should be to run, not to fight."

"That's grim."

"It's realistic. I don't want to kill anyone, but if we get recaptured, I'm gonna fight them with everything I've got."

"Let's hope it doesn't come to that."

"Okay, so when do we do it?"

"I don't know if we can plan that ahead of time. We haven't seen what mealtimes are actually like, yet. So it might be that my idea wouldn't work anyhow. Let's plan that tomorrow, we just watch closely and gather data. After that, if it looks like it might work, we look for our opportunity—and run with it the first chance we have."

~

I was pretty agitated after my nighttime conversation with Dan, but I must have slept, because it seemed like I closed my eyes for a second and the next thing I knew, the door was opened, letting in the pearly light of dawn.

One of our guards—a man who looked like he was about Dan's age, but if the leader had been telling the truth, could have been my great-great-great grandfather—stepped in, and spoke without any preamble, and without so much as a smile.

"Come with me. The morning meal will be ready shortly."

Dan sat up, blinking and yawning, then slid out from under his blanket and started pulling on his clothes. The man watched both of us dress—privacy was apparently not a high priority here, although what he thought we could do when we were weaponless and he was standing in front of the only exit from the cabin, I don't know. Then I thought of Dan's comment about fighting and possibly killing for our chance to flee and realized our guard's caution was warranted after all.

Even under the trees, it was evident it was going to be a beautiful morning. The coolness was refreshing, with a light breeze ruffling the branches and allowing quick glimpses of a crystal blue sky above.

I wish it had lifted my spirits, but nothing could have done that but freedom.

As the guard led us out into the center of the camp, I was reminded of another thing Dan had said—to act uncooperative enough to be realistic and cooperative enough to look like we were taking their threats seriously. The young man took my upper arm to propel me to a seat, and I snarled, "I can find my way if you just point."

Hope that struck the right balance.

Breakfast looked like some kind of cooked cereal, perhaps oatmeal. Filling but uninteresting, and undoubtedly provided by *Them on the Edge*, since there was no sign of anything like farming, or even a garden, in the gloom of the forest. They ate while seated at two long tables with low benches, and mostly in silence. I guessed that the tables were taken apart and stashed somewhere out of sight when meals were over. I didn't recall seeing them when we came through camp the previous evening.

I watched the people of the settlement eating their breakfast. The leader was at the end of the other table, but other than that didn't seem to take precedence over anyone else. Once they all had served themselves from a communal pot, there was little movement and little noise.

It was as strange and somber a breakfast as I could imagine.

The fact that everyone was seated gave me some hope that Dan's plan might actually work. If there had been cooks or servers who stayed standing, they'd be quicker to give pursuit should the two of us suddenly leap up and run. On the other hand, there was no telling how ready to respond these people were. They gave every sign of being quietly cautious, every move calculated and deliberate.

Despite their odd garb and solemn, old-fashioned demeanor, I got the sense that they were a more formidable foe than their appearance would suggest.

In any case, we docilely finished our breakfast, asked if they wanted help cleaning up and were summarily turned down, and our guard conducted us back to the cabin. Before we stepped in, he said, in a subdued voice, "Do you have bodily needs to take care of before you go back inside?"

Dan snorted laughter. "No, I took care of my bodily needs against the wall on the way to breakfast."

Two spots of color rose in the guard's cheeks. You'd think people who lived in the woods wouldn't be embarrassed about taking a piss outdoors, but he gave every sign of discomfort. He turned to me, shifting from one foot to the other. "What about you?"

"I'm fine. If I need a wall to pee on later, I'll pound on the door to let you know."

The guard's blush deepened. He looked relieved to usher us into the cabin. There was a low *thunk* as the crossbar was lowered on the outside, trapping us once again.

"How long do you think we'll be cooped up like this?" Dan gazed at me through the gloom of the interior. The air was musty, like an old basement.

"I don't think they've set a duration for our sentences."

"Probably until the Winter Solstice. I don't think they'll make a mistake with us like they did with Uncle Brad. They'll wait until that thing in the temple rapes us and turns us into zombies, or whatever the hell it was that happened."

"That sounds pretty accurate to me."

"In any case, I don't plan on waiting around to find out. It's pretty clear that I was right that the only time we'll be out and about is during meal times and to take a piss. My guess is for the latter, they'll be savvy enough to let us go out only one at a time. So it's during meals."

"When, then?"

Dan sat down on the edge of his bed and frowned. "I think I'd suggest breakfast. The problem with dinner is that it leaves us less time to get out while it's still light. I'm not entirely convinced that they're that much better in the woods than I am, but they'd sure as hell have an advantage in the dark, and that's even if Uncle Brad's cryptic comments about how our senses will improve once we're part of the cult aren't true. They know the place, we don't."

"Not lunch time?"

Dan grinned. "Anxious to get out of here?"

172

"Just a little."

"Lunch could work. I think we'll have to be on our toes, and ready to bolt the moment we have an opportunity. It's got to work, and work the first time. If we escape and are recaptured, they'll either put us in complete lockdown or else kill us outright. I'd bet on the latter."

"Me too."

"So it's one and done. We have to throw ourselves into it full-bore as soon as we see an opening."

"How do you want to signal each other?"

"I don't know. We can't shout something, because the less attention we draw the better. If we jump up and bolt, at first only the people near us will see and respond. If we shout out 'Now!' or something like that, everyone in the camp will turn and look. The best thing is if we can take off so suddenly and unexpectedly that for a moment, most of them aren't even sure what just happened. Then use that moment to put as much distance between them and us as possible. As soon as we're out of sight from them, double-back to camp to throw off the pursuit. Give it maybe ten minutes, more if we think we can do it. Then haul ass in the right direction, toward that cave in the embankment."

I nodded. "It's a good plan."

"You don't sound very optimistic."

"Honestly? I'm not. They've got numbers on their side, and their familiarity with the forest. Not to mention whatever weapons they can grab. We'll be running like hell with nothing but our clothes."

Dan grinned at me. His smile in the shadows looked almost predatory. "Yes, but we have the advantage of our determination. No fucking way am I going to let myself be captured. If it happens, there will be a few people limping their way back here with serious injuries."

"God, Dan, I'm sorry I got you into all this."

"I got me into all this. And I'm not sorry at all. I wanted to help you get your answers, and you did get them. They weren't the answers you wanted, but at least now you know what happened to Uncle Brad and Cara. We'll get out of here, don't worry. Brother Enoch and his tribe of lunatics aren't going to get the better of me. They'll have to kill me first."

I looked at my strong, vital son, sitting on his bed, his posture radiating athleticism, power, and confidence, and it made my heart ache. My fear was that he was right—but that our both ending up dead before all this was over was the likeliest outcome.

~

As I expected, the next time we were released was at lunch. Dan seemed to take pleasure in making the guard uncomfortable, and as soon as we left the cabin he said, "Hang on a moment," turned around, unzipped, and peed on the wall. He shook off in an exaggerated fashion, and was still zipping back up when he turned around and said, "Thanks, much better."

Sure enough, the guard blushed again. His reaction made the leader's story of their being nineteenth-century holdovers strangely plausible. Coupled with their odd, old-fashioned garb, the strait-laced attitudes seemed right out of the pioneer days.

But if Brad had been telling the truth, their view of sex was anything but puritanical. Not only did the induction ceremony sound like some kind of supernatural orgy, the leader had apparently encouraged Brad to screw as many women as he had the time and stamina for. Once the ceremony had happened, he'd been happy to do exactly that.

These people were a weird amalgam of archaic morality and something close to outright debauchery. The combination was like nothing I'd ever heard about before.

Which made Brad's story of their being controlled by an alien entity have the ring of truth. What Azrok had done was to leave behind the parts of its hosts it found useful—their obedience to a leader, strict adherence to rules, acceptance of their place in the community—while removing inhibitions about sex, and most likely, violence.

The group assembled at the tables, quietly eating their midday meal, looked anything but violent. They could have been a gathering of men and women from a contemplative religious order. Conversation was carried out in near-whispers. Only a few heads turned as we approached one of the long picnic-like tables, and were seated and served.

Apparently curiosity was another thing Azrok discouraged.

Dan and I ate our meal in silence. For the first few minutes, our guard frequently looked up from his own food, eyeing us suspiciously as if we were suddenly going to flip the table and start a brawl. He seemed to relax after a while, and by the end of the meal was talking quietly to the woman seated next to him.

This boded well for our escape plan. Perhaps their inherent obedience to the rules made them quicker to assume we'd fall into line as well. Despite their experience with Brad—which, after all, had been ten years ago—they'd be quicker than I'd thought to lull into the assumption that we weren't going to cause trouble.

I finished up my meal, and glanced up at Dan. He caught my gaze and gave me a minuscule shake of the head. When I looked around, as unobtrusively as I could manage, I saw why. The leader was obviously discussing us with several of the older—or older-looking, at least—community members, and several of them were staring in our direction, their glares decidedly unfriendly. If we jumped, the alarm would be sounded instantly.

Moments later, the guard turned toward us. "Back to your cabin," he said, his voice stern. He was clearly fed up with us. I wondered how long he'd be assigned to watch our cabin and escort us.

As long as the leader told him to, probably.

We rose, which attracted some attention, but once people saw that we were in the guard's care and didn't look ready to flee, they turned back to their own food and conversations. There was a flash of fear in the man's face when he put a hand on Dan's upper arm to guide him toward the cabin, and Dan shook it off angrily, turning to glare at him.

"Don't touch me."

"You're in no position to tell me what to do," the guard said, but his voice sounded less certain than his words.

"I'm in the position to tell you to keep your goddamn hand off me unless you want to lose it."

The guard's eyes widened. I was fairly certain Dan wasn't going to fight with him then and there—after all, it'd been his idea to keep a low profile—but there was no doubt that he wanted the guard to know he wasn't to be trifled with. It was the truth. My son had at least four inches on him and outweighed him by a good thirty pounds of solid muscle.

The young man swallowed. "Fine." He couldn't hide the tremor in his voice. "Just go."

Dan gave him a little nod as if to say, *Don't provoke me, we both know I could kick your ass into the middle of next week*, and turned back toward the cabin.

Moments later, we were locked in again for an afternoon of the boredom of captivity.

~

Over the course of the afternoon, even shut in a windowless cabin we both felt a change in the air. There was a preternatural stillness, an oppressive weight, and I was not surprised when we were released from our confinement for dinner to find that the bright sunshine had been replaced by a low pall of gray clouds. The overcast and humidity told me was rain on the way.

Dinner was an even more subdued affair than lunch had been. Whether that was because of the threatening weather or not I couldn't be certain, although these people had to be used to the vagaries of the upstate New York climate. I doubted a little thing like a summer rain shower would discourage them.

About halfway through eating—some kind of stew with chunks of meat and mixed vegetables, that actually wasn't bad—I half-turned to the woman seated next to me and said, "What do you do about mealtimes if it's pouring rain?"

She jumped as if she'd been stung, then swiveled her head toward me, eyes wide. At first, I thought she wasn't going to answer—and I suppose running into one new person every ten years made strangers a frightening novelty—but she finally said, in a low voice, "We dine in our cabins."

"Food and drink brought to you?"

A stiff, twitchy little nod. "The men and women whose turn it is to cook and serve go from cabin to cabin. If the weather is really inclement, the Patriarch allows them to have double rations if they wish. During heavy rain or biting cold, such duties can be very unpleasant, and he doesn't wish to have people avoiding necessary tasks out of concern for their own comfort."

"That's reasonable enough." I gave her a smile.

All this elicited was wider eyes. Her lips tightened, and she turned back toward her food.

Conversation was ended, apparently.

After dinner was over we were told to prepare ourselves to be locked in for the night, taking turns emptying our bladders, still under watchful eye, although a different man than the morning's guard. This man was older and had a serious glint in his eye that brooked no nonsense. He was square-built, with steel-gray hair and broad should-ders. Powerful musculature wasn't common among the residents—they didn't seem to get a lot of exercise, although Brad's mention of the autumn chores of hauling and splitting firewood probably strengthened a few muscles. Most of them were thin and a little frail-looking.

This man, on the other hand, would have been a formidable foe in hand-to-hand combat. Something to keep in mind once we attempted escape.

Here was someone it would be better to avoid altogether.

Even Dan sensed the guard's demeanor, and didn't taunt him as he had the morning's guard. After we'd both peed and then confirmed we didn't need anything else, he docilely went up the steps into the cabin and I followed.

The *thunk-chunk* of the door closing, and the bar being lowered across it, told me we were once again locked in.

I undressed in the dark, slipped under the covers, and tried to relax. Dan was already snoring long before I dropped off. The thought kept coming back to me that if our plan for escape went wrong, we might both be dead soon—and it wasn't the possibility of my own death, but my son's, that made my heart ache.

III

The rain started to fall in the middle of the night. I awoke to the thrumming beat of the drops hitting the wooden roof and runnels of water pouring onto the ground. Thunder growled in the distance, and the wind had picked up, making the branches overhead creak.

I sat up and stretched, then glanced at my watch. Three in the morning. Still a good two hours until first light, and three until they brought us out for breakfast. If there was to be a breakfast gathering— if the rain continued, we'd be dining in our cabins.

Dan evidently heard me move, and said in a hushed tone of voice, "This could be a good omen."

"How? We'll be stuck inside."

"No. Remember what they said, that when the weather was inclement, they brought meals to the cabins? This means two things. First, that the entire community won't be out and about, and potentially witnessing our escape. Second, there will be only one or two people to overpower. We need to be ready as soon as we hear the bar across the door lifted. The door starts to open, we barrel out. Knock them down and take off. They might chase us, but we'll have a head start. It'll be a few minutes before they rouse the rest of the camp, and at that point, it'll be impossible to tell what direction we've run."

"So do we keep our original plan of running in the wrong direction to throw them off?"

He didn't answer for a moment. "I think we'll have to make that decision on the fly. It depends on whether I'm right that no one will be out and about except for the servers. If it really is only one or two of them, I'd say we make a beeline for the cave as quickly as possible. I don't know, if it doesn't seem like we're being pursued, maybe even continue and try to get clear of the forest. If it's raining hard, they won't be able to track us by our footprints, so although they might suspect we'll take off toward where the car is parked, they won't be certain. If a lot of people are out—if the weather clears or if there are more servers than I'm anticipating—we stick to the original plan."

"I think I'm just going to follow you. You're the one with the sense of direction."

Dan gave a low laugh. "I hope I don't let you down. I guess we'll find out if my bragging about orienteering is justified."

"I hate to say this, but we probably shouldn't go back to sleep. We fall into a deep sleep, then suddenly wake up when we hear the bar being lifted, we'd have to jump out of bed and be alert enough to knock down the guards and take off. Plus, what are you wearing?"

Dan laughed again. "A smile."

"Yeah. Me too. I'm not so keen on a naked sprint through the forest. We should get dressed, boots on, anything that's light enough to take along in our pockets. We're only going to get one chance at this."

"Agreed."

We both slipped out from under the light blankets. The air was warm and heavy with humidity. We dressed silently in the dark. After lacing up my boots I plunged my hands into my pack, trying to identify the contents by feel. I located some energy bars and a plastic bag containing peanuts, and stuffed those in my pants pockets. If Dan was right, we might be in that cave for a day or more—we'd need whatever food we could carry.

I checked my watch again. 3:23. It was going to be a long wait. The adrenaline was already coursing through my veins. I wasn't a fighter. Other than a couple of scuffles in middle school, I'd never been in a fight in my life. I wondered if I would be able to do it, if when the moment came, I could hit someone with the intent to hurt, to disable, possibly to kill.

No way to tell. I'd have to find out once it was time.

Which, if Dan was right, was going to be in less than three hours.

~

The rain and thunder continued unabated.

I sat on the edge of the bed, head nodding as I tried to fight off sleep. The weather helped—I was jolted awake more than once by the sound of something, probably a tree branch, falling onto the roof. I consulted my watch. 5:45.

It must be getting light outside, not that we could tell. Breakfast, if it was served at all in such a storm, would be coming soon.

The thought made my heart pound.

Why had I gotten myself and Dan into this? What the hell had I thought I was accomplishing? After ten years, either Brad was dead or was absent from his home voluntarily. The idea of being held captive for all that time was absurd.

In either case, my blundering in, and worse, bringing my son along for the ride, was a fool's errand from the beginning. Dan had tried to tell me. Alban Bishop and Melvia Shields had warned me away, and both of them paid for it with their lives. Even Cyndy Evans, the pretty young assistant librarian, had been frightened enough of Lem Stutes that she'd stayed away from her job on account of it.

And who knew? I didn't even know if Cyndy was alive. Lem had said he'd only warned her to stay away, to take a couple of days off, but I had no doubt the skinny, sullen Edge-dweller would lie if he had harmed her. After all, he was almost certainly behind the deaths of old Alban and the head librarian. A third murder was not just possible, but likely.

I cupped my face in my hands. Foolish, right from the beginning.

If I was being completely honest, the whole stupid enterprise was more to assuage my own guilt over not having been there to protect my twin brother from harm. He'd always been the one who felt like he had something to prove, both to me and to our parents. He teetered between wanting to be seen as capable and mature and as daring and reckless, never certain of himself, and doing things that were foolhardy just to impress the rest of the world that Bradley James Ellicott was as tough as anybody.

The first few times, when he'd told me about solo back-country camping trips and rock climbing and scuba diving expeditions, I'd tried to caution him gently to be careful, to take precautions and be smart, but my gentle remonstrance only served to make him furious, as if I didn't trust him or thought he was a child. I stopped doing it the third or fourth time I was rebuffed—so the time that he was actually in mortal peril, I hadn't said anything.

I couldn't even remember how long I'd known he was planning the camping trip to Devil's Glen. I remembered his laughing about a friend challenging him to spend a night in the woods, and how it'd take more than a few scary stories to keep him away. I didn't think much about it, given his reputation for thrill-seeking—and only realized the actual danger later, after he had already disappeared.

Blaming myself was ridiculous, but sitting there in the dark cabin, waiting for what was likely to be our only chance to escape, it was all I could do. Maybe if I'd checked up on him more often, knowing how reckless he could be. Maybe if I'd talked to our parents—they'd evidently known what he was planning, which was why my mother more or less died of the guilt she heaped upon her own head.

I was supposed to have my brother's back, always. And the one time it mattered, I'd let him blunder off into the woods. As a result, his girlfriend was dead and he was some kind of brainwashed slave. Even in a best-case scenario, our escape wouldn't help Brad. My earlier thoughts of returning in force to rescue Brad now seemed ridiculous. Brainwashed or not, he was staying here by choice. Part of it might have been because of his fear that he'd meet Bethiah's grim fate, but I knew that mostly, he *liked* it here. Whether it was because of the supernatural influence, or the life of idleness, or because of the overpowering, orgasmic effect of being penetrated by Azrok, was impossible to know. My negligence had allowed Brad to be captured. My stupid, selfish obsession led myself and Dan to suffer the same fate.

I knew then that even if we did get out of this alive, I'd never be free of the guilt.

A creak on the front step yanked me out of wallowing in self-recriminations. I was suddenly alert, every sense stretched to the breaking point. I heard Dan stand up and move toward the door, and I did the same.

"You ready?" he whispered.

"I have to be."

A low, grinding noise as the bar across the door was lifted. It opened a crack, letting in a gray, sullen light and curl of warm, damp wind.

"Now!" Dan hissed.

We threw ourselves forward against the door. The heavy timbers flew open, and a gray-clad person carrying a pair of plates went airborne, landing flat in the mud. We plunged down the steps, looking around wildly.

Only one other person was nearby.

My brother.

His eyes locked mine for a moment, and he took a step toward us.

"Don't, Uncle Brad," Dan said. "I don't want to hurt you. I really don't. But if you get in our way, I'm going to hit you with everything I've got."

There was a suspended moment when he hesitated, and the three of us stood in a crooked triangle as the rain pelted down. He looked over at his fallen comrade, who still lay prone in the mud. The fall must have knocked him? her?—it was impossible to tell—out cold.

The rain continued to sluice down from skies the color of dirty cotton. Every item of clothing I wore was already saturated.

Brad, wide-eyed, gave a vague gesture with one hand.

"Go," he said in a low voice, barely audible in the storm.

Dan and I turned and ran.

Over the next hour, my confidence rose, and the dark thoughts of the previous hours fell away. Part of it was finally taking action. The die was cast. No more waiting. Now we were deer running from the wolves, back to our animal origins, just a pair of prey trying to outrace the predators. Dan's path ahead of me was also unhesitating. I followed him as best I could, although I lacked his stamina and nimbleness as he plunged between trees, leapt over logs, and scrambled up muddy, branch-strewn slopes, never slowing for a moment.

There was no sign of a pursuit, but I recalled how we'd been followed through the woods on our way in by a half-dozen men and women who had remained inaudible and out of sight the entire way. They could be right behind us and we might not be aware of it. We couldn't afford to relax, or even stop to look around.

There was nothing for it but to trust Dan's sense of direction and make as quickly as we could for the cave, and shelter, where we would regroup and decide what our next move would be.

A clap of thunder, this one nearby. The storm seemed to be right on top of us. Water cascaded down my face, blurring my vision. The wind howled through the trees like one of the Furies looking for her next victim. When a branch broke free and landed only a few feet from me, I shouted an obscenity and yelled ahead to Dan, "We need to find shelter!"

Without turning, he shouted, "No! This is our storm! We need to use it!" He seemed almost exultant, as if the violent weather was sweeping down on Devil's Glen with the intent of foiling our enemies.

I recalled that when Azrok destroyed my house, the first sign I had of its approach was a noise like a high wind. But I didn't say that. I was breathless enough that Dan probably wouldn't have heard if I did. The effort of shouting to him once, added to the exhaustion from running for what seemed like hours, was all I could manage.

That, and continuing to put one foot in front of the other.

Later—I have no idea how much later, my brain had long since stopped paying attention to anything but the aching in my lungs and my legs—Dan slowed as we approached a rocky bank that sloped steeply downhill. Water sluiced over the rocks, making them slick and dangerous.

But that wasn't the only reason he slowed. He grasped my arm and pointed.

"The cave!"

We scrambled down the bank, then stopped cold.

The stream that had been a bubbling little rill only a few inches deep was now a roaring torrent of water the color of café au lait. It was not only impossible to ford, it would be suicide to put one foot into it.

Dan's storm had set an impassible barrier in front of us. Any possibility of reaching the car that day was gone.

Thankfully, the cave was on our side of the stream, and Dan grabbed my sleeve and pulled me toward it. As we ducked into the narrow cleft in the rock face, another clap of thunder shook the hillside, so close it made my guts vibrate.

Once inside, Dan stood panting and dripping on the dry, rocky floor. I, on the other hand, collapsed to my knees. If the people of Ulthoa stormed our hideout, I wouldn't have been able to fight back, run, or do anything but lie down and let them take me.

After a moment, Dan reached in his pants pocket, and pulled out a little headlamp, slipped the elastic around his forehead, and turned it on. The cave extended into the hillside farther back than we could see, and Dan stepped carefully into the shadows, one hand on the wall. It seemed to widen as it went back, the floor angling upward slightly. Good thing, or it would probably be full of water now. As it was, the cave was warm and dry. Tight quarters, and a little musty-smelling, but as good a hideout as we could have hoped for.

After moving a little farther in, Dan sat down with his back against the wall, and said in a tired voice, "Dad, you should move away from the cave mouth."

"You really think they'll be out looking for us in all this?"

"I'm not making any bets about what those people might do."

There was no arguing that. I made my aching legs move, and went another twenty feet into the cave, then collapsed again.

"You think they'll harm Uncle Brad for letting us go?"

"How will they know? He'll probably tell them we overpowered him. I didn't see anyone else around."

Dan nodded, and the beam of the headlamp bounced crazily in the dark. "I hope so. I wonder why he did it?"

"Who knows? I'd like to think it was out of love. Maybe despite his talking the party line, he secretly hoped we'd escape all along. Or maybe he just knew he was outnumbered. No way to tell."

There was silence for a while, and I sat there, forehead against my knees, trembling from exhaustion and chill.

"We should get these wet clothes off," Dan said. "I know it sounds weird, but you'll be warmer naked. First rule of water-based hypothermia."

Once again I forced myself to stand, groaning and wincing, and we both stripped, taking each piece of clothing and wringing pints of water out it. He was right—once the clothes were off, the warm air seemed to reach into my bare skin. It wasn't long before I stopped shivering, and at that point, fatigue completely overwhelmed me.

I lay down, curling up on one side with one elbow under my head. The last thing through my mind before my consciousness faded away was that this was the experience of our ancestors for millions of years, living in caves, nothing between our skins and the elements, beset by dangers from all sides. Despite those odds, some had survived, even thrived.

With those oddly optimistic and comforting thoughts, my brain slipped downward into a sleep so deep that even dreams could not find me.

~

I woke with a painful crick in my neck. At my age sleeping on hard surfaces was no longer as easy as it had been when I was in my twenties. I sat up, groaning, and felt around until my hand blundered on Dan's headlamp and my questing fingers found the switch.

The beam was painfully bright to my dark-adjusted eyes, but after a momentary wince, I aimed it at my wrist. A little after four in the afternoon. Everything was silent, but we were far enough from the entrance that it was impossible to tell if the rain had stopped. Dan was still sound asleep, curled up on his side, his face completely relaxed.

I was ravenously hungry and thirsty. I felt in my pants pockets—still clammy and damp, in the close cave air our clothes would be slow to dry—and found an energy bar and a bottle of water. I only drank enough water to quench my thirst, and ate half the bar. Heaven alone knew how long we'd have to make our food last. Afterward I switched off the lamp and returned it to the narrow rock ledge where Dan had stowed it, then sat down cross-legged on the rock floor, and tried to stretch and ease my sore muscles.

Perhaps a half-hour later, I heard a rustling noise as Dan roused, then a yawn.

"Hell of a camping trip, Dad," he said in a groggy voice. "We done yet?"

"I wish."

"Did you get any sleep?"

"Yeah. More than I thought I would. But my back feels like I've been hit by a truck."

A rueful chuckle. "I'm not much better. I was hoping I'd be back in my apartment by now. Once I get there, I'm climbing into bed and sleeping for days."

"I'd settle for your couch."

There was a pause. "Have you checked to see if it's still raining, or if the creek's still too high to cross?"

"No. Didn't feel like moving any farther than I had to."

"Once the creek is low enough, we need to get our asses across it. But I don't want to misjudge. Six inches of rapidly-flowing water is enough to knock a man down. I know it means we'll be stuck here longer, but better than one of us drowning or meeting a rock face first."

"What do you think our captors are doing?"

"Unknown. I will say that as hard as the rain was falling, it'd be impossible to tell what direction we went. And even if they deduced we'd head back the way we came, the forest is big enough that it'd be impossible to search the whole thing with as few people as they have. They're what, two dozen?"

"Something like that."

"Then I think luck is on our side." Another pause. "Fuck, the clothes are still wet."

"I know."

"I guess it'd take them days to dry in here. Oh, well, we'll have to put 'em back on even if it's uncomfortable. I'm not hiking naked even though I'm not very shy about people seeing my bare skin."

"Not very shy?" I chuckled. "I remember when you were in high school, you were like the captain of the coed skinnydipping team."

That got a laugh. "You found out about that?"

"Your mother told me. She was half amused and half mortified. Said you and your friends were on your third time getting a warning from the cops not to skinnydip in the old millpond on Quincy Creek. She said next time they were going to cite you for public indecency."

"We just found another place to swim."

"I figured. You never did like being told what to do."

"I like that even less than I like wearing swim trunks."

We slowly pulled on our cold, damp clothes. Even in the warm, dry air in the cave, I was immediately chilled again, and rubbed the backs of my arms. After lacing up our boots, we made our way to the mouth of the cave.

What we could see of the sky, up through the narrow slot of the gully and between the branches of the trees, was low and gray, but at least the rain had stopped. The creek was still high, but wasn't the roaring torrent it had been when we arrived.

"Still not passable," Dan said. The frustration was obvious in his voice.

"How much longer?"

"I don't know. I'm not sure how big this stream's watershed is. I can't even come close to figuring out a rate for the water level dropping because I was asleep when the rain stopped." He squinted up at the top of the high bank on the other side of the gully. "It's already late afternoon. If we wait much longer, we won't be able to clear the forest before it's dark." He gave a harsh sigh. "Fuck. I think we're stuck here in this cave for the night."

"Oh, well, it could be worse. We could still be captives."

There was a low laugh from somewhere nearby.

Dan's posture stiffened, his eyes wide, nostrils quivering like a deer that's just scented a wolf.

Coming out from behind trees, rocks, from both directions along the creek, even scrambling down the bank of the gully behind us—it seemed like the entire population of the settlement was there. It was the leader who laughed, and he approached us with a grim smile.

"You honestly thought we would let you escape?"

I looked around wildly, searching for an opening, any opening. There was none. I registered Brad's presence, and our eyes met for a moment before he turned away, grief-stricken.

His was not the only unhappy expression. It seemed as if the leader's determination to keep us from getting away was not shared by the entire settlement.

Maybe they weren't as unified a front as it had appeared at first.

"How did you know where we were?" Dan said, in a strangled voice.

"Your uncle told you that we are guided by a being that is free of the human limitations of time and space. You wonder that we knew where you had hidden? We knew the creek would prevent you from going forward, and we had our people posted to stop you from backtracking and trying a different path. It was only a matter of waiting for you to show your faces."

"You motherfuckers," Dan snarled.

The leader frowned, but gave a quick, dismissive wave of the hand. "Your abuse means nothing. Your ignorance and insolence is beyond curing. You've come to the end of your run. We are done dealing with you and your father. You will come with us back to the settlement or be dragged. It is your choice."

With a loud cry of anger and frustration, Dan burst into a run. He didn't get far. Within seconds he was brought to the ground, struggling wildly, the tendons on his neck standing out, screaming with fury but helpless to free himself.

The leader turned to me. "Are you as foolish as your son?"

There were plenty of pairs of hands available to take me down, and I was nowhere near as strong as Dan was. I hated myself for my cowardice, but I couldn't face a probably futile attempt either to help Dan or to fight my way out. My heart was wrung out, my muscles unstrung. I said nothing, and moments later, I was grasped from behind, my arms pinioned.

"Bring them," the leader said. "We will return them to captivity for now. But tomorrow, we will have done with them both, for once and all. There will be no second chances."

IV

They bound us hand and feet with cloth strips, and we were dumped unceremoniously into our cabin, the door barred behind us.

Twelve hours of frantic flight, and we ended up right back where we started.

Dan hobbled on his knees over to where I sat on the floor, my back propped uncomfortably against the bed frame, and turned so his hands could worry at the knots that bound my wrists together. It was impossible for either of us to see—not only were our hands tied behind us, in the windowless cabin it was almost completely dark—and within a few minutes, he gave up with a harsh sigh.

"They cinched these down too damn well, and the canvas is too tough to tear." The frustration was evident in his voice. "I don't think I can untie these."

"Even if we did, I don't think they'll be as careless as they were last time."

"You're probably right."

"So we're in for it."

Dan swiveled around on his butt so he was facing me. I could see his eyes gleaming in the shadows. "Yes, but what do you think we're in for?"

"The leader didn't sound like he was taking any further chances. I'm guessing they're planning on killing us both. I have no idea how, but I'm guessing it will be something pretty unpleasant."

"There are pleasant ways to die?"

I gave him a grim chuckle. "Well, there are certainly better and worse ways, don't you think? I'm hoping they're not going to go back to their Puritan roots. Hanging and burning at the stake have always struck me as singularly horrible."

"Can't argue with that."

"I'd say they're going to have their evil demon eat us. Given what it did to my house, seems like it could dispatch us without even breaking a sweat."

"Demons sweat?"

"Figure of speech."

He gave a low chuckle. "But you're right. Look at the scar on Uncle Brad's chest. It's a wonder it didn't cave his chest in."

"He was lucky. Twice."

"If you can call being brainwashed and stuck in a forest-dwelling cult 'lucky.'"

"True."

Dan shook his head. "I can't believe we're having this conversation. I don't even believe in evil spirits and the paranormal and whatnot, and here we are chatting calmly about being eaten alive by a devil-monster from outer space."

There didn't seem to be any good answer to that, and silence fell in the little cabin.

I must have dozed, despite my worries and the ache that was developing in my back from the awkward position I was seated in, because the next thing I was aware of was a creaking noise as the bar on the door lifted. It sounded loud in the omnipresent dead silence of the forest. My eyes popped open, trying to focus, but no light came in through the crack of the opening door. It was evidently in the depths of the night.

A stealthy footstep moved closer toward us. Every muscle in my body tensed. Were they planning on murdering us in our sleep?

Dan snapped awake, too—I heard him move, and when he spoke his words were sleep-slurred. "Who's there?"

The response was whispered, and the sibilant tones could have been male or female, young or old. There was no way to tell. "Shush. Quietly. I'm someone who means you no harm."

"If you actually mean no harm, then let us go," Dan snarled.

"I can't do that." There was a pause. "There's not a lot I can do to stop the Patriarch from ordering your execution tomorrow. But I...I don't know. I couldn't let you die without knowing the truth."

Dan still sounded furious. "This is supposed to help us how?"

"I'm not sure. But I thought...maybe, somehow, if you knew...you could use it. I don't know how, but...I know the Patriarch doesn't want you to know, so maybe it could be important."

"Stop dithering and tell us," Dan snarled. "I'm not in the mood for playing games."

"All right." There was the sound of someone swallowing hard. "But first I have a question for your father. What do you know about yours and Bradley's parents?"

Whatever it was I'd been expecting him? her? to say, it wasn't that. "Our parents? What the hell do they have to do with it?"

"Everything." The voice became more confident. "So tell me. What do you know about them?"

"They were ordinary people. Ron and Nancy Ellicott. My dad was a general contractor, my mom an elementary school speech therapist. They both died last year, about six months apart."

"That's what I thought. So you really have no idea."

Dan snorted. "No idea of what? Will you just tell us straight up?"

"All right." The voice continued, even lower. "The Patriarch had six children. Abel, Catherine, Mariah, Isaiah, Cora, and Ethan. Catherine died of a terrible fever when she was only six years old. The Patriarch's wife, who was born Tabitha Craig, followed not long afterward, some thought destroyed by grief at the loss of her eldest daughter. The others...when Azrok came, all were dedicated, as your brother Bradley was. The youngest sister, Cora—she was a wild and disobedient one. She was dedicated with the rest, so she knew the gifts and the perils of rejecting her place here in Ulthoa, but it did not stop her. At first she would not leave the forest, fearing the outcome, but then she took to meeting with men from the Edge, and giving her body to them. She sought it, saying that if she was trapped here, never to leave, at least she would find pleasure wherever she could, and that the men she met were far better lovers than any she could have had here. She believed, too, that she would not have the outcome of bearing a child from it, as all thought that the dedication to Azrok caused infertility. This was wrong."

"She got pregnant."

"Yes. She would not tell the Patriarch whose child she was bearing, if she even knew herself. She boasted of how many men she had made love to, as if such behavior merited praise. She maintained that she was pleased with what she'd done. Then she told him she would not see her child raised here, in Ulthoa, to become the property of Azrok and the temple. They argued about it, over and over again, until when Cora's time was close, he had her locked in this very cabin, and here she gave birth."

There was a long pause, and silence in the little room.

Finally the voice added, "To identical twin boys. Joshua and Aaron, she named them."

When I was able to speak, I could hear the strangled tone as the words forced their way from my throat. "What are you saying?"

"I think you understand quite well."

"That's impossible."

"No. You and your brother, whom you call Bradley, are the sons of Cora Bishop. Who your father is, we do not know, but he was certainly one of the men on the Edge with whom Cora had dallied. But when you were only two weeks old, Cora decided to follow through on her pledge to save you from the Patriarch, who is your grandfather. She persuaded one of the others to help her escape, and the door was secretly left unbarred. In the middle of the night, she fled with the two of you, taking only what she could carry, and slipped off unnoticed. But when she came out from under the protection of the trees…" The voice trailed away.

"She died."

"Yes. The withdrawal of herself from Azrok's place of power meant that she was no longer shielded from time. When you were born, Cora was well over two hundred years old. Her body transformed from that of a young woman to a withered skeleton in a matter of minutes."

"What happened to the babies?" Dan asked.

"You should be able to guess. While we may not leave the protection of Ulthoa, the men and women of the Edge are under no prohibition from entering here. They are afraid of us, and terrified that they will come under Azrok's power, but have the means to shield themselves using talismans that prevent any of that power from affecting them."

I heard the sudden understanding in Dan's voice. "The necklaces."

"Yes. Their great-grandsires, when we first settled here, delved into ancient knowledge and found a way to ward off Azrok's influence. Foolish, really, as they could have eternal life and health, but were afraid to reach out their hands to grasp it."

"At the price of never leaving again."

"Small price, though, is it not, for what you receive in return? In any case, when Cora's absence was noted, we sent word to the people on the Edge to find what had become of her. It was not long before they came on her remains—and the two babies, hungry and cold but unharmed. Their instructions were to bring the children back, but one of the men of the Edge took them—you and your brother—and felt sorry for them. They spirited the two of you away to a childless couple, people they knew who lived far enough away to be out of the Patriarch's reach. You were given new names, new identities. And there you stayed, until now."

"So Ron and Nancy Ellicott..." I stopped, unable to complete the thought.

"Are your adoptive parents."

I felt the weight of it all descend upon me. It sounded absurd, but in my heart I knew it to be the truth. "How do you know all of this?"

"You have not guessed it? My name is Mariah Bishop. The Patriarch's third child. I am your aunt."

I was bowled over by what she had told us, by the thought of being in the presence of someone who herself was over two centuries old. And that gaunt, harsh-visaged man, the leader of Ulthoa...he was my grandfather? I choked out, "Why are you telling us all this?"

"You deserved to know. Perhaps...perhaps tomorrow, if you can remind the Patriarch of his kinship to you, that you are his grandson and great-grandson, he will repent of his anger and spare your lives."

"You could just untie us and let us go," Dan said.

"I dare not. If I did so, and it was discovered, I would be whipped, if not worse. I cannot risk that. I am not brave like your mother was. She would have borne any danger to see you to safety. But I...I felt sorry for you, and I thought perhaps you could reason with the Patriarch. He is not an evil man."

Dan snorted. "You know what he's planning on doing to us, and you say he's not evil."

"You don't understand."

"Then why don't you explain it to us."

She sighed. "He is our protector."

"Your jailer, more like."

"No. Think of what happened to my sister. Think of what happened to Bethiah Craig, who befriended your brother ten years ago and died trying to help him escape. Azrok has given us a great gift, but at a price. And it...it is a capricious master."

"It's the mark of Cain," Dan said quietly.

"What?"

"It's marked you. That thing has put its imprint on your soul. You'll never be free of it."

"Perhaps not. But none of us did this unwillingly. When we were dedicated, we made that choice."

"Did you know the whole picture, though? Did you know you could never leave the forest? That it would keep you trapped here? Did you even know how dangerous it was, that it would unhesitatingly kill if it could?"

Mariah sounded as if she were becoming agitated. "But the Patriarch knows how to control it, to keep it at bay, to shield us from the brunt of its power. Without him, without someone standing between Azrok and us, it would overwhelm us, destroy us body and soul, that is true. Then it would be loosed upon the world. But with the Patriarch as our intercessor, it is benevolent, not evil."

"Not evil?" I said. "That's the second time you've used that phrase in a pretty sketchy manner. We saw what Azrok can do when it gets out. It destroyed my house. We were lucky to get out alive."

"My father was trying to stop you from prying, to keep you away from here. In his own way, he wanted to prevent all of this from happening. First by sending those on the Edge to stop those who were giving you information…"

"Kill them, you mean."

"He did not ask the men of the Edge to kill. That was their decision."

That sounded like splitting hairs to me, but I let her continue, and she went on in calmer tones.

"When you would not be dissuaded, and were drawing others in to this misguided enterprise, my father thought that if you were killed, it would stop the contagion from spreading further. No one else would think to look into your brother's disappearance. It would be ended, like removing a diseased limb to save the body."

"Kind of would have sucked for me, though."

Again her voice rose in frustration. "You persist in misunderstanding. What if your curiosity had resulted in not just you and your son coming here, but dozens of men with arms? What if you had found our place, killed us all? There would be no one left to control it, to stop

Azrok from leaving where it is caught, deep in the temple. It would have taken *Them on the Edge* first, sucking the life from them one after another until it was strong enough to escape the Temple. After that there would have been nothing stopping it from spreading death and ruin everywhere. The Patriarch—my father—is all that stands between it and your world. As long as he is there, it can be controlled, at least enough to prevent it from destroying. You think your life is more important than that?"

"How does he do it?" Dan asked suddenly.

Mariah, who sounded as if she were near tears, said, "What?"

"Keep Azrok at bay. How does he do it? This thing is incredibly powerful. How does he stop it from getting out?"

"I'm not...I shouldn't be here. I shouldn't have come. I'm sorry you're going to die, I truly am. I should leave."

"No!" Dan shifted, and groaned in discomfort, but his voice was steady. "You need to tell us. If he can stop Azrok, others can."

She gave a long, wavering sigh. "It's not that simple. My father endured...he learned how at great cost. When he came upon the temple in the woods, when I was only a child, when we first came here. At first, none were brave enough to enter the temple...it stood as a symbol of fear to us. It is why many, even of our blood kin, shunned us. Even my father's brother would not come here to see him, once he found that words would not convince my father to abandon his homestead. But there were books of old learning he found...he found them when we were still allowed outside of the forest, before..." She trailed off.

"Before you were taken over," I supplied.

"Yes. Before we were dedicated. But my father is a curious man, and after delving into such matters, he thought to enter the temple and see what dwelt there. Azrok was there, dormant, sleeping. Someone— we do not know whom—had trapped it behind a charmed door, a stone slab that had carven upon it the same design that is on the talismans worn by *Them on the Edge*. My father thought...he thought he could master it, and he opened the door."

"So he's the one who set it free?"

Now the anger was clear in her voice. Criticizing her father was apparently not allowed. "It was not his fault. He was curious, he lusted after knowledge. He never intended to cause...all this."

I was in no mood to cut any of them slack, least of all the leader. "But that's exactly what he did. His intentions don't mean a damn thing."

"That is why he set himself up as the barrier. When he opened the door, Azrok was upon him in a moment. It flung him back, and blasted the charmed door to rubble. For seven nights, it roamed as it would, venturing farther and farther outward. At first it killed cattle and other livestock, leaving them drained of blood. Then a child from the village went missing, then a farmer who lived alone, and each time, the next night their bodies were found—bloodless, and showing signs of having been dropped from a great height." She paused. "The men of the town suspected my father of having caused it, and prepared to come for him in force. He knew he had to do something."

"None of this made it into the history books," I said. "Even the ones that mention the rumors about the woods and the Bishop family."

"They wouldn't. Some things are too frightening to put onto paper, they can only be hinted at if people wish to stay sane. But my father knew Azrok had to be stopped. Each day, it came back near sunrise from its fearful visitations, and was quiet for a time. And my father underwent a horrible ordeal to learn how to contain what he had loosed. He learned how to fashion a talisman with the symbol that was on the charmed door, the same that is on the talismans worn by *Them on the Edge*. He is never without it, and he cautioned *Them on the Edge* to wear theirs faithfully, acting as a fence should his own power flag. As long as he wears it, it turns him into a barrier, replacing the one that Azrok had destroyed. He cannot completely contain it, as the door could, but he can in some way block it, keep it bound here." There was a pause. "He has made himself into a dam holding back the flood to keep the rest of the world safe. He, and the rest of us, went into hiding, permanently, disappearing into the deepest part of the woods. We took steps to make certain we would not be found."

"And that's why he wants to kill us?" I said.

Now she was nearly yelling. "He cannot allow anyone to jeopardize what we have here. Over time he has learned to control it. He made a bargain with it. It enters our bodies, giving us health and life for so long it might as well be called immortality. It feeds from us sufficiently to sustain itself, but not enough to overpower my father and break its bonds. We must remain here, and remain vigilant, protecting the temple and keeping my father safe. It is a fragile balance, and nothing must disrupt it, to the peril of all."

"And you convinced my brother of all this."

"He was willing to see reason. He has accepted his identity and his place here. Since his dedication he is truly Aaron Bishop, not Bradley Ellicott. The man who went by the latter name does not exist anymore. And you...you, Joshua, if you do the same, perhaps my father—your grandfather—will spare you both."

There was a suspended moment of total silence in the dark room.

"You think he'll relent?" Dan's voice was harsh, his sudden words making me jump. "After saying there were no second chances, and he'd have done with us once and for all? I don't believe it for a moment. And I'd rather die with my dignity intact than grovel before a cult leader." He snorted. "We'll make sure to thank him for his selfless devotion toward the safety of the human race before he has us both killed."

There was a clatter as she stood up suddenly. "My father was right." Something in her voice had changed, some door that had been opened a little was slammed shut. She now sounded impossibly distant, making her pronouncements from on high, and I could hear her father's self-righteous tone in hers. "I should never have come here. He said rightly that your ignorance was beyond cure. I should have listened, but I was driven by pity." The door opened. "You are my blood kin, and I will mourn tomorrow to see you die, sacrificed to the god you scorned. But you have brought your fate upon your own heads, and I will not lift a finger or say a word to stop it."

The door closed, and there was a clunk as the bar was dropped into place.

"She seems nice," Dan said, after a long pause.

This got a laugh. I marveled at my son's ability to retain his sense of humor when in a few short hours we were both likely to die. "You think she was telling the truth?"

"I think *she* believes it. She didn't sound like she was lying. Whether everything she told us is right—that's another matter."

"I can't believe these people are my relatives."

"*Our* relatives," Dan corrected. "You don't believe in any kind of genetic predisposition toward evil, do you?"

"You were the one who brought up the mark of Cain."

"Well, I didn't mean it literally."

I shook my head. "So. Joshua Bishop. That'd take some getting used to."

"I'm not changing my name," Dan said firmly.

"Moot point anyhow."

"You sound resigned to our fate."

"I'm not." Despite our situation and the conversation we'd just had with—my aunt?—my mind was clear. It might not make a difference to the outcome, but I was not going to simply lay my head on the block and wait for the axe to fall. If they wanted my life, they'd have to fight me for it.

W hen the door opened again, I squinted against a faint line of
pearly gray that signified it was maybe six in the morning. I
suppose I slept some, because it seemed only minutes earlier that
Mariah Bishop had locked us back in. This time, however, it was four
men—probably the four strongest men the encampment had—who
came in and without saying a word, untied our hands and loosened the
bonds on our feet. All they did, though, was give us enough slack to
walk, leaving us hobbled and unable to run even if we could have
somehow overpowered them with our hands tied behind our backs.

The leader was indeed taking no chances.

We were yanked to our feet, and forced to walk to the door and
out, each of us flanked by a pair of guards. My mind started running
over what Mariah had told us. In the cold light of morning, still groggy
from fatigue, it all seemed dreamlike and surreal. Enoch Bishop was
my grandfather. The couple who I'd thought of all my life as my
parents were actually the adoptive parents to me and my brother. Our
birth mother was over two hundred years old when we were born, and
died trying to get us out of the forest and away from Azrok.

And now Enoch Bishop was acting as a human dam, holding back

Azrok's power, starving it to keep it weak, lest it break free and wipe out humanity.

I thought back on the beginning of my quest to find my brother, on the hints and whispers about the people who settled in Devil's Glen. Allegations of Satan worship and pagan rituals. The truth—if this *was* the truth, and a part of my mind still rebelled against accepting it all—was stranger, more complex, and more terrifying than anything that had shown up in hesitant mentions in histories of the county or sly half-truths by the locals.

Alban Bishop had said we should stop investigating, and he paid for warning us with his life.

Now, it seemed, we were to meet the same fate. Or worse. Because the whole encampment had turned out to watch. They were assembled in front of the stone temple, silent and staring. I was reminded of the fact that public executions had been the norm for centuries, and people turned out by the hundreds to watch malefactors die.

Apparently that was another tradition from the past the people of Ulthoa had maintained.

Seated in the stone chair in the portico of the temple was the leader. He held his gaunt, rawboned frame rigidly upright, hands clasping his knees, his countenance stern. Two men stood behind him, one on each side.

Bodyguards? Why? They'd done their job well—there was no way we could run. Whatever they had planned for us, my night's pledge to fight for my life with all I had seemed like an empty promise.

I peered at the shadowed figures behind the leader, and was shocked to see that one of them was Brad.

Had my brother risen through the ranks so high that he was chosen to stand at the leader's right hand?

Finally we stood at the base of the steps, looking up at the leader. I gave a quick glance around at the somber faces watching us. One of the women, surely, was Mariah Bishop, my mother's sister, who had spoken to us last night. But which? We never saw her face. The woman who finally gave away the secret of the cult of Ulthoa could have been any of them.

The leader spoke, his voice low but penetrating.

"It grieves me that it has come to this. Your actions have left me with no choice. My first responsibility is to the safety of this community."

Dan glared up at him. "And maintaining your position as the cult leader."

He didn't even flinch. He was evidently prepared for defiance. "You only show how little you understand the situation."

"What are you planning on doing with us?" I asked.

"You know of the being in the temple, who gives us our lives and is the source of all our power. I believe your brother told you that much."

"Azrok."

A stiff nod. A tiny narrowing of his eyes was all that indicated he was displeased with my using the name of their demon god.

"Our virtual immortality comes at a price. One you know of. We must never leave Ulthoa, or we will die. The other is that the connection takes as it gives. We gain extended life and health. We give to Azrok some of our own life's blood, and its life is also sustained. Each year we renew that link, and both Azrok and the people of Ulthoa are able to persist. Perhaps forever."

"We know all that," Dan snarled.

One of the leader's thin eyebrows lifted a fraction of an inch. "Then it will not surprise you to find that our decision is that you will be given to Azrok. In withdrawing your life force, it will be sustained and will draw less from us for a while."

I smiled at him. My guess was right. "So as long as you keep it hungry, give it only enough to keep it alive, it's controllable. Are you sure two strong humans aren't going to be too much food? You don't want the tiger growing powerful enough to escape from its cage."

"I know what I'm doing," the leader snapped.

"Do you? I think you blundered into this, starting with your breaking the door down and freeing Azrok in the first place. Now you're blundering around trying to control it. But you've got yourself cornered, don't you? You starve it too much, it dies, and so do all of you. You can't leave the woods because you're dependent on it. You give it too much food, and it grows too strong, escapes, and wipes out everything in its path. You're not a leader, you're a zookeeper."

There was a susurration of gasps from the people watching. Evidently no one had ever spoken to the leader that way.

"Who told you this?" His voice betrayed outrage.

"You know I've spent the last months trying to find out what was going on here, and you have to ask?"

"I should have killed you on sight."

"But you didn't. I'm not sure why, but thanks. Because you came damn close to killing me and Dan both when you sent Azrok after me last week. Why didn't you try again? I'm guessing it's because you knew it was at the limit of what it could do. It's the problem with keeping the attack dog too hungry. It can't go very far, runs out of energy quickly, and has to come cringing back home to be fed."

"That is enough," he hissed. "You fools. You shall find out how much power it has, and learn the error of your mind as you die, drained of every drop of blood, every spark of energy."

I decided to launch my last salvo. If this didn't work, we were minutes from dying a very horrible death.

"So your loyalty to that demon is greater than your loyalty to your own grandson and great-grandson?"

Now the gasps were louder, and there was an undercurrent of anger to them—directed not toward me, but toward the leader.

His face blanched. "Who told you this?"

"That's irrelevant, because it's the truth, and you know it. My brother and I are the twin children of your daughter Cora. Named at birth Joshua and Aaron Bishop. Your blood flows through our veins, and you are going to give that blood to a creature with no semblance of humanity. All to save your scrawny ass and maintain your position here." I turned toward the assembled people of Ulthoa, a crowd of two dozen pale, aghast faces, looking from me to the leader as if unsure where their allegiance lay. I shouted toward them, "If we die today, keep in mind what that means. He is willing to sacrifice his own kin without thought or remorse. The next time, it could be you. It could be any of you." I turned back to face the leader and the portico of the temple. "And what about you, Brad? I'm sorry, I'm not going to call you Aaron, you'll always be Brad to me. Are you just fine with standing there watching while we are sacrificed to the devil-god?"

Brad didn't answer, but his eyes were huge, locked on mine with an unreadable expression.

"So. I guess we've said all we have to say." My gaze turned back toward the leader, who was still frozen, as if carved from granite. "If you truly want to feed your own flesh and blood to a monster for the simple fact of our defiance, then go ahead. Do it. I *dare* you."

I heard Dan's voice next to me say, in a reverent tone, "God *damn*, Dad. I didn't know you had it in you."

The leader and I stared at each other, our eyes in a contest of will. Then his lips tightened in an unmistakable expression of fury at being thwarted. He said, his voice at first low and rough, "Iä Azrok!"

"Look at him!" I shouted. "He'll crush dissent any way he can, even if it means killing his own grandson!"

"Iä Azrok!"

"Is this who you want to follow? A man who sides with a monster not even of this Earth over his own kin?"

"Iä Azrok!"

I was losing, I knew it. I could feel the power building up behind the leader, its pressure beating against me. I smelled the rancid odor of sour milk, the same as when the thing had destroyed my house.

"Iä Azrok!"

A smoky cloud filled the portico of the temple, roiling its way up from the depths behind. The leader was right about one thing— however they kept it in a weakened state to protect the source of their own power, it was easily strong enough to kill Dan and me at a touch.

We were seconds from death.

I looked away from the leader, who was still chanting his words summoning the creature to do his bidding, and glanced up at my brother. He was still staring at me, but his cheeks were wet with tears.

I mouthed, "Goodbye, Brad," to him.

He was galvanized into action. Pulling a knife—Dan's razor-sharp hunting knife, taken from his backpack the day we were captured—he took two quick steps toward the leader, grabbed him by the hair, yanked his head back, and slit his throat.

Enoch Bishop died without making a sound, but his dark eyes were filled with shock and outrage. He tumbled out of his chair and rolled down the stone stairs until he lay right at my feet.

I was glad the last thing he saw before dying was my face looking down at him.

Then the inevitable dissolution began. His skin grew taut and dry as two hundred and fifty years of aging caught up with him all at once. It split like tissue, graying on the edges, then collapsing inward. His face became a gaunt skeleton, then that too crumbled, and the leader of Ulthoa—the Patriarch, my grandfather—was reduced to a powder the color of dust.

Someone amongst the onlookers screamed. I thought it was because of their leader's death, but I looked up. The face of Azrok filled the portico of the temple, slate gray like thunderclouds, but with glittering black eyes showing a malign intelligence. It was not looking at the two it had been summoned to kill—my son and me—but at my brother, standing alone on the top step, still clutching the hunting knife. The others who had stood at Enoch Bishop's side had fled. I stumbled toward him, but the canvas straps still hobbling my ankles made me stumble and fall to my knees, nearly on top of what was left of the slain Patriarch.

Now Brad's face turned toward mine, and in his expression I saw the face of the twin brother I had known and loved. He was once again wholly himself, the parasitic connection between him and Azrok severed. He gave me a crooked smile, and in a bizarre reversal, he was the one who mouthed the word *Goodbye* at me just before the monster struck.

The cloud creature swept his body into the air and sent him flying backwards. Brad hit the stone wall, the sound of his body crashing against the solid surface making a noise I knew would haunt me for the rest of my days. But in a moment, Azrok had turned toward me, Dan, and the rest of the people of Ulthoa cowering behind us. I could feel the thing's gleeful hatred aimed toward me like a laser beam, and I knew what Brad had told me was true, that this was a creature somehow trapped here on Earth but born in the frozen wastes of interstellar space. It was utterly different from humankind and would never be anything but hostile.

We were food and playthings. Nothing more.

It reared up, ready to strike us as it had struck and killed my brother.

Then I remembered what Mariah Bishop had told me about how her father kept the thing at bay.

He learned how to fashion a talisman with the symbol that was on the charmed door, the same that is on the talismans worn by Them on the Edge. *He is never without it, and he cautioned* Them on the Edge *to wear theirs faithfully, acting as a fence should his own power flag. As long as he wears it, it turns him into a barrier, replacing the one that Azrok had destroyed.*

I reached into the leader's clothes, collapsed on the ground like a deflated balloon, shuddering with revulsion as my fingers sunk into the dust that was all that was left of his body. My hand contacted something hard, solid, and I pulled on it, lifting out a chain with a pendant made of gray-flecked stone. The surface had a carved pattern of spirals surrounding a gap. What had Dan called it? A *strange attractor.*

How fitting.

It was larger than the ones worn by *Them on the Edge*, and I could feel its power vibrating through me as I held it in front of me. I clambered awkwardly to my feet, but then stood as tall as I could, holding the pendant swinging between me and the hideous face.

"Stop!" My voice held thunder I didn't realize I was capable of. "You know this sign. You are helpless against it. My grandfather is dead, but the power in this talisman, and in the one holding it, is undiminished. Return to your den. You will do no more damage here."

Azrok's glossy black eyes regarded mine for a moment, as if it were considering attacking anyway. The hatred for the talisman, and for the person holding it, was piercing as the bite of ice in January. But it had become a pendulum, breaking our lines of sight like the ticking of a clock, and each time it did the creature winced and retreated a little.

"Go!" My voice echoed from the lower chambers of the temple, rooms and caverns that went down to unknown depths, built eons ago to house this thing that had somehow fallen to Earth like a meteor. "You will do no more damage here. You know this."

As if it were smoke being sucked out of a room, it swirled backwards, the shining eyes closing after one more hate-filled glance at me. Down into the ground, leaving only an acrid odor behind.

I waited for a few moments, but the only noise was someone weeping in the crowd behind me. I slipped the chain over my neck. With a vibration like a plucked string, its power sank into me.

I understood why Enoch Bishop had wanted never to be without it. Azrok was not an adversary that would miss an opportunity to overcome its master, break out, and kill.

There was a tug on my bonds, and I looked down to see Dan cutting the cloth strips around my ankles with the hunting knife. His were already cut, and he quickly freed my hands and feet.

"Dad," he said. "That was fucking amazing. How did you know what to do?"

I shrugged. "From hints of what Brad and Mariah told us. Other than that, I don't know. Maybe it just runs in the Bishop blood."

"I want nothing of it."

"I understand." I walked over to where my brother had fallen. But there was to be no opportunity for a tearful farewell. Brad was gone. His body was broken, but his face was peaceful. He might have lived for ten years as a Bishop, but he had died an Ellicott. I closed his eyes.

"I'm sorry, Dad."

I nodded. "It's hard to lose him twice."

"He came back at the end, you know."

"You saw that?"

Dan nodded. "Not just because he killed Enoch Bishop. It was him, totally. He broke free somehow."

"I know. I'm glad." I would grieve later, but for now, I was so exhausted no tears would come.

"It was a near-run thing. When he killed Bishop, I thought that creature was going to pulverize us all."

"Me too. What I did...I thought it had about a two percent chance of working. Maybe I knew what to do because the amulet told me. I felt its power when I picked it up." I gave him a wan smile. "But you know what this means."

He looked at me with dawning comprehension. "You can't be serious."

I thought about what my life had been—a meaningless job, living alone, almost no friends, not even many good acquaintances. My presence had made hardly a ripple in the world's fabric. But here— here I could make a difference, even though no one but my son would know about it.

I cleared my throat. "My grandfather was not a good man. He was ambitious, ruthless, and could be cruel. But for two hundred years he stood as the barrier between Azrok and the rest of humanity. Someone has to do that now that he's dead. Someone has to be that."

"But why you?" He gave a short, sharp gesture toward the onlookers. "Why not one of them?"

I let my gaze travel over the people of Ulthoa, who were still staring at the scene in front of the temple as if they were too horrified to comprehend it. And, after all, they were facing a situation they hadn't been in for two centuries—leaderless, their entire social order overturned. It was no wonder they didn't know what to do.

I lifted the amulet in my right hand. It felt heavier than its size would have suggested. "Will one of you take this?"

I was met with nothing but wide, terrified eyes.

"I'm not one of you. Which of you would the Patriarch have chosen?"

A man spoke. It was the square-built, muscular guard who had conducted us to our cabin from dinner the night before our escape. Before, he had looked formidable—now he seemed shrunken, as if his actual age suddenly showed through the smooth, youthful skin of his face. "We dare not."

"Why?"

"We were warned...the Patriarch warned us never to touch it. It was too powerful for any of us to wield, he said, without years of sacrifice and study. He told us the amulet had an intelligence of its own, and for any to handle it who had not been tried and found worthy would be fatal."

"I'm holding it and have come to no harm."

"You are of the Patriarch's blood."

"So are some of you. Some of you are his children, right?"

There was an uneasy movement, but no one answered.

"None of you will take this?"

"It has chosen you." The man who had been our guard, who had handled us as dangerous outsiders, now was gazing at me with a sort of fearful reverence. "We cannot usurp that."

"Even if I give it freely?"

Once again, I was met by silence.

Dan spoke beside me. "You can't turn a follower into a leader by handing them an amulet."

"Then that leaves me no choice."

"But you won't be able to come home."

"Maybe not for now." I looked into the empty maw of the temple. Even wearing the talisman, how far down could I go into the depths and still be safe? What was the limit of its power—and Azrok's? "But if Enoch Bishop could learn how to control it, so can I. Maybe I can rebuild the door that he broke down, and trap it permanently. Until then..."

"You are going to stay here." His voice sounded incredulous.

"Is there another choice? I don't doubt now they were telling the truth. Brad, Mariah, and even Enoch Bishop. Without a barrier, we're laying the whole world open to being attacked."

Tears were in Dan's eyes. "But Dad. I thought...over the last few days, you know? I never got to know you when I was a kid. I know that was part my fault and part Mom's..."

"...don't forget mine."

He shrugged. "Okay. But when I agreed to help you, part of it was because I wanted to get to know you. And you know, you're a pretty cool guy. So I thought..." He choked, looked down.

"I'm sorry." It sounded pathetically weak, but I didn't know what else to say.

"How will I tell people? They'll want to know where you went."

"No!" My voice was sharper than I intended. "My grandfather was right about that much. No one can know where we are, and no one can know what happened to me. I didn't tell anyone where I was going this weekend—my house is a pile of rubble, but I don't even think I told my boss I was staying with you. So they won't even know where to look. We took your car, so you hike out and head home. You didn't tell anyone you were going backpacking with me?"

He shook his head. "I told my boss I was going hiking, but I do that all the time. I didn't mention you. And I sure as hell didn't tell Mom what I was doing. I thought the whole idea was crazy, then." He gave a fleeting smile, there and gone in a second.

"So it shouldn't be a problem. It'll probably be days before anyone thinks of searching, and who would come looking out here?"

"We were seen together..."

"You're my son. No one will question that."

"Maybe I could...visit you? Here?"

"I wouldn't. The prohibition against coming here was smart. The fewer people who disturb this place, the better." I paused, glanced up at the now-quiet temple, then down at the two dozen onlookers, still deathly silent, waiting to see what would happen.

Who would become the new Patriarch.

I looked back at Dan's strong young face. He had an entire life to live, and he sure as hell wasn't going to spend it here. "Who knows? I don't plan on sitting idle. If my grandfather can learn about how to control Azrok, I can. If I rebuild the door and lock it back permanently in the temple, I might just reappear one day."

"What about them?" Dan nodded toward the people of Ulthoa.

What about them? What would happen if I sealed Azrok back up in the depths of the temple? Cut off, would they wither and die? Or would they simply start to age again, beginning where they had been frozen, slipped into stasis?

Impossible to tell. Could I seal Azrok away if it meant killing them all? Even Mariah, whose help allowed me to stop Enoch Bishop and defeat Azrok?

And I still didn't even know which one of those pale, terrified faces she was.

But if the answer to that was no, I could well be condemning myself to staying here in these dark woods for an eternity. I would stop where I was, in place and in time, as the rest of the world around me continued to turn. My son would age and die as I stayed here, as if Ulthoa was the pivot of reality, never moving as the universe whirled about it, the still point in space. Anchored by an alien entity that was trapped, that must remain trapped and hungry forever.

So I would have to commit myself to that fight. Because Azrok, whatever its gifts to its followers, was still implacably hostile. It would be looking for a means to escape. Enoch Bishop had learned to manage it, even to use it, as he had done when he sent it against me.

Something in me stiffened, and I felt a resolve I had not experienced in a long while. Perhaps ever. I had lived my life aimlessly, without any thought, simply putting one foot in front of the other day after day with no destination in mind. Now I had a purpose, one that was critical to the Earth's survival—even if no one but me and my son and a handful of people here in the woods ever knew about it.

I looked at Dan. "I don't feel that I owe these people anything. I'll protect them if I can. But the critical thing is to do what the

Patriarch did. To become the barrier between Azrok and everything and everyone else."

Suddenly I found myself wrapped in a tight embrace, Dan's strong arms around me.

After a time, I said quietly, "You'd better go. I'm not going to feel easy until you're safely out of these woods."

He nodded and stepped back, dashing the back of one hand against his wet cheeks. "I didn't think it would end this way."

"I thought it would end with us both dead. At least this is an improvement, right?"

"Yeah. I guess it's all a matter of degree."

"So all we can do is take the ending that's offered to us. That's all anyone can do. Nothing worked out how I wanted it. My brother is dead, and I'm now trapped where he was." I looked into his dark eyes for a moment, held them. "But at least I was lucky enough to recognize it, and make it a conscious choice."

"Jump off the cliff or be thrown."

I gave him a solemn nod. "Exactly. Cara made that choice, literally, to end her life on her own terms. At the last moment, so did Brad. My dad used to say that it was okay to be afraid, but it wasn't okay to let fear pick us up by the tail and whirl us around. In the end it might be the only real choice in life, the only one that makes any difference."

VI

I have no desire to recount my son's departure from Ulthoa. It was deeply painful for both of us, a pain I feel still. How many years later is it now? I've lost count. I've been tempted to leave, to toss aside the amulet and flee the forest, to hell with what happens afterward. But I'm frozen in time, and now I've been through the yearly ceremony of dedication more times than I can recall. I still feel like a healthy man in his mid-forties, but what would I be outside of the forest's shadows? Would I crumble to dust as my grandfather did, as he fell to earth with his throat cut, and time caught up with him at last?

It's too late anyway. I feel it in my bones. The outside world has gone on without me. Any stir made by my disappearance is probably long over. No one came into the forest searching for me, that was certain. The people of Ulthoa kept close watch for a few weeks after Dan left, waiting for the search parties, or—worse—armed police attempting a rescue. I was glad when neither came. Evidently Dan was successful at keeping anyone from connecting my disappearance to the forest, although someone had to think of the dark irony of my suddenly vanishing, just as my brother had ten years earlier.

Them on the Edge continued to provide us with food and other necessities as they had for two centuries. If they noticed or cared that the leader of the encampment was now a different person, and was in fact the man who had troubled them earlier, I never found out about it. My sense was they felt that whatever had transpired in the woods was over, and order had been reestablished. The affairs of *Them Inside* were their own, as long as the balance of power was maintained and the Edge was kept safe, a boundary hemming in the entity that dwelt in the woods.

Other than that, there is little more to be said. There are still occasionally curious thrill-seekers who make their way to the withered end of Claver Road, who have heard whisperings of the haunted forest, or who perhaps haven't heard enough to keep them away and are simply looking for a walk in the woods. The oppressive silence is usually enough to dissuade them from staying long, but we keep our eyes on them just to be sure.

Now that I've written this down, I'm not certain why I did. It is unlikely any shall ever read it. No one comes here, and I've given up any hope—even any desire—of leaving and returning to the outside world. So here this account will stay. Perhaps I will bring it with me one day into the depths of the temple. I have been down three levels, and each set of steps I descended felt closer to the center of the thunderstorm, the eye of the hurricane, the maw of the volcano. I could feel the raw energy surging up from below, but the amulet kept me safe. How much farther I could go, I do not know.

I will bring this manuscript down into the deep, as I descend into Ulthoa, bringing with me the accounting of what I know, and leave it there. It will be my final sacrifice of my old life on the altar of Azrok. The only way anyone will ever find it is if the world changes eons from now, if the balance of power is thrown awry. Then either Azrok will be locked away or destroyed—if that's even possible—or it will burst forth and wreak death and destruction on the face of the Earth.

But until then, I stand in the gap, like a dam holding back a great river.

My name is Joshua Bishop, and I can only hope I am strong enough to face that task for as long as it is required of me.

Even if it's forever.

ABOUT THE AUTHOR

Gordon Bonnet has been writing fiction since he was six years old, with a passion for storytelling and a deep love of the written word. He has always been fascinated with the paranormal, but his love of science, languages, and history also shows through in his writing.

He also writes the popular skepticism and critical thinking blog *Skeptophilia*, as well as producing the weekly YouTube *Skeptophilia* video. You can also follow him on Twitter *@TalesOfWhoa* and Instagram *@skygazer227*.

When he's not writing, he can usually be found running, making pottery, or playing music. He lives in rural upstate New York with his wife and two dogs.

STUDY/BOOK CLUB QUESTIONS

These chapter-by-chapter questions are ideal for a Literature Class or a Book Club. They are thought-provoking, and help offer additional insight to the characters of *Descent Into Ulthoa*.

Part 1: Devil's Glen

Chapter 1

1. Why do villages like Guildford often want to suppress any information about "less-than-savory things that had been done by ancestors who died over a hundred years ago"?
2. What sort of people is the main character referring to as "the Guildford aristocracy?"
3. Why do you think Melvia Shields is hostile, and "outright stonewalling" the main character?

Chapter 2

1. Why did Melvia Shields's attitude change when the main character told her why he was researching the history of Guildford?
2. Why does she say, "You will not tell him I sent you" when she hands him the piece of paper with Alban Bishop's name on it?
3. Why does Alban Bishop explain the lack of information on the settlers on Claver Road by saying, "Any time you talk to someone could be the last time you'll ever see 'em, but no way to know that when it happens."?
4. Why does Alban tell the main character, "...soon as I could, I moved from my daddy's house to one on the other side of the village. His front windows faced west, y'see."?

Chapter 3

1. Why do you think Alban Bishop relented and sent the main character the box of books?
2. Who do you think Alban meant when he wrote, "Them that lives

in the woods aren't the only ones who are dangerous"?

3. In one of the books, the main character reads the line, "Afterward, you will wish you had fettered your curiosity and remained in safe and secure ignorance." Do you agree with what this implies—that there are some things it's better *not* to know? Why/why not?

Chapter 4

1. Why is Dan dismissive at first of his father's attempts to figure out what happened to Brad and Cara? What eventually changes his mind?
2. Why does Dan suggest going into the woods, when he's obviously still dubious about there being anything to the stories?
3. When the main character says to Alban Bishop, "What I read scared the hell out of me," why does Alban respond, "Good."?
4. Alban tells the main character that curiosity and stupidity "can sometimes be the same thing." Do you agree? Why/why not?

Chapter 5

1. Why does the main character blame himself for the deaths of Melvia Shields and Alban Bishop?
2. What does the main character mean by, "I've been in stasis, as if I'm waiting for something or someone to shake me up and show me it's all worth it."?
3. Why does Dan call the trail cam "Chekhov's Gun"?
4. What does Dan mean by, "…sometimes ignorance is willful. If you're ignorant of something, it absolves you of any responsibility for fixing it."?
5. What do you think the significance is of the necklaces worn by *Them on the Edge*?
6. Why did Mrs. Stutes tell the main character, "You don't know what you're gettin' into."?

Chapter 6

1. Why does Dan bring up the quote from Niels Bohr, "…a

horseshoe brings you good luck whether you believe in it or not."?

2. Why do you think Joe Overby is reluctant to believe what happened to the main character's house—even after he has an opportunity to see photographs?

3. What does Dan mean when he tells his father, "You flail around looking for some possible explanation until there's no way you can do that anymore."?

Chapter 7

1. Why do you think Dan—who is a practical-minded scientist—says he wouldn't drink the water in the creek "even if it was boiled"?

2. The main character obviously believes what Alban Bishop told him enough to venture into the woods with his son. Why does he then describe Alban's story as being like an urban legend?

3. Why do you think the main character and his son are so surprised to see the steps up the cliffside, when they'd been told more than once that there were human inhabitants of the woods?

Chapter 8

1. Why does the main character say, "All the other outcomes I had considered seemed more likely than the one I found myself facing."?

2. What does Dan mean when he tells Brad, "It looks like you've had to get used to a lot of things."?

3. Why does Brad act as if leaving the outside world for life in the forest was a "not unfavorable tradeoff"?

Part II: The Instruments of Darkness

Chapter 1

1. Why do you think Brad, an experienced hiker and mountaineer, suddenly felt reluctant to go into the woods?
2. Why do Brad's parents treat him and his brother differently? How does that affect Brad's relationship with all three of them?
3. Why do you think Ron and Nancy Ellicott tried to talk Brad out of going into the woods? If they were so concerned, and (as Brad thought) knew more than they were telling him, why didn't they give him specifics about the dangers?
4. Why do you think the inhabitants of the woods decided to kidnap Brad and Cara rather than killing them?

Chapter 2

1. What finally impelled Brad to attack the man in the chair?
2. What is the significance of Brad's dream of entering the temple, while he was recovering from his injuries?
3. Why does Bethiah decide to tell Brad the truth of what happened to Cara?

Chapter 3

1. Why does Ethan tell Brad, "What I want has nothing to do with it."?
2. Why does Brad reject Bethiah's attempt at seduction?
3. Why did the Patriarch ask Bethiah to go to Brad's cabin at night?
4. Why does the Patriarch tell Brad he blames himself for what happened to Cara? Do you think the Patriarch is telling the truth about that?
5. Why does Brad think the Patriarch is lying about whether any other children have been born in the encampment since Ethan?
6. What does the Patriarch mean by, "such an action is not prohibited, it is only foolish."?

Chapter 4

1. Why is Bethiah so concerned for Brad with regards to his participating in the Ceremony of Rededication, when she has been through it many times herself?
2. Why do you think Bethiah died when she left the forest?
3. Why do you think the Patriarch didn't punish Brad for attempting to escape, or kill him outright?

Chapter 5

1. Why does Brad call the agreement between *Them on the Edge* and *Them Inside* "détente"?
2. What does Asenath mean by comparing the Ceremony to "standing upright in a windstorm"?
3. What does the Patriarch mean by "we are become the instruments of darkness"?
4. Why does Ethan treat Brad so differently after the Ceremony is over?

Chapter 6

1. After the Ceremony, Brad thinks back to his attending church with his grandparents when he was a child, but then he realizes that the two aren't similar, but opposites. Why does he conclude this?
2. What is meant by, "The realization that the being in the temple was evil didn't affect Brad on an emotional level. It was purely an abstract mental construct."?
3. Why is Brad healed of his other injuries, but still has the scars on his cheek and on his chest?
4. What is meant by, "...the geometry of Brad's relationship with the people of Ulthoa had changed."? Why and how did it change?
5. Why is the Patriarch's name such a shock to Brad?

Part III: The Mark of Cain

Chapter 1

1. What causes the main character to think, "I wanted to strike him. This wasn't my brother. It looked like him, sounded like him, even moved like him, but the creature who sat on a rock outcropping across from me was nothing more than a flawed copy of the boy I'd grown up with and the man I knew."?
2. What does Dan mean by "jump off the cliff or be thrown"?
3. Why does the main character think, "I had the unsettling impression of people who were only mimicking humanity, but whose wills and motivations came from somewhere unimaginably distant."?
4. What does Dan mean by, "their confidence is their fatal flaw"?
5. Why does the main character ask Dan, "Did you really think that was Brad talking?"

Chapter 2

1. What about Dan's plan makes his father think, "He'd been a scientist pretty much from the cradle."?
2. Why does Dan recommend trying to escape in broad daylight?
3. What is the relevance of what Dan tells his father about the advice from his martial arts instructor?

Chapter 3

1. Why does Dan call the rainstorm "a good omen"?
2. When the main character is waiting during the night for their chance to escape, he recalls the relationship he had with his brother while they were growing up. Why does he blame this for his failure to discourage Brad from going to the woods ten years earlier?
3. Why do you think Brad let them go rather than sounding the alarm?
4. What does Dan mean by "This is our storm! We need to use it!"?
5. How did the people of Ulthoa know where they were hiding?

Chapter 4

1. Why does their informant tell them "maybe, somehow, if you knew [the truth], you could use it."?
2. Why do you think Cora was willing to defy her father?
3. Why do you think Mariah told them what she did? And why does she eventually regret it?
4. What does Dan mean by calling the dedication ceremony receiving "the mark of Cain"?
5. Mariah makes it clear she thinks her father is not evil, but has made terrible decisions because he's caught in a dilemma—without him maintaining the status quo in Ulthoa, Azrok will escape. Do you agree with her? Do you think this justifies killing Dan and his father, who are determined to break the Patriarch's hold on the settlement?

Chapter 5

1. Why does the main character say to the Patriarch, "you're not a leader, you're a zookeeper."?
2. While the Patriarch is summoning Azrok, it's obvious that some of the people watching the execution think what the Patriarch is doing is wrong. Why don't they interfere?
3. Why does Brad do what he does, even knowing he'll die?
4. How does the main character know how to stop Azrok?
5. Why does the main character say that Brad had "lived for ten years as a Bishop, but died as an Ellicott"?
6. Why does the main character decide to stay in Ulthoa?
7. Why does the main character describe Ulthoa as "the pivot of reality...the still point in space"?
8. What does the main character mean by, "[it's] okay to be afraid, but [it's not] okay to let fear pick us up by the tail and whirl us around"?

Chapter 6

1. Why does the main character think that *Them on the Edge* only care about maintaining the balance of power?
2. Why does the main character decide to bring his manuscript down into the temple and leave it there?
3. In a way, this entire novel is about a man trying to find his place and identity. You probably noticed that nowhere in the book is his name ever mentioned (although we know his last name is Ellicott). Why do you think the author made the choice to leave the main character nameless until the very end? Why do you think the main character in the end accepts that his name is Joshua Bishop? How does that choice change who he is?

CPSIA information can be obtained
at www.ICGtesting.com
Printed in the USA
BVHW082208101021
618658BV00001B/99